The Ones Who Survive

Victor Manuel

ISBN 978-1-956010-25-1 (paperback)
ISBN 978-1-956010-26-8 (digital)

Rushmore Press LLC
1 800 460 9188
www.rushmorepress.com

Printed in the United States of America

Someday, this pain will be useful to you.

—Deana, *The Walking Dead*

Prologue

Dawn breaks, washing the horizon in crimson twilight. The owls perched on the nearby hawthorn tree watch him with their piercing yellow eyes. Oddly, this gives him great comfort, as if nature has come to pay respects. Traditions must be kept, so he says a prayer, "I may have the gift of inspired preaching; I may have all the knowledge and understand all secrets; I may have all the faith I need to move mountains—but if I have no love, I am *nothing*" (Cor. 13:2).

Willing his pain away, Cole digs his hands into the cold ground and pushes himself up, looking at the hills above. The trees are covered in a dusting of white; he pretends they're snow-covered hills, but the acrid air and bitter taste in his mouth tell him it's ash.

Tears running down his face, he steps back and takes in the grave. Cole knows he has buried the last remnant of his past. The last person who knew him, all of him. He doesn't know if he has buried the final page of a chapter in his life, or if he has buried the entire book.

Shovel in hand, he walks away and mumbles, "Endure. Adapt. Evolve."

It's something he had heard in his tenth grade biology class, a lifetime ago—the three things humanity must do to avoid extinction, according to Charles Darwin. The journey has been long and tortuous. He has seen and done things no one should ever have to.

But this is the world now, he tells himself. *This is what surviving looks like.*

Cole knows he must show a strength he has never known. He knows he'll need to become something different—something more. Or perhaps something less. Difficult choices lie ahead, and survivors live with their choices.

Don't they?

Part I

ENDURE

Every new beginning comes from some other beginning's end.

—Semisonic, "Closing Time"

Chapter 1

The universe is vast and ancient, its mysteries measured in incomprehensible quantities. We break down the incomprehensible by putting it in categories and giving it names, such as dark matter and black holes, hoping the name and science sticks. We do this with the big moments in our lives too, all in an attempt to relate to our world—find reason and purpose. Understand. We call the controllable *choice* and the uncontrollable *fate*. So where does this story, my story, really begin? What determines my journey? The choices I make now or the mistakes and circumstances of my past.

I sat on the bleached-wood bench and fiddled with my gold claddagh ring—its heart pointing toward me, constantly spinning it in place. Not sure if it was a nervous tic or because I wasn't used to how loose it felt ever since moving it from my middle to my ring finger.

The light gray sky looked unsure, as if it couldn't decide whether it wanted to be a happy, sunny October day perfect for pumpkin picking with the kids or a bleak, wet autumn day made for reminiscing old regrets. The sky leaned toward the latter. This town was named Stormville for good reason. The arctic cold is unusual for this time of year though. We went from a spring that waited for a summer that never came, straight back to winter.

The icy wind cut daggers through my face. I moved to pull the hood of my black sweatshirt over my head, but I stopped. I needed to be aware of my surroundings.

The infection was omnipresent—a menacing shadow blanketing the horizon.

Its official name is ACRES, an acronym for acute cellular rabid encephalopathy syndrome—fancy words that say nothing and an acronym that sounds like a cemetery in New Jersey. Most people just call it "the Infection." The baser among us prefer the racially charged name Latin Rabies.

The various news outlets have been reporting conflicting information pertaining to how ACRES is transmitted and infection rates. The *E* in ACRES had recently been changed from *Ebolic* to *encephalopathy* since the former implied a relation to Ebola and its lack of effective treatment. Bad business when a new cure or vaccine is peddled every day. All agree on three things: ACRES has a 100 percent infection rate, the infected are extremely violent, and the contagion originated in South or Central America.

Another gust of ice snapped me out of the media-induced rabbit hole my brain had become. I looked around expecting—hoping—-to see a person, but the streets were empty. The feeling of being alone was palpable, oppressive, like being alone at midnight in a poorly lit parking lot and your car is a nowhere in sight. Not that I expected a parade or a carnival; after all, I was at a bus stop on a Monday morning in front of Green Haven Correctional Facility. However, there wasn't even a civilian going to work or a person coming to visit a loved one in prison.

I clutched the large Manila envelope and hugged it close to my chest, as if it were a stuffed animal or a safety blanket. It carries the only things I wanted to take with me:

- a bachelor's degree in psychology
- Department of Corrections certificate for sign language interpreter

- pictures
- some of Alex's letters
- composition notebook
- a cute purple "Congratulations" pen—its click top is a smiling emoji wearing a graduation cap with a tiny yellow tassel; and
- a copy of Stephen King's *Pet Sematary*

The Department of Corrections DOCCS also provided me with a few items—a New York state ID; a debit card with all the money I had in my account, plus the forty bucks they issue every person released from prison; and a blue nylon fanny pack carrying legal papers and two doses of the nasal spray Naloxone, in case I happen to witness an opioid overdose. These items compose my scrapbook of the past ten years. The CDC pamphlet warning against ACRES is new though.

I was spared the state-issued "please join our cult" outfit consisting of formless khaki pants and white, one-size-fits-all long-sleeve button-down shirt. Mom had sent me going home clothes—black-on-black Prada hoodie; tight black Guess jeans; and heavy-duty, all-weather black leather boots, the ones with the steel toe. I'm wearing one of Alex's white Hanes T-shirts. I made him sleep with it on for a week. His scent is my safety blanket.

I've spent ten years envisioning what my release date would be like. For the first two years of my incarceration, I'd picture Brian Jameson, the boy who plagued my high school existence, in his silver Lexus waiting for me at the gate. Now he's a memory of a bygone era; my only concern being the man who stayed inside, counting down the time until I see him again.

In later years, I'd picture running into my parents' awaiting arms. We'd hug, cry, and know my banishment is over. After the death of my father, Jeffrey, two years ago from a massive heart attack (a "widow maker," the doctor called it), I'd picture the same homecoming; but my father was replace with my brother, Marc;

sister-in-law Pilar; and niece Bar. But no matter how I envisioned it, I never imagined it would be like this—alone at a bus stop.

My family would've met me at the gate, had they not flown down to Florida eight days ago for Daniel's wedding. It was supposed to have been a four-day trip. The infection wasn't being reported as it is now, just a few stories about civil unrest in Peru and Venezuela. The closest it got to the States was a story about a slain family of American tourists in Mexico. A young couple from California and their twelve-year-old son were found dead in their trailer—shot in the head. The couple's eight-year-old daughter was reported missing. This would've been labeled another tragic tourist story, except the son had a small bite mark on his left leg. The mother and father had the same bite marks on their hands. The bites matched the missing daughter's dental records.

It meant nothing at the time; it might as well have been another alien abduction story. However, five days ago, the CDC shut down all flights in and out of Florida, Texas, Arizona, and New Mexico. Two days later, all US flights were grounded.

Cellphone service has been spotty at best, but I was able to talk to my mom, Laura, last night. She said things aren't how the news portrays them—it's worse.

"Army trucks carrying machine guns patrol every street," Mom said. "But what scares me the most is the look on their eyes. Some soldiers just have a blank stare. And all of them have blood splatters or some sort of splatters on their faces and uniforms. We've decided to leave Biscayne and head to the Keys to Janet's—Daniel's wife—uncle who lives in Summerland Key. It's one of the further islands, more isolated."

"When are you leaving?" I asked, knowing the entire country was under an 8:00 p.m. curfew.

"I don't know, Cole. Your brother and Daniel are the ones making the plans," she said.

Her voice sounded high-strung and tight, like a copper wire ready to snap.

"Oh, Cole, I wish you could have seen Janet's wedding dress, it was beautiful—classic Alexander McQueen. It looked like a replica of Kate Middleton's wedding dress," she said, trying to change the mood. "I feel so bad for Janet. Poor girl hasn't been able to enjoy her special day. But what I really should feel bad about is not being there with you. I'm so sorry, baby. I didn't know—"

The copper wire snapped, and tears choked her words.

I heard the terror in her tears, the confusion, the guilt. Anyone who comes to prison gets to know guilt—intimately. I've learned it's good, necessary even, to carry guilt. It reminds us of the people we've hurt and the prices we've paid for the choices we've made.

However, guilt can also be self-righteous in a way that destroys. There are some people whose pain you've caused that no amount of atoning will ever wipe clean. And it is this guilt that is sometimes necessary to bury deep down, past the periphery of our subconscious, to a dark place we didn't know existed—necessary because guilt can trap us like quicksand, killing any forward motion.

My mom's guilt was not needed. God knows she needs to conserve all the mental and physical energy she has. Besides, I knew she wouldn't want to be anywhere but here with me.

I tried lightening her mood by bringing up the one person who can always bring a smile to her face—my dad.

"Mommy, please don't cry, you have nothing to feel guilty about. You've been with me every step of the way for the last ten years. This isn't how either of us envisioned tomorrow, huh?" I began, a smile already touching the corners of my lips in anticipation. "In the words of the great Jeffrey Trent, 'If you want to make God laugh, tell him your plans.'"

My mom laughs a small restrained laugh. But it's enough. And for those few seconds, the world is right again—the skies are blue, summer makes a late appearance, and a cure is found. My dad's affinity for shopworn aphorisms was infamous. He would always say to me, "Cole Trent, you better get all your ducks in a row."

"Cole, I miss him so much," Mom said. "All this would be much easier if he were still alive, wouldn't it?"

My mom had been a wreck after his death—an echo of the woman I knew. She drowned her pain in Xanax and wine. After six months of blackouts and crying spells that could last for days at a time, my brother intervened.

He convinced her to enter a woman's rehab center in Utah. She spent months among other women in pain—mothers who've lost children, widows, neglected housewives, abused women, and lost teenagers. Her favorite were the sweat lodges, she told me. I wasn't comfortable with that, seeing a lot of news stories of people passing out and dying from the heat.

"Those are different," she'd assure me.

We spent a lot of time on the phone during this time. She'd cry for hours at a time, and for the most part, I'd just listen, adding my opinion when asked.

Eventually, her tears dried, and she found a new normal, a new way of being. She became independent and determined to be there for her family.

"I know, Mommy. I miss him too—"

The call dropped, and my heart sank. No matter how often that happened, it never failed to feel like someone punched me in the throat.

I saw the cab long before I heard it, the familiar golden yellow and thick, black lettering made it look like a silent giant bee circling Green Haven's thirty-foot concrete wall—the tallest prison wall in the state.

The cab pulled up a few feet away. I walked toward it and looked back over my shoulder.

"This is not goodbye," I whispered.

A piece of me was staying in there—for now. I also knew that as soon as I stepped into the cab, it would mark the end of a long chapter in my life and the beginning of the next.

The threshold of this impending change electrified the air. It tingled my senses like the moment when the first lightning bolt cuts the stormy sky open, releasing its rain.

Where did this chapter begin? I wondered as I entered the cab. Let it rain.

Chapter 2

The last time I saw Brian Jameson was the day after my nineteenth birthday, nine years ago, when he came to visit me. We weren't dating anymore, of course. It had been an amicable breakup—whatever that means—the baggage is never shared fifty-fifty.

I entered the visiting room at the Riverhead County Jail and spotted Brian near the back. I smiled and made a beeline toward the reception officer. He took me into a tiny room on his right, patted me down, and cleared me.

"Seat number 58," he said, never making eye contact.

I shuffled toward Brian at the awkward speed to which I'd become accustomed, not fast enough as to appear desperate but not slow enough as to waste the two hours allotted on a visit.

"Damn, you're beautiful," he said, wrapping his arms around me and pulling me over the Plexiglas border into his tight embrace.

My five-foot-eight frame melted into him, and I took in his scent—beach sand and cinnamon. I wondered what my scent must be to him and became painfully aware of my worn, shapeless, dull-green prison slacks. I broke the embrace first.

Brian H. Jameson, six feet two, was ex-captain of our high school's basketball team. His green eyes, sandy blond hair, and head-to-toe Abercrombie & Fitch reminded me of an afterschool PSA against smoking. He always hated my smoking.

We sat on stainless steel stools and began sharing the Twitter version of what we had been up to since his last visit, two months earlier, when he came home for Spring Break.

"I really love Arizona. The people are the best, and the weather really agrees with me," he said, although his sunburned skin might had disagreed with the latter.

"So you're really enjoying Arizona. That's great. I love that I can use the word *haboob* when I talk to you," I said, hoping humor would mask my jealousy.

Not much goes on when one spends twenty-two hours locked in a six-by-eight cell, so I decided to tell him about the fight I broke up between a Latin King and Blood.

"They were in each other's face, yelling and pointing," I began. "I saw the Blood balling up his fist, getting ready to swing. Without thinking, I jumped in between them."

Brian's interest was piqued. He placed his hands on the counter and pulled himself closer to the Plexiglas, filling the empty space between us, his eyes fixed on mine.

"I placed my hands on their chest," I continued, "pushed them apart and said, 'No, use your words!'"

"No f—ing way," Brian said, his concern giving way to humor. "What did they do?"

"I think they were shocked. They looked at me, then looked at each other, then looked at me again, sat down on the stainless steel bench, and used their words."

Using both hands, Brian covered his mouth and began to laugh. Sounding as serious as if I were reading a court summons, I continued.

"See, the argument was over peanut butter and jelly. We get a bowl of peanut butter and a bowl of grape jelly every morning for breakfast. Some people, yours truly included, refrain from eating it. Can you imagine fifteen–eighteen people serving from the same bowl?"

Brian's facial expression let me know he could imagine it. Underneath his disgust, I saw sadness in his eyes.

"So Killah—whose real name is Shawn—felt Flaco—whose real name is God only knows—was being selfish since he's always served first."

"It sounds like Killah had a valid grievance. What was Flaco's counterclaim?" asked Brian, fully committed to the story.

"Well, Flaco said it wasn't his fault because he's in the first cell and the officers feed him first."

"Another valid argument. So, what was your decree, Judy Justice?" His sarcasm escaped me.

"I came up with a new system. Instead of sharing, every morning, a different person will keep all the peanut butter and jelly. We started with Killah since he was the most disgruntled, then Flaco, and so on. I felt like Michelle Pfeiffer in *Dangerous Minds*. And storing peanut butter and jelly has dramatically cut down the amount of empty plastic containers we throw out. Green living. Boom," I said as I dropped the invisible mic.

The absurdity of this life—my life—engulfed us, and we broke out in stomach-grabbing, teary-eyed laughter.

Still laughing, Brian ran his fingers through his hair and said, "Shit, I love you so much. God, how aren't we together? I think you are the one."

"Oh, Brian, what are you saying? I mean, I've loved you since I was twelve, I know you're the one," I told him. "But you know why we're not together—you have school and a life to live. I, well, you know what I have going for me. It could never work."

Could it? I foolishly pondered.

The change in Brian was subtle but profound like noticing, for the first time, a nervous tic that has always been there.

He lowered his head to meet my gaze and, with all the love in his eyes, said, "Oh, Cole, I'm sorry. I wasn't saying—I didn't mean to lead you on. I love you. You're so special, you know that, right? But what kind of life could we have? What would people think? What would my parents say?"

Ouch.

I don't remember what my response was. I remember making a joke about misunderstanding *were* with *are*. I remember burying my pain under a complacent smile and high-pitched laugh.

And I remember thinking, *So this is how* that *feels.*

I don't know how long the visit lasted after that, neither do I know what we talked about. I did know that Brian made it perfectly clear I wasn't one of *them* anymore. I was banished to a new *us*. But which?

When the officer announced visiting hours was over, I rose first, extending my arms to Brian. He wrapped his arms around me and kissed me on the lips. I surrendered to him, cupping his face with my hands.

"See you later," we said.

I called my best friend, Christina, that night and told her about Brian's visit. I cried, remembering the humiliation. She decided I needed "breakup-music therapy," and I agreed since any type of music system wasn't allowed in county jail. She put me on speaker and blasted music for an hour and a half—no small deed since it cost five dollars for a fifteen-minute call and she was a jobless soon-to-be nineteen-year-old.

She played Avant's "Separated," No Doubt's "Don't Speak," "Lauryn Hill's "Ex-Factor," Mary J. Blige's "Not Gonna Cry," Michelle Branch's "Goodbye to You," Natalie Imbruglia's "Torn," and Stevie Nicks capped the night off. The landslide indeed brought me down, Ms. Nicks.

Two months after Brian's visit, I was sentenced to ten years for vehicular manslaughter in the first degree. And two days after sentencing, I was put in a white Ford van and sent to Downstate Correctional, a reception facility.

Driving up the Long Island Expressway—the concrete artery that gives the island life—I envisioned my life as a book and clearly saw the last page of a chapter being turned. I felt a strange, almost guilty sense of hope. My old life had burned down in a horrible way, leaving only half-burned ashes of moments, memories, and relationships. But as fire destroys, it also cleanses, renews. I was no longer restricted by the expectations of my old life. I'd become a paradox, a prisoner in life, but gained the freedom of unknown possibilities.

Even though I never saw Brian again, we remained friends for years after, communicating through phone calls and the occasional birthday card. I was there when he graduated Arizona State University. I was there when he married a pretty girl named Jen. I was there when he moved to Scottsdale, Arizona, and opened his own real estate agency. I was there for the birth of his son, Jason, almost six years ago. We lost touch soon after his birth, allowing life to take us where it wanted.

So I was not there the day his wife and son disappeared. And I was not there the day Brian Jameson took his own life.

Chapter 3

"Where to?" the driver asked.

His eyes are dark and reflective like black diamonds. I can see myself in them. His complexion is the color of burned olive oil. Short, curly, black hair and thick, black eyebrows frame his apple-shaped face. But his dimples give an innocence to his boyish, good looks. He's of Middle Eastern descent and much too young to be a cab driver.

Shouldn't he be at school? I thought. *Have I reached the age when every twenty-four-year-old and under looks like a high school senior?*

He stared deep into my eyes, and I recognized that look at once. I've seen it my whole life—he was trying to figure out my ethnicity and if my eyes were real.

My eyes are a bright baby blue, a gift from my Caucasian father. However, they're also almond shaped, and my eyebrows are arched and sharp. My cheekbones are high, and my skin is the color of dark caramel mixed with milk. All a heritage passed down to me from my Peruvian mother. My long, thick, wavy hair a mixture of hazel, chestnut, and natural copper highlights—as if my parents' genes had battled over dominance and neither had conceded.

"The Pines Gated Community, Smithtown, Long Island," I said, but he needed an exact address.

It felt like a lifetime since I've said my address aloud.

"Fifty-two Southside Lane, Smithtown, New York."

Hearing those words in that order was like hearing a song I'd forgotten I loved. The young driver entered my address on the screen in his dashboard and gave me an ungodly high cab fare.

"It's not just gas that's expensive," he explained. "But to get to Long Island from Hudson Valley—Stormville—we must pass either through New York City or around it. A lot of the main roads are either jammed with traffic or closed. The detours add extra milage and tolls."

"Thank you for the geography lesson," I mumbled under my breath and swiped my state-issued debit card on the meter.

His tight smile suggested he doubted I could afford it, but I did have enough—with ten cents to spare. He nodded and put the car in drive. His smile relaxed, flashing teeth made for a whitening-strips commercial. I noticed a shadow behind his eyes, a shadow I couldn't quite put my finger on but felt so familiar.

"Don't worry, I'll tip well when we get there," I assured him.

I had no idea if there was cash at the house; my parents used to keep twenty-dollar bills in the kitchen's cutlery drawer. I was sure that hadn't changed.

He kept the Hudson River to our right; and on our left, the razor-wire roofs of Downstate's concrete housing buildings peered over a sea of amber, brown, and red foliage.

We stopped at a red light, and through the foggy horizon, I spotted a monumental milestone—the Newburgh Beacon Bridge with its perpetual "WARNING! CONSTRUCTION UNDERWAY!" sign flashing orange.

If the Long Island Expressway, LIE, marked the end of a chapter, then the Newburgh Beacon Bridge marked the beginning of the next. I've crossed it twice; first when I was sent to Clinton Correctional Facility from Downstate reception and then when I left Clinton for Green Haven five years ago.

The driver stepped hard on the brakes and jerked the car forward.

"I didn't know they added tollbooths at the bridge," I asked.

"They didn't." His face a blank slate.

The New York Thruway has a total of six car lanes, three lanes in each direction. There were two officers for each lane—twelve machine gun–toting officers in total.

"Are they military or NYPD?" I asked.

"Don't' know. They're dressed in all black. I think it's an ID or DUI checkpoint," he answered, his license, proof of insurance, and registration appearing on his lap like magic.

Taking my state-issued ID out of my pocket, I wondered if they were going to notice it's a prison ID.

Will they judge me? Clutch their guns and give me a hard time? I thought.

I tried taking a good look at the driver's officer, but I was enthralled by the man at my window. He looked like a cross between KFC's Colonel Sanders and the *Monopoly* guy. His tiny frameless spectacles was a sharp contrast to his black uniform and machine gun—like a bear on a unicycle.

"Where you two headed?" Monopoly Sanders and his partner asked simultaneously.

"Home," I answered.

"And where is home?" Monopoly Sanders asked as he stared into my eyes and flashed a black light on my face, arms, body, and around the car's interior and exterior.

"Smithtown, Long Island."

I don't know if it was my answer or something in his partner's eyes, but Monopoly Sanders's white mustache twitched like a rabbit's nose as he exchanged a smile with the driver's officer. Smiles that hid oceans behind them.

"All clear," said the driver's officer.

Monopoly Sanders waved us through but not before saying, "You two be safe now. Remember, it is your civic duty to report any cases of ACRES. And do try to avoid the city and the Long Island Expressway. It's jammed with traffic and checkpoints. A lot of civil unrest."

The sharpness in those last two words made us lose all interest in asking any questions.

I saw the same shadow that I noticed behind the driver's eyes pass the eyes of Monopoly Sanders, and I remembered what it was—fear.

In prison, fear is everywhere and nowhere. It's common currency; some people want to use it, some want to hoard it, and everyone wants to hide it. To survive the first years in prison, one must either learn to sense fear, however subtle it may be, or protect it behind a bodyguard of lies. After a while, sensory adaptation kicks in, and one becomes numb to fear.

The sky opened up, creating pockets of light as we drove away. I felt a pang of sadness; I couldn't picture any other homecoming than the LIE. It's like coming home through the cellar door. Although, I didn't hate skipping the Queens–Midtown Tunnel.

We were clearing the checkpoint traffic when we heard a scream coming from behind us. The officers moved with military precision. Every driver-side officer stood in the middle of his or her lane, machine guns in hand, stopping all car movement. The passenger-side officers rushed the middle lane, heading north toward the bridge and away from the city. They surrounded a cherry-red Porsche, pointed their guns, and ordered the passenger and driver out of the car.

The driver seemed to be pleading with them, but I couldn't tell. The passenger came out first. She was a tall redhead wearing blue jeans and a gray sweatshirt that was clearly three sizes too big. Her arms were up, but she was holding her sleeves up with her hands. Her right hand let go of the sleeve; and her bandaged, blood-soaked arm became clear for all to see. We turned at the next exit toward New Jersey.

After half an hour, the silence in the car became stifling like a humid summer day.

"What's your name, young man?" I asked, sounding ancient—"gaycient," really—but breaking the proverbial ice.

"Faysal. You?"

Faysal, twenty years old. He was attending seminary until his dad was diagnosed with stage 4 lung cancer. The doctors gave him a few months to live; he was on his fourth month. Faysal decided he was going to work as long as he needed to give his parents a comfortable life. He has a younger brother, Michael, who's a track star in his high school and has an athletic scholarship to Cornell, where he'll be attending next year.

"So how did you decide on seminary school?"

"I was a skinny Iranian kid, growing up Muslim in post 9/11 New York—not easy. I wanted to understand where all the . . . the hate came from, how people can do horrible things in the name of religion."

"Did you find your answer?" I asked.

"I'm still searching."

Thought so, I told myself.

I sensed he was getting ready to ask me questions, so I changed the subject.

"So, Faysal, what have you heard about ACRES? Who do you believe?"

"The government is definitely hiding a lot. What was that at the checkpoint? Anytime they can't explain something, they just call it civil unrest. But I'm not sure about the news either. Have you seen the videos and pictures people are posting online? That shit's crazy— it can't be real. Oh, sorry," he said, his face turning different shades of red. "Of course you haven't. I know they don't have internet in there. I mean—I'm not assuming anything. I've just worked this job a while. Not that it matters. I'm sorry for—"

"Calm down, Fessy," I interrupted, searching his face for any sign that he didn't appreciate my giving him a nickname. I saw nothing, so I continued. "No offense taken. Besides, you assumed right. Don't ever apologize for assuming correctly. Truth is too precious."

He smiled, and his face returned to its natural tone.

"My dad used to say, 'When you assume, you make an ass out of you and me.'"

"Mine too!" I shouted, and we both laughed.

While laughing, I noticed the tablet on the passenger seat.

"Hey, does your tablet have internet access? If it does, may I please use it?"

"Uh, sure. Let me set it up for you. Do you know how to use it?" he asked, poked at the tablet, and handed it to me.

"Yeah. We have tablets in there. No real internet access, though, just the ability to send emails and download content from their secured server. I only used my tablet to buy music."

I googled "Brian Jameson, Arizona." I skipped his social media sites and clicked on the "Help Find Jen & Jason" link.

Chapter 4

It began ten days ago when I called Christina.

Christina De La Cruz and I have been friends since we were zygotes. We used to tell people we were twins—fraternal twins since she's one hundred percent Puerto Rican. We mastered the art of perfectly comfortable silence that is born from true friendship. We'd stay on the phone from sunup to sundown, most of the time not saying much, except to tell the other of a funny thing on TV, a good song on the radio, a scandalous rumor, or we'd make a funny noise to remember we're not alone. It's a phone habit that not even prison could fully break; although it did take its toll.

Her visits were sporadic, almost nonexistent. I understood though. The world may be frozen in time for someone in prison, but it doesn't stop for everyone the incarcerated leaves behind. To them, we become painful reminders of how the world used to be—or ought to have been.

Some prisoners have a hard time accepting this; I didn't. Life goes on with or without you, best we can do is find our own ride. No matter how long Christina and I went without contact, there was always the unspoken knowledge that we would see each other again as if no time had passed. She's family, and there's an invisible force in family. Like gravity, it pulls.

We hadn't seen each other for the last six years but remained in touch through the phone. It was during one of these calls, ten days before my release date, when Christina got a news alert—Brian's family was missing.

His wife, Jennifer, and five-year-old son, Jason, had gone to her parents' abandoned ranch in Yuma County, Arizona, on the Mexican border and had vanished. Brian waited two days before reporting his family missing.

At first, the theory was that Jen had taken Jason and gone to inspect the property before selling it and had gotten lost. Then, the circumstances around their disappearance began to cast a shadow on Brian.

He was demonized for taking two days to alert the authorities. Brian explained that, without telling him, Jen had taken Jason and had one of her friends pick them up and drop them off at her parents. Once Brian got in contact with her, Jen had asked Brian to give her space. He agreed. Now their marriage woes were public fodder for a nation that wanted to ignore the real evil on the horizon.

Half the country believed Brian had killed his family. People carrying "Tell Us Where Jenny Is!" signs hounded him. The other half believed Jen had taken Jason and ran away from whatever evil Brian must be inflicting on his family and Jen was happy to let the world see the monster she married. I didn't believe any of it. Brian Jameson was no Scott Peterson, and Jen was no *Gone Girl*.

There has never been any love lost between Jen and me. She hated my phone calls with Brian. He swore Jen didn't know about our history. I doubted that, but I let him believe whatever he wanted. To Jen, I must have been an inconvenient truth she had to sweep under the rug every morning and every night and probably every time she had one too many—a constant reminder her husband used to fuck a guy. If I were her, I'd hate me too.

It's impossible to know the inner workings of someone else's marriage. I won't even pretend to know why they were sleeping in separate beds. What I do know is, Brian loves his son and would never hurt him. And he wanted the world to know that as well.

He hired special investigators, search parties, famous TV psychics—anyone who might be able to help find his family. He posted every search, interview, and family video on his site. He also had a live feed, and in a few days, the streamed videos got shorter and stranger. It became clear Arizona was being overtaken by *something*.

I asked Christina to describe the videos to me, but she couldn't bear to watch them. Christina is a sweet, kind girl, not afraid to stand up for what's right. She's a survivor; however, conflict, gore, and death do not become her. We've never been able to watch a horror film together. Last time we tried watching *Cabin Fever*, she turned it off not even a minute into the movie—the ominous music and leaves rustling in the wind were too much for her to bear.

Yesterday, she told me Brian had killed himself, and it was all online.

Chapter 5

Brian's page background was a picture of him and his family at the Grand Canyon. He's holding Jason who's caught midlaugh while waving at the camera. Brian is kissing Jen's cheek; she's smiling. They looked happy.

I went straight to the live-feed videos. The first posting to catch my attention was from a week ago.

—◊◊◊—

October 3, Monday
10:30 p.m.

Walking on my property when I was stopped by two U.S. soldiers in a black Humvee. They had been parked with their lights off. The soldier in the passenger seat pointed a black light on my face, then up and down my body. At first I thought they were border police—heavily armed border control. Thought I must've lost track of time and walked right up to the Mexican border. But I looked at my watch, and I'd only been walking for a half hour—no way I made it that far. So then I thought they were part of the search party, but they didn't even know who Jen is.

The soldier in the driver's seat looked to be right out of high school. He said their night-vision cameras had spotted me a long time ago and they could've shot me had it not been for their infrared. This made the passenger-side soldier, the one with the flashlight, put one hand on the driver's shoulder. The driver didn't say a word after that.

He asked me what I was doing out in the desert at night. I explained I've been taking these walks since my family went missing. I asked him what they were doing out there—after all, it's my family's property. He said they weren't authorized to say.

He said it wasn't safe and I needed to head home—ASAP. I told him I wasn't scared of the wildlife or coyotes. He said, "There are *worse* things out there." He didn't elaborate. I gave them a picture of Jason and Jen and asked them to please keep their eyes out for any signs of them. He assured me they would, and then they were gone.

I walked back to the ranch, and even though it was dark, I could feel those soldiers following me. I don't know why they didn't turn their lights on. I could've used it. Guess they didn't want whatever they were looking for to spot them first.

Okay, so here's a map of all the places we've searched. The blue circles are the caves we'll search tomorrow.

October 4, Tuesday
9:40 a.m.

I f—ing knew it! I don't know how we could've missed it. Only twenty minutes from the ranch. My heart dropped when I saw Jen's gold hoop earring, the ones I got her last Christmas, next to a dried-up pool of blood. Chief Juez said it looked as if something or someone had bled to death there. He must've seen the expression on my face because he quickly added that jaguars often hunt cattle and drag the kill up a tree. I don't know how putting

25

a jaguar attack anywhere near the realm of possibility was any better—I didn't even know Arizona had jaguars!

Anyway, it seems Jen must've gotten hurt, somehow—maybe it was a jaguar—but she got up! There are clear tracks, Jason's and Jen's, leading to the cave. She must be badly hurt because her tracks were uneven, as if she dragged her feet.

I think what happened was, Jen got hurt, and Jason got scared and ran to the cave. When Jen recovered, she went after him. Those caves are part of an ancient dried-up aquifer connected to the ranch's well system and the Cocopah Indian Reservation. The underground structure is miles deep in all directions. Right now, it's impossible to tell how far they could've gone. We're waiting for all the gear to arrive. I just know they're okay. You guys don't know Jen, she's a tough girl. She grew up playing in this desert. And she always takes precautions when she goes on her nature walks—especially if she's going with Jason.

Jennifer, Jason, please be strong. Help is coming. You guys are my world. Just hold on.

—⟋⟍—

October 5, Wednesday
11:07 a.m.

My wife is dead. My son is dead . . . I'm sorry. I can't—

—⟋⟍—

October 5, Wednesday
4:15 p.m.

We split into four groups of two. Not even ten minutes into the search, the smell hit us. It smelled like rotting meat and sulfur. We heard a scream echo through the cave. It was impossible to pinpoint where it was coming from. I felt like I was in a funhouse, but instead of mirrors reflecting distorted images, it reflected screams full of terror. And there were these . . . these guttural groans, like a dog that was trying to snarl with food in its mouth. It was maddening.

My search partner Paul and I tried following the screams as best we could using the digital map and GPS trackers to guide us. Paul got there first. He stopped so abruptly that I ran into him, almost knocking him over. I tried going around him, but he held me back. He couldn't stop me from seeing Jen's face though.

She was on top of Chief Juez. His headlamp had fallen off, making grotesque shadow figures on the cave walls. Jen's clothes were torn, dirty, and soaked in blood. Her skin didn't look pale or dull—it was gray with a bluish-green tint. She didn't look like Jen. She didn't look human. She looked like something pretending to be Jen. She had Juez's left forearm in her mouth, her teeth almost through the bone.

He was trying to get her off him, but she wouldn't let go. Her fingers tore his flesh, leaving bloody holes on his back. I called out to her, told her to stop. But she wasn't listening. She didn't even look at me. I pushed Paul aside and ran toward her. That's when they came.

I put my hand on her shoulder. She was cold, so cold. As soon as I touched her, she let go of Juez's arm and turned toward me. Before I could say her name, Jen's body flew backward, like a rag doll being thrown by a kid.

Everything's a blur after that, as if it happened all at once or never at all. Six, maybe seven, soldiers rushed past Paul and encircled us. Their rifles were equipped with black lights, which they flashed in our faces. Three soldiers ran over to Juez. I haven't seen him since.

They ordered Paul and I out of the cave, their rifles still pointed at us. I pleaded with one of them, told her my son was still missing, that her people had just shot my wife in the head. She told me my son had been found. I asked her if he was okay. She just kept repeating, "They will tell you more." I asked who *they* were. She wouldn't say.

I ran outside, hoping to see Jason, hear from Jason. Instead, Paul and I were escorted into separate white tents that weren't there when we had entered the cave. The spectators were gone, but I heard the other search party members. They were answering questions.

A short man who looked to be in his fifties came into my tent. He was holding a clipboard and a small flashlight. He wore a white lab coat over his military uniform. He introduced himself as Dr. Smith. He didn't feel like a doctor though. He felt distant, more concerned with asking questions than hearing answers. I asked him if Jason was okay, if I could see him. He said he'll inform me as soon as he heard anything and continued asking his redundant questions and checking boxes on his clipboard.

When he was done, he thanked me and said someone will be seeing me shortly. I wanted to ask him about Jason, ask him what the fuck was wrong with Jen— if I was gonna catch whatever she had. But he was gone before I could open my mouth.

I waited for less than a minute to go out and look for answers. Two soldiers ordered me back in the tent, but I refused. They had killed my wife and for all I knew infected her with something. Someone was going to tell me where my son was. I was ready to punch one of the soldiers in the face when a tall woman wearing clear-framed glasses stopped me and told me that she's sorry, that Jason was dead. She apologized for not telling me sooner—she wanted to be sure it was him. I asked to see him, but she said I couldn't or shouldn't. I don't remember. She said Jason was attacked by a wild animal, only pieces of him remained. The world started spinning. I threw up on her shoes and fainted.

I woke up in bed, at the ranch, in a hospital gown. What kind of government agency shoots your wife, tells you your son has been butchered, and tucks you in bed?

They've taken all our gear, including the body cams we wore in the cave. And they also took my computer. I'm sure the only reason they didn't take my phone is because the battery had died so I left it in the dresser.

I'm going into town today. I need to know if Chief Juez is okay and find anyone who can help me get answers. I'm gonna keep posting videos because the world needs to know what's happening here. Someone needs to hold them accountable. This is for you, Jason, Jen. I love you guys.

October 6, Thursday
2:16 p.m.

I tried visiting Chief Juez, but the top four floors of the Yuma Regional County Medical Center have been closed off. There's military everywhere, and medical staff is being ordered not to speak to civilians. I have a source on the inside—I sold him his first house—he says they found tissue from Jason inside Jen's stomach. The contents of her stomach were undigested. God, Jenny, what happened to you?

October 7, Friday
7:13 p.m.

Arizona, New Mexico, and Texas have been put under martial law. An eight-o'clock curfew has been established. I tried heading to the police station, but a perimeter has been set up around the center of town.

The authorities are saying it's because of rioting—civil unrest. I don't think so. I think whatever infected Jen has gotten out.

—⟁—

October 8, Saturday
4:35 p.m.

They're calling it ACRES, but what I've seen has no name. I went back to the hospital, hoping to learn anything about Chief Juez's status. The usual receptionist at the main desk—Carla, I think her name is—wasn't there. In her place was a soldier. He didn't look older than twelve. He said the hospital is under military supervision and asked—ordered—me to leave. I called my inside guy, but his phone went straight to voice mail. So I sat down in the ER's waiting area and waited. I don't know what or who I was waiting for. I just waited for answers to come, any answers.

I don't know how long the man had been there. The man's skin had been a little sallow and clammy, his eyes a little sunken and dull, his hand constantly reaching for his left leg. But he had been lucid. He had been . . . human.

We made idle talk, the man and I. He said he had been fly-fishing when he slipped and fell in the water, hitting his shoulder on the side of the boat. But what had scared him the most was whatever had tried to take a chunk out of him. The water had been too "murky to see your own dick," he said. But he felt it, the bleeding wound on his left foot proof of it. I lost track of him when he started rambling about catfish. He left to go to the bathroom, and I didn't think of him until a few hours later when I heard the scream—a primal, blood-choked scream.

It echoed through the ER, silencing all other noises. People looked at each other, trying to figure out where it had come from. I found it first.

I walked into the men's bathroom. The metallic scent of blood suffocated the room. There was a pool of bright red blood forming under the last stall, the handicap stall. I heard a weak gurgling underneath a monotone, almost mechanical gnawing. I got on my hands and knees and looked under the door. The boy looked to be about ten years old. His face was covered in blood, his eyes wide, and bubbles of blood formed on the side of his mouth. Our eyes met, and he blinked a slow, heavy blink. As if it had taken all the strength he had left to do it. Then a dull glaze fell over his brown eyes.

The man atop of the boy turned to face me. I froze, thinking how much it resembled how Jen had looked before she was killed. Its stench snapped me out of it. It smelled like rotting meat, sulfur, and shit. I turned toward the exit, tried getting on my feet, but it were as if I had no knees. I crawled to the door, pushing it open and throwing myself out onto the hallway. A soldier rushed toward me—all I could do was point at the bathroom. She kicked the door in, splintering it on its hinges. The thing crawling on the floor didn't even flinch. It just kept coming. I looked past it, to the dead boy in the stall, and he moved. He was convulsing, stopped, made that guttural groan the other thing had made, and then began to crawl toward me.

The soldier's gunshot roared in my ears. I got on my feet and ran.

"What happened to him?" Faysal asked, his voice pulling me back to the now.

I sat the tablet on my lap, and blood rushed back into my white knuckles. My brain felt like a traffic jam—too many competing thoughts for anything to get through. I had been too wrapped up inside Brian's final days to notice the tablet's volume was on high or that Faysal had stopped the car at a Citgo gas station.

"There's one video left. You ready?" I asked.

Faysal nodded his head *yes*, but his eyes said no one is ever ready for any of this.

—m—

October 9, Sunday
3:13 a.m.

The power has begun to fail all over town. The internet is down, but I hope this video posts itself when the connection returns, if I can't post it myself.

I've lost a lot of blood. Damn those fuckers bite hard. After the hospital, I drove straight to the ranch. I started to pack the car with whatever I could find—food, water, clothes, guns. As I finished loading up the car, one of those things jumped me from behind. It sank its teeth into my shoulder. I spun really fast and pushed it as hard as I could.

It flew over the hood of the car. It was wearing a blood-soaked white hazmat suit. And its throat—its throat had been ripped open.

I stared at it—its eyes were fixed on me. It got back on its feet and came for me. It moved slow, clumsy. Its arms were stretched out in front of it. Its hands looked like claws. I think it was a woman. It had a diamond ring on its wedding finger.

I had it follow me toward the house. I wanted to know what it was. I picked up a shovel and hit its knee, caving it inward. It fell on its side, but it didn't even flinch. It didn't stop coming. I broke its arms, punctured its lung, severed its spine. It never took its eyes off me. Even as it lay on the ground, unable to move, it still snapped its teeth at me—it was still trying to bite me? Eat me? I pushed the shovel through its eyes, into its brain. That did it. It stopped moving.

I'm not leaving this ranch, I know that now. I feel the fever burning through my brain. I feel the infection coursing through my veins. It feels like . . . death. My body is cold, and the bite mark hasn't stopped bleeding. It's the bite. The bite kills you, and the bite brings you back. Except, you won't be you.

I was bit about six hours ago, and I already feel the change coming.

The boy at the hospital turned soon after taking his last breath, but the man who infected him had been bit at least four to five hours before he turned. I think it depends on the size of the bite and the size of the person being bitten—the closer you are to death, the sooner you'll turn.

I won't become one of those things. I'm gonna go see my family. If you're watching this, run, get away. God help you . . . God help us all.

Brian walks off screen, and the sound from the gunshot explodes in the background. And then silence . . . until the video cuts off ten minutes later.

"Fessy, please tell me you have a cigarette" was all my brain could formulate into words.

Chapter 6

"No, sorry. I don't smoke. I'm sure the gas station has some," Faysal said while looking at the red-and-white Citgo sign but not really seeing it.

It were as if his eyes could see through it and were focused on something far, far away.

"That's okay," I said, becoming painfully aware that I had no money left.

I didn't really want a cigarette. I quit years ago. My asking was just a regression, an echo of a thought my jarred brain had misfired.

"How well did you know him?" Faysal asked.

I told him everything I knew about Brian. I chose my words carefully, as if I was reading his eulogy.

"I need to call my family," he said in a monotone voice—devoid of emotion but full of certainty.

He fumbled for his phone, pressed the screen, and held it close to his ear. Faysal's eyes burned a hole through his steering wheel while he spoke a language I didn't know. I think it was Farsi or maybe Arabic. It could have been Hebrew for all I knew. I didn't understand his words, but I understood his language. It was the universal language of love and concern.

Faysal's phone conversation felt far too personal for a stranger to listen to. I felt awkward, exposed, as if I were caught outside his dining room window watching him and his family eating dinner. It made me yearn for my family, for Alex. I rolled down the window and stuck my face out, breathing in the cold air.

I searched my Manila envelope for my purple graduation pen. I placed it between the index and middle finger of my right hand and brought the pen to my lips. I took a drag as if it were a cigarette. The fresh air filled my lungs, and I exhaled the fake cigarette smoke. I started doing this when I was trying to quit smoking—a way to curb the cravings while I wore a nicotine patch. I continued the habit long after I stopped wearing the patch and quit smoking; it helps calm my nerves and clear my thoughts.

I took another drag of my pen cigarette and thought about my family. Remembering my last conversation with my mother felt like shards of glass passing through my heart. Alex's face flashed through my mind's eye—Alex, with his deep blue-green, round eyes; short, reddish beard; and kind face. I felt so far away from him; he might as well have been in Mexico. No, not Mexico. That's where the sickness is at its worst. With my thumb, I spun my claddagh ring in place. Alex was safe. I knew that—told myself that. He was safer than I was. He had a thirty-foot concrete wall to keep the infection at bay.

"Do you want to call someone?" Faysal asked, handing me his phone before I could answer.

I called my mom's, brother's, and niece's phones. They all went straight to voice mail. I left them identical messages: "Hi, it's me. I'm okay, in a cab on my way home. I'm calling from Faysal the driver's phone. I'll be home in a couple of hours. Please be careful. Stay away from the infected. They can't be reasoned with. I love you. Talk to you soon."

I thanked Faysal and handed him his phone back. Faysal tried speaking, but the words got stuck in his throat. I dreaded what he was going to say. I figured it was something along the lines of "I'm sorry, but I must go home, board up the doors and windows, and protect my loved ones. I'll give you half your money back and help you call someone to pick you up."

Instead, he cleared his throat and said, "Okay, we're halfway to your house. I suggest we don't make any stops and avoid main highways when possible."

My relief must have shown in my face because Faysal smiled at me as he put the car in drive. Of course he wouldn't leave me stranded. Faysal—no, *Fessy*—is a good guy. From now on, he'll be Fessy to me. Experiencing hardships together bonds people in a way that the good and beauty in life could never do. Hardships force us to question our own survival for the well-being of another. This shared pain gives us the unspoken permission to call each other whatever we please. He will always be Fessy. His last name is irrelevant. (It's Singh. His last name is Singh.)

We drove through the rural parts of the Garden State. The dread of knowing we'll eventually have to enter the urban areas to get to Long Island by way of the Verrazano–Narrows Bridge became the other passenger in the car.

"So, Fessy, anyone special you fancy?" I asked, hoping idle conversation would distract us.

I wanted to say *girl* instead of *anyone,* but one can't assume such things these days.

"Nah, don't really have time for girls nowadays. After leaving school and my father's health deteriorating, I'm kinda just trying to figure things out, you know?"

"Oh, I know, "I said. "The 'struggling twenties'—it's such a transitory period in life, but for some reason, it is rarely spoken about, leaving a person feeling like a lonely island. I think it's because of society's obsession with youth. Twentysomethings have it, so it's like we shouldn't have anything to complain about."

"Exactly! How about you, Cole? You got a special someone in your life?

"Yeah," I said, flashing him a smile and my ring finger. "His name is Alex. He's my everything. Wanna hear something funny? My name was supposed to be Alexander, but my dad's favorite aunt, Nicole, died two days before I was born. To honor her memory, my dad named me Cole instead. A simple deviation with momentous consequences. I could never date—let alone marry—someone with the same name as me. Call it a personal quirk. Alex would have been friendzoned on the spot. My future was determined before I was even born by a two-day time span. Funny how life works, right?"

That story has always amused me, and sharing it with Fessy helped me knock down some of my walls and open up to him. I told him about my childhood, my family. I told him about Christina and Susan, the girl I considered a sister but hadn't talked to in ten years because she hated me. I told him about how Alex and I met and what our plans for the future are. I even told him about Brooke Leeman's party and how Brian and I hooked up that night on her dad's boat. I purposely omitted anything about prison and what I did to get there. I was baiting him, wanting him to ask.

It took half an hour for Fessy to cave.

"I'm sorry, but if you don't mind my asking, why did you go to prison? No offense, it's just that you look so innocent."

I put my index and middle finger to my lips, close but not quite pulling on my imaginary cigarette. Newport Lights 100s was my choice of poison . . . once upon a time, oh so very long ago.

"Fessy, let me tell you a story."

Chapter 7

Ten years of my life are anchored by one late August night. It's a colossal black hole in my timeline—pulling and devouring everything around it. I have buried the memory deep within, only to excavate it later, study it, and try to solve the cosmic formula "If *this* didn't occur, then *that* wouldn't have happened."

My black hole began with a broken promise and a lovely party. The universe likes to conceal the tragedies within the beauty.

"Co-Co, if you leave, you'll be sorry!" my five-year-old niece Bar said in that sweet but stern voice all toddlers are infamous for.

Bar was upset because she had been dropped off at my house under the pretense we were going to watch cartoons—a night we had planned two weeks earlier when I promised my brother I would babysit her for the weekend. Thankfully, my mom had agreed to cover for me. My dad had protested against letting me go, wanting to teach me the value of keeping my commitments. But my mom, seeing how much the party meant to me, eventually convinced my father. Besides, it was only one night.

"I'll be back tomorrow, cuteness. We'll get ice cream and watch *anything* you want, okay?" I said and blew her a kiss from the doorway since I knew any closer would lead to her throwing her sippy cup at me.

I kissed my parents on the forehead, thanked them for watching Bar, and grabbed my car keys. As I walked out the door, I knew everyone in the house was disappointed with me.

I'll buy them their favorite ice cream, I thought, fully convinced a sweet gesture would solve everything.

The night sky was clear, the full moon washed in a blue-white glow.

"On my way. Be ready," I texted Christina and turned my car on, enjoying the roar of the RX8's engine.

It was a two-minute drive from my house to Christina's. I parked outside her window and honked my horn. As usual, she had me wait, so I turned the interior light on and lowered the music. I reached under my seat for the lime green plastic clipboard I had bought in the beginning of senior year and placed it on my lap.

I held a small packet made of white wax paper up to the light and flicked it with my finger, watching its contents settle neatly at the bottom. My mouth watered as I ripped open the top and poured the brown powder on the lime green surface.

Using my old high school ID, I cut up the heroin into two equal lines. As soon as I turned the light off, Christina opened the passenger door.

"Turn the music up!" Christina said, closing the door and throwing her bag on the backseat. "You still haven't put this Rihanna song in a mix for me."

"I'll do it tomorrow. Promise," I said, and she handed me a short, red straw she took out of her purse.

I snorted a line. My salivary glands tingled, and I tasted copper and hamburger.

The heroin coursed from my head to the tips of my nails, enveloping my senses in warmth. I passed the clipboard and straw to Christina.

"Ugh, I wish you didn't have to leave tomorrow. I don't want to spend a weekend at Brooke's, especially without you. I love her, and as much as I enjoy her extravagant stories, her house is just too *gaudy*," she said, snorting her line.

"This baby grand piano was owned by Frank Sinatra," I said as I rolled down my window and lit a cigarette. "And the keys are made from virgin elephant ivory, which is super rare, since, you know, elephants are such sluts."

We laughed at my exaggerated version of Brooke (but not by much), and I passed Christina the pack of cigarettes and lighter.

"Exactly!" she said, lighting her cigarette. "I'm scared to touch anything."

"Pretend the elephants weren't real virgins," I joked and put the car in drive.

"You can leave with me if you want, but, Liz, Susan and the rest of the girls are staying over too. Besides, we're staying at her guesthouse, not the main house."

"Her guesthouse is almost as big as your house or mine," she said, blowing smoke out the window. "I'll see how I feel in the morning."

"Correction—it's *bigger* than your or my house," I said and drove off.

Brooke Leeman had been our friend since freshman year, and she was throwing a graduation party at her Nissequogue mansion—a prestigious neighborhood in Smithtown. Nissequogue is nestled between St. James and the Long Island Sound. It's where old money lives.

The summer had been one long festivity, but Brooke's party was special because it was the last one before everyone left for college. I had two missions that night—have a romantic moment with Brian onboard Mr. Leeman's yacht and make up with Susan.

We arrived at around 9:00 p.m., and I parked on the curb. Before getting out of the car, I stashed my Newports in the glove compartment and fought the urge to smoke another. Brian hated cigarettes, and the night had to be perfect.

"I'm gonna go find Susan," I said while Christina and I trekked through Brooke's golf course–sized front yard. "I gotta end this stupid argument."

Susan O'Connell was the nurturer in our group—the friend you called at 2:00 a.m. to help you stalk a cheating boyfriend, the friend who brings over your favorite food after you dump the aforementioned cheater.

She was also the most conservative of the group—quick to righteous ire, slow to forgive, and *never* forgets. We hadn't talked in weeks. The seed of the argument was planted months back when Susan and I got accepted at SUNY Oswego and I decided not to attend. And then I made the radical (according to Susan) decision not to attend *any* schools as a spite to higher learning when NYU turned me down due to a lack of extracurricular activities.

"Your idea to take a gap year is immature and, frankly, selfish to your parents who have worked so hard to see you succeed," Susan said over the phone the last time we talked. "You're acting like a spoiled brat who's too busy getting high and shopping for clothes in the kids' section."

In turn, I called her a control freak who only wants me to go to school with her because she can't make friends on her own. I made fun of her clothes; however, mine are tight by *choice*, while hers, well . . . that's a different story.

I regretted all of it but especially the last part. She's a beautiful girl—bright hazel eyes; long, wavy, brown hair; lush eyelashes; and a heart-shaped face. At five feet eight, she excelled in lacrosse and soccer while keeping her feminine hourglass figure. The truth was, I *envied* Susan. Her determination and ambition were admirable; she knew what she wanted and how to get it. I wasn't worried she couldn't make new friends; I was afraid she would replace me.

At least, that's what I had planned to say. When I saw her watching a game of beer pong by the pool, my brain went into damage control—find a resolution taking the path of least resistance so we won't draw a crowd.

"Susan, I know you don't want to be bothered with me, but I just want to say I'm sorry."

I looked for any sign of acceptance. Her face was stoic, but she was white-knuckling the red cup in her hand.

I flinched, thinking she might throw her drink at me—which I would have welcomed if it meant she forgave me. She didn't, so I continued.

"I'm lost, Susan. I don't know what I want to do with my life. I've always been the *Good Times* person, the partier, and I don't know how to translate that into adulthood."

It was more than I had intended to say and wasn't willing to take it any further that night. We could—and would—talk about the deeper issues, like the real reason I wasn't going to college, on a different day when we were alone. After all, we were at a party, which is not the appropriate place for a heart-to-heart sit-down. Right?

Thankfully, my mea culpa was enough.

Susan grabbed my arm and said, "I'm not mad at what you said, I'm worried about you. I . . . don't want this 'gap year' business to lead you down the wrong path. You're so smart, Cole. Don't waste it."

I saw her expression tighten and a shadow pass behind her eyes. I wasn't the only one holding back. The subtext to her words was the drugs.

She wasn't wrong to worry. Opiates had begun to take over our lives. It had started with prescription drugs like Vicodin and Oxycontin. However, heroin had been a line none of us thought we'd cross. Yet here we were.

We hugged, shed our tears, bit our tongues, and saved our issues for another day. Our friend Liz Anderson took a picture of the moment—Susan embraced me so tightly it looked as if our faces were melting into each other.

The rest of the night was a kaleidoscope of moments and selfies with apparently everyone at the party: Pictures of Christina and I playing beer pong against Susan and Mike (we won). A picture of

Liz and Brooke doing a keg stand—Danny, Liz's boyfriend, is seen scowling in the background.

The last picture I took that night is of me and Brian on Mr. Leeman's yacht, which was actually the main reason why I "needed" to attend the party. I wanted us to have a memento before he left for college. My arms were around Brian's neck, I was kissing his cheek, and he was smirking into the camera; the full moon reflecting on the water offered the perfect backdrop. That picture—unlike the previously mentioned ones—was never presented in court.

"I gotta get my phone charger from my car," I said to Brian as we walked back to the party.

He offered to accompany me, but I told him I was fine going alone. The truth was, I was dying for a cigarette and had left them in my car because he hated when I smoked around him.

Passing the mansion's tall, thin metal gate, I heard someone crying. I found Liz sitting on the curb. Her eyes were bloodshot, and strands of hair were plastered to her face from her tears.

"Liz," I said, running to her side, "what's wrong?"

She looked as if someone had kidnapped her family and just called her for ransom, but it did nothing to diminish her beauty. Liz Anderson was a statuesque blonde-haired, blue-eyed beauty; she reminded me of those models on the front of hair-dye boxes.

"I'm fine. Sorry. I-I'm trying to get a signal so I can call a ride." Her hands trembled as she fumbled with her phone.

Worried, I sat next to her and held her shaking hands. "No. You're not fine. Tell me what happened."

"Danny—he's being a dick, Cole. We started arguing about. It doesn't matter what the argument was about. It's always the same issue, he thinks I'm going to forget him when I go to California."

Liz and Danny had been dating since sophomore year. She was going to attend Cal State, and her grandfather, who had been a prominent actor in the silent film era, had rented Liz an apartment in the condo made famous by the MTV show *The Hills*. Everyone agreed that Liz was destined for greater than Danny Toole.

"I told him to stop. That I *love* him," she said through tears. "He brushed me off, so I grabbed him by the arm, and he fucking shoved me! He didn't even offer to help me up. Just left me here."

"That's it," I said, picking her off the ground. "He's been treating you like shit all summer. I'm gonna kick his ass—we'll get Brian to do it!"

"No, Cole. I just want to leave. Can you please take me home?"

This was Liz—the girl who taught me how to hack into a boyfriend's phone and would help me cover up any lie, maybe even a body if circumstances called for it.

She lived on the border of Nissequogue and St. James, an eight-minute drive. Of course I would take her home; it wasn't even a question.

Nissequogue streets were narrow; two cars can barely drive side by side. The thick, deciduous forest enclosed the roads on both sides. There were no streetlights, only the moon and headlights to ward off the dark. Eerie shadows hid around every tree, leaving an anxious driver feeling as if the Headless Horseman was going to jump out and drag you to hell.

The moment was still a blur. My mind locked it away, believing it too traumatic to watch in its entirety. If I did, it might shock me into oblivion. So instead, my brain allowed me to see it in fragments, as if I were looking into a poorly lit room through a keyhole.

"Liz, isn't the beeping annoying you? Just click your seatbelt on so it'll stop," I said.

She ignored me and curled up in the passenger seat smoking a cigarette, which only made me more desperate to help her since she detested cigarettes.

Amy Winehouse's *Tears Dry on Their Own* came on over the speakers, and I fumbled with the radio to turn the music up when she grabbed the steering wheel and screamed something. I think it was "Watch out." I know it must be a trick of the mind, but when I try to remember this moment, I see Liz's eyes wide and scared.

They're blue pools frozen in time, and inside them there's a shape—a ghostly white figure like a marble statue of a priest in a cemetery.

The statue was a man in the middle of the road. I swerved around him. I don't remember hitting him. I don't remember flipping the car. I don't remember rolling downhill into the Nissequogue River. All I remember is the noise my car made going through the trees and branches, like a sledgehammer crushing bones.

I woke up two days later in the hospital, handcuffed to my bed. The doctors told me I had fractured my skull, but it was a miracle I hadn't broken anything else.

My parents told me not to say anything to anyone other than my attorney.

My lawyer told me the man I hit had a broken hip but was recovering.

But it was the detectives who told me Liz had been decapitated when she was ejected out the passenger window.

That night, I wriggled out of my handcuff and left my hospital room. I walked to the stairwell and headed upstairs. The alarm went off when I opened the door to the roof, and two officers tackled me to the ground.

The newspapers said I tried to jump, and the cops said I tried to escape. Truth is, I just wanted to scream.

I was labeled an escape risk and denied bail. In court, my lawyer attempted to shift some of the blame on to the man on the road—Mr. Jackson, an old widower who was suffering from dementia and had a penchant for late-night walks wearing his favorite white tuxedo.

I didn't want to hear any of it. After several months of legal proceedings, the DA offered me ten years and five years parole, and I took the plea deal. I would have jumped on anything he offered.

I wanted to be punished. I wanted to feel the pain. I was poison.

Chapter 8

"So," Fessy said, scanning my face over the rearview mirror, "have you figured out the 'this' that would've changed everything?"

"Don't drive under the influence," said everyone alive, I thought as I contemplated his question.

That was the obvious answer, the one Fessy probably expected. But as I watched one nondescript apartment building after the other pass us by, I knew that wasn't quite my truth.

"It's easy to look at it through an adult mind and say 'I wouldn't have gotten behind the wheel,'" I said after a long silence. "But I wasn't an adult, I was a teen. At that age, we believe we're immortal and bad things only happen to a friend of a friend. No, back then, the only thing I could've changed was my obsession with having a *Dawson's Creek* moment and just smoked a damn cigarette in front of Brian."

His name hung in the car as Fessy and I consolidated the past with the videos we had watched, until the checkpoint ahead stole the air out of us.

The officers waved their black lights, asked their questions, and made their comments, same as before. Everything seemed routine, as if it were the everyday process of crossing the Verrazano–Narrows Bridge from Staten Island into Brooklyn. After a short drive along the shore through Queens, we got on the Northern Parkway, and my heart skipped a beat.

The Northern Parkway is to Smithtown what Oz's Yellow Brick Road is to Emerald City—the front door. There was no evidence of the infection, no CDC flyers, no people with signs warning about the end of days, or frantic traffic threatening to overload the highways. And as the lanes got narrower, signaling we were about to enter my home, all cares and worries left my mind.

How could I put aside watching my first love kill himself after describing—in detail—an unimaginable sickness heading my way? Context.

We underestimate our ability to adapt and get lost in any given situation. In prison, I never put too much—if any—thought into who I was living among, be it a serial killer, rapist, or gang hitman. Now that I'm out, I'm not sure how comfortable I'd feel living next to them. Although the sickness and all its tragedies were very much present, being home—the feeling of belonging—overrode everything.

The memories of the place I had known merged with the town in front of me, making it impossible to discern what had or hadn't changed. We past the park where I had my first kiss. (*Are those new benches?* I thought), the parking lot everyone used to meet at before and/or after a party (*Was that gas station always that big?* I asked myself), and it hit me. It doesn't matter how something looked, what we remember is how it made us feel. Yeah, my hometown is different, as I am too, yet deep inside we're still the same.

However, not all change was so easily accepted.

Fessy turned onto Southside Avenue, and, as if magic, the Pines Gated Community wasn't there.

It was a trick of the eye, of course. The Pines' south entrance (there's four—north, east, south, west) was closed off by a tall, heavy gate made of ancient-looking wood and bronze hinges. The pines encircling the community's perimeter—the trees I grew up playing in—were now bigger, taller, less inviting, and more protective. It didn't look like a neighborhood; it looked like an enchanted forest with the gate to Noah's Ark.

"I don't see a buzzer," Fessy said while parking on the curb.

"There isn't one," I responded, sure of that much. "The Pines is a gated community as Rhode Island is an island—in name only."

Confused, I stepped out of the car and walked up to the entrance. It looked like something out of *Lord of the Rings*. I was ready to say "Open Sesame" or "You shall not pass" when a thin slab of wood slid open.

"Hello. What can I do for you?" the man asked.

His tone was kind, but there was a sharpness behind his words.

He had appeared so abruptly, so seemingly out of nowhere, that it had shocked my senses. But recognition returned soon after.

"Mr. Hemburry, it's Cole. Cole Trent. Remember me?" I asked politely, although I would have been very much offended if he didn't remember who I was.

John Hemburry was my neighbor and had been the Pines' hottest dad. He played and was good at every sport. He even made hunting—his favorite sport—look good. A proud NRA card–toting member and staunch supporter of the Second Amendment has never been my type. But when someone looks like a cross between Ryan Reynolds and Thor, the sensible thing to do is forgive and overlook personal shortcomings. I had also made the bulk of my teen income from babysitting his eldest daughter, Braelyn. I had even watched his twin girls, Arissa and Gianna, a few times when his wife, Jessie, returned to work and Mr. Hemburry needed to catch up on sleep. The twins were born a few months before Brooke's party—they had no idea who I was.

"Oh my god, Cole!" he said and went in for the hug, smelling of sweat and aftershave. "Let me take a good look at you."

He kept his hands on my shoulders and stepped back.

"You look great, Cole. You still have youth on your side. I can't say the same for me" he said, patting his stomach.

Mr. Hemburry did look about twenty pounds overweight, his face more sun damaged, his shoulders rounder. But he was still handsome in an "overworked, tired dad" kind of way.

"Nah, John," I said, testing the change in age dynamics.

Last time he saw me, I was a kid. I wanted him to see me as an adult—as his equal.

"You're probably still the fittest dad in the Pines."

"Damn right I am!" he said, laughing and enjoying the compliment. "Okay then, let me help you with your luggage."

"It's fine. I don't have any, but I still have to tip the driver. Can you please open the gate so he can drive me to my house?"

"I'm sorry, Cole, I can't. No one is allowed in without previous permission. The board voted on it a few days ago. I was supposed to have informed them of your arrival so it could all have been approved, but I forgot. Sorry. Things have just been crazy around here—everywhere, actually. ACRES has everyone on edge, you know? Here, let me pay," he said, pulling out his wallet and handing me his credit card.

"Thanks," I said as I took it and walked toward Fessy.

I was confused. Mr. Hemburry's tone had been amiable but resolute, leaving no room for debate. And after Brian's videos, I understood the precautions. Still, my mom is a member of that board. This was my home too. Shouldn't I be granted permission? But all that was a superficial reaction to the insecurity of not being completely accepted by the community, by the *us* of whom I had been a part. What had really bothered me was that I wasn't ready to say goodbye to Fessy.

"He's paying," I said, sitting on the passenger seat, a mischievous smile on my face as I held up Mr. Hemburry's credit card.

Fessy reached back over his seat and grabbed my Manila envelope and blue fanny pack. I swiped the card and gave him a triple-digit tip. He handed me my property, and our eyes locked. There was no need to say it; our expressions could spell it out—friendship.

"Fessy, please be safe. Call me as soon as you get home, or if *anything* happens. The number's in your phone," I said, extending my hand out.

He held it in both hands and said, "I will. Thank you. You be safe too. Good luck, Cole."

I watched him drive away until he was out of sight, and I swear I saw his eyes watching me from his rearview mirror. It was hard to see Fessy leave. In the time we spent together, we had shared lifetimes' worth of memories. He wasn't just the usher of this new chapter in my life; he was the common thread that connected my present with my past; and I hoped I hadn't seen the last of Faysal Singh.

"How's Jessie?" I asked as John led me up Southside Avenue.

It was a quick walk.

The Pines is cross shaped, and my house is near the corner of the intersection where it becomes Northside Avenue.

"She still works at Nassau Medical Center?" I asked.

"Yup. She was promoted to head ER doctor last year," he said with a sniffle.

"She's home sick with the flu. I think the twins may be coming down with it, and now so am I. Occupational hazard of being married to someone in the medical field."

I laughed, half absentmindedly. Nostalgia had begun to take over again, filling me with a giddy glee. Every bush, driveway, and lawn triggered a memory from my childhood. All the houses looked just as I remembered, except there were no Halloween decorations. In my time, there would have been pumpkins and jack-o'-lanterns on every porch by now.

"We're worried about Brae. She's away at school in Texas."

His words were full of anguish and instantly stopped me in my tracks.

"I know how that feels, John. My family is in Florida, and I haven't heard from them since yesterday. Braelyn is tough. Like her father, she excels at everything athletic. I'm pretty sure she could have kicked my ass back in the day when she was eight and I eighteen. Trust me, if anyone can beat this shit, it's Brae."

"Thanks, Cole," he said with a strained smile. "Let's hope the government figures this shit out soon."

Like they figured it out in Arizona, I thought.

When we arrived at my house, time stopped. The past melding with the present was strange, like watching a movie projector playing two films layered atop each other. Mr. Hemburry understood I was having a moment, said something about rotating shifts at the entrances, and left. (I don't know if he was asking me to volunteer.)

Home sits on top of a short hill, in a white ranch with a blue door and blue window shutters. The front yard is beautiful in its simplicity and the elegant giant willow in between mine and Mr. Hemburry's property still demanded all the attention.

The asphalt driveway had recently been redone, making it look like a frozen black river. My father's white Ford F-250 pickup truck was parked next to Marc's silver Jeep. I assumed my mom and Pilar had parked their cars in the garage.

I walked up the stone steps and opened the front door, stopping to smile at the words on the doormat, "Home Is Where You Make It."

The alarm went off, and I rushed to disarm it. The system was new, but the code was as familiar to me as my name—2325112. Liz showed me that password when we were fourteen years old. We used it for everything, and over the years, due to its easy pattern on the keypad, it crept into all aspects of my family's life. But only I know its true origin. Funny, the intricate small ways we find to keep a piece of the departed with us.

I walked through the living room, touching and inspecting everything. The decor, for the most part, was unchanged—a mix of sleek surfaces and sharp edges—my mom's interpretation of modern minimalism. The kitchen was completely redone though. Aside from all the appliances being stainless steel and state-of-the-art, the wall separating it from the dining room was knocked down, and an island was built in the middle of the kitchen, which is where I found the phone.

It had no buttons, just a screen flashing Play in red letters. I pressed it and listened.

October 10, Monday
8:33 a.m.

Baby? I don't know when you'll be getting home. Hope all went well.

We left Biscayne last night. I thought the army was going to turn us around, but they actually encouraged us to leave, even helped us get to the Seven Mile Bridge.

The ride was awful, Cole. The infected—they're everywhere and there's no reasoning with them. We had a close call with one, but thankfully everyone is fine.

Don't worry about us, honey. We're at the Tomsons' place, and the only way in is through the bridge, which the army has well secured.

This mansion has everything we need—including an orange orchard! We're safe. Please take care of yourself. Be careful, stay indoors as much as possible.

Call as soon as you can. If our phones don't work, try this number, it's the Tomsons'. I miss you. We'll be together soon. I love you, Cole. Marc, Pilar, and Barbara love you too.

October 10, Monday
10:02 a.m.

This is William Golding from the Department of Corrections. I'm calling for Cole Trent, I'm his parole officer. Due to health concerns, our offices will be closed until further notice. I'll call again at 6:00 p.m. to schedule a home visit. Your presence is required.

October 10, Monday
1:15 p.m.

You have a collect call from Alexander Oz, an inmate at Green Haven, a New York correctional facility. If you wish to accept, press 1.

Chapter 9

I grabbed the phone and pressed 1, realizing I was an hour too late and it was just a message. Salty tears stung my eyes from the utter futility.

No, I thought.

This wasn't the time for crying; it was the time for clarity—before the pain turns into fear.

I called my family, but none of their numbers went through. Loneliness flooded the house, and it felt as if the temperature dropped by ten degrees.

The dial thermostat that was next to the bathroom door was replaced by a small screen on the wall.

When did everything become touchscreen? I wondered as I raised the temperature to a toasty 78 degrees and dialed Christina's number.

"Oh my god! You're home," she said. It sounded as if she were in a wind tunnel. "How does it feel to be back?"

"Strange. I don't know. Before, you know, I went away I used to get this feeling of not belonging, like I was taking someone else's place or something. But now that I'm back, I feel I belong because I made it through the storm and I'm still me. Like I've earned my spot now."

I was embarrassed by my outburst, so before she could respond, I added, "You sound far away. Are you driving?"

"Yeah, my dad has me and my brother driving all over town picking up supplies. He's stockpiling everything, Cole. It's like he's getting ready to sequester us for the duration of this sickness. Anyway, what are you doing? You want to grab something to eat? Curfew is not for another five to six hours, and I *really* want to see you before the day is over."

"I can't leave the house, gotta stay by the phone," I told her. "But I'd love it if you could come over?"

The thought of seeing her after six years and hanging out like we used to made me dizzy with nostalgia—with wanting.

"I'll be over in an hour or two. I'm starving though. Is there food at your house or do you want me to pick something up?"

"Yeah," I said without checking the fridge.

Although I was sure we had food, it didn't matter. There was only one thing I wanted.

"Is the Taco Bell still open?"

"Yes!" she exclaimed, reading my mind.

"Cheesy Gordita Crunch!" we said simultaneously and broke out laughing.

Memories of late nights at Taco Bell inundated my mind: greasy tacos after a party, comfort food after a fight with a boyfriend, or simply the choice food for a Saturday night spent watching movies or TV. The laughter died down, replaced by a deep sense of camaraderie built on a shared past.

"I'll call up front, let them know you're coming," I said. "Chris, do you remember the Pines having a huge wooden gate? All it's missing is a moat."

"I know, right? It appeared two days ago, never seen it before then. I'm not going that way though. Taco Bell is on the corner of Eastside Avenue, remember?" she said in a tone that reminded me of a kid explaining a universally known fact to a grandparent suffering from Alzheimer's.

"Of course I remember," I said, sounding more defensive than I intended. "Don't they have a gate at that entrance as well?"

"Yeah, but it's a simple toll gate—without a toll—and Simon Green will be manning the post. He knows me."

"Okay. I'm gonna take a hot bath. You have no idea how much I've missed it. The door is unlocked in case I'm not out by the time you get here. See you soon."

I wondered whom Christina had been visiting to be so well acquainted with the workings of the Pines—a lover perhaps?

I made a mental note to find out and entered the master bedroom, what I used to know as my parents' bedroom. I don't know what to call it, now that my father is dead, and "Mom's bedroom" sounds evasive, as if I'm trying to erase or change its history. But I suppose I'll get used to it.

The room smelled like perfume and velvet. I fought the urge to jump on her bed and headed into her bathroom. Cozy heat tingled my feet, and I remembered she had a heated tile floor installed a month after my father's death—a "grief-driven impulse buy," my brother had called it. I liked it. The heat balanced out the coldness of the marble surfaces. It made the room feel inviting.

Everything else looked the same: The trims and metal fixtures are still bronze. The towels are still fluffy and white. My father's sink also looks the same—almost. His toothbrush and razors are gone, but his colognes and aftershaves remain. I wondered if my mom breathes in his scent when her longing becomes unbearable.

I undressed, taking Alex's shirt off and sinking my face in it to enjoy his scent.

The bathtub filled up fast, the rising steam fogging the room. I looked through the bottles neatly lined around the jacuzzi and chose lavender-scented bath salts and oil, pouring a generous amount of both.

I took my hair out of a ponytail and let it fall past my shoulders. It had been a decade since I've taken a bath. I slowly entered the water, savoring every nuance. My ring slipped off my finger, so I placed it next to the phone.

"You need to get it sized," I said aloud to remind myself.

My muscles melted, and the lavender scent dulled my senses.

I closed my eyes and began to think—or perhaps dream—about Alex.

Chapter 10

Think doesn't do Alex justice. It sounds detached, as if it's done explicitly by choice. Like breathing, he's in everything I do, shaping the things I say—the words I use. And when we're apart, he's a phantom limb I'm constantly reaching for.

Bethink sounds more fitting, as if *being* and *thinking* had a baby.

Most prisons in New York State are referred to as gladiator schools. But Clinton Correctional Facility has the portentous honor of being known as "the Colosseum." It's where men find what they're really made of.

I got lost in bad choices, bad experiences, and bad relations or, I suppose, found myself. I learned from those hardships. However, thriving in prison—or any harsh environment, for that matter—comes at a price. You can't swim dirty waters and expect to stay clean. Every challenge was a battle I needed to win. But seeing life in those terms, win or die, cheapens it. After four years, I wanted that part of my humanity—the part I had compromised in the name of survival—back.

I put in for my transfer in March, and by August, I was crossing the Newburgh Beacon Bridge, ready to start anew. Clinton marked the beginning; Green Haven marked the end. I had five years left on my sentence, and I was to spend them healing and preparing.

Love and relationships were the furthest things from my mind. I enrolled in American Sign Language, ASL, to become an interpreter for deaf inmates. I also enrolled in college and pursued a degree in

Psychology. I met Alex a year and a half after arriving at Green Haven when I walked into the library looking for a book on ASL.

He had never acknowledged my presence before when we would pass each other in the yard, but on that snowy January morning, I could feel his gaze on me as I perused the bookshelves. I knew what everyone else knew about him—he had been in Green Haven for ten years, worked in the library for four of those ten, worked out in the yard five times a week, and ran poker games Saturdays and Sundays in the gym. I didn't know his name, although I had heard people call him *Ayo*. But it sounded like "Eh, yo!" As if whoever was calling him didn't know his name either.

"Do you need any help?" he asked, his tone a mix of kindness and concern with a hint of amusement.

"Yes. I mean, no—sorry," I said, stepping over my words.

He was handsome, like "music video" handsome: Tall with a complexion the color of milk and honey. His eyes a blue-green only seen in a hot spring on *National Geographic*. He kept his hair military short, and his neatly trimmed beard was a palette of New England fall colors, red, brown, gold.

"ASL is kicking my ass. I'm not having a hard time remembering signs, it's incorporating body movement and facial expressions I can't seem to get right," I said.

"I knew it was ASL related," he said. "Only people taking the sign language class look in this section. I have a book up front. It's the best ASL book we got. I use it to help me remember some signs."

"You've taken ASL?" I asked, intrigued.

"Nah, it's too much work. I know the basics and this." He closed his right hand into a fist, his thumb resting on the side of his index finger. It was the sign for the letter *A*.

He held the *A* sign up to his face and rubbed it on his beard.

"Is that the sign for apple?"

"It's my sign name. A deaf person assigns it," he explained. "It's usually the first letter of your name on a distinctive feature. Mine is

A for Alex on my beard. The deaf guys come to the library a lot, and I like to be able to understand them when they ask questions."

"That's really nice, Alex. My name's Cole," I said, realizing he hadn't asked and embarrassed when I said it.

I quickly added, "Last name Trent. What's yours?"

"Oz." A crooked smile touched the corners of his lips. Sexy.

"Are you related to Dr. Oz?" I asked, half joking, half serious.

"Ha-ha. Never heard that one before. So where are you from, Cole Trent?"

"Long Island, born and raised. And you, Alexander Oz?"

"I knew it!" he said, biting his lip and hitting his hand with his fist as if he had gotten the correct answer on Jeopardy. "I could tell by your accent. I'm from Gowanda."

"Wow, you're from Africa?" I asked, genuinely excited to meet a white person from Africa, like meeting Charlize Theron. I could ask him about apartheid.

"Uh . . . Gowanda is in Western New York, near Buffalo," he laughed but not in a judgmental way.

His laugh was inviting, warming the space between us. I didn't feel dumb; I felt proud to have made him laugh. I wanted to do it again.

We met every Friday after that day. He enrolled in the same college program as me and set up a table at the back of the library, behind the classical section, away from prying eyes, where we could study. We talked about everything, trading our secrets and sharing our scars. I saw the real Alex, and he allowed me to show him the real me. And he never flinched; he never judged.

No matter what was going on in our lives, we never missed our Friday sessions. It's hard to say when love actually bloomed because falling in love with him was like learning how to read—one word at a time, then everything makes sense at once, forgetting there was ever a time I didn't know how.

But I can pinpoint two occasions that demand attention.

It was May, fifteen months after our first meeting. I had turned twenty-six five days earlier, and Alex was turning thirty-two in two weeks. (We're both May babies, but I'm a Taurus and he's a Gemini.) I had just received my associate's degree and was getting ready to pursue a bachelor's. The day was humid, and there was only one other person besides Alex and myself in the library.

Alex hugged me in celebration of my hard work. I placed my hands on his upper back and rested my head on his chest, his heart beating in my ear. We locked eyes and kissed. His lips were soft—albeit, cold—as if he hadn't used them in a while, which only made the moment sweeter. Feelings, wanting, I had been ignoring took hold; and I ran my hand over the front of his pants, massaging his hardness. I sat him on the chair, pulled down his zipper, and got on my knees.

It was on after that, never missing a chance to hook up. We carved a bigger place for us to exist within the confines of our penitentiary, living on hidden affections and stolen moments. He made me feel how I used to, before prison happened. He made me feel clean again. And a month and a half later, on June 29, two became one.

The summer heat turned the library into a slow cooker, and Alex and I were the only ones there. I opened my *Abnormal Psychology* textbook and waited for him to finish work so he could join me in our oasis.

"Your favorite show, *Buffy the Vampire Slayer*, comes on every morning. Did you know that? I liked her in that movie . . . what's the name? The one you're always quoting?" he said as he walked in and leaned back against a bookshelf.

"*Cruel Intentions*," I said, suspicious of his randomness.

Alex tends to ramble when he's anxious or nervous.

"Yup. That's the one." His face was serious, his hands trembling.

He took a deep breath, got on one knee, and pulled out a gold ring from his back pocket.

My mind locked, and seconds stretched into minutes.

That's the same claddagh ring Angel gave Buffy, I thought as my brain connected the pieces.

Then, witnessed by Wilde, Shakespeare, and Hugo, Alex spoke.

"I keep thinking about how much I enjoy talking with you, how great you look when you smile, and how smart you are. I daydream about you on and off, all day, replaying pieces of our conversations, laughing again about funny things you said or did, or smiling to myself thinking about the things I'll do to you the next time we're alone. I've memorized your face and the way you look at me . . . it melts my heart. I don't know what the future holds, but I'm certain that you're the best thing that has happened—and will ever happen—to me. I'm in love with you, Cole. And I just want to know one thing. Will you marry me?"

I know I said *something* but can't remember what. And I won't ask Alex for fear he'll overthink my forgetting. I don't know why my mind has erased the moment; I suppose it doesn't matter.

Obviously I said *yes*, and over two years later, it still feels like the first time.

We had to keep our relationship secret, so I wore my ring on my middle finger. Any type of romantic or sexual interaction between inmates is against Department of Corrections policy. I don't know if people suspected though. Whether they did or didn't, no one said a thing. It was all very *Romeo + Juliet* meets *Orange Is the New Black*.

Alex quit the library a few days before my release date. He said the place wouldn't feel right without me. He took a job as an aide in the Hospice Unit, which will help him when he sees the parole board the next year. We'll get married then, although he *hates* it when I say that.

"I have no problem doing the paperwork—I *want* to do it," he always says. "But people have been getting married long before our courts and laws existed. I don't need a piece of paper to tell me we are one."

That sounds good, but I need the paperwork. Call me a traditionalist.

Chapter 11

How is it nighttime? I thought, waking up in a pitch-black bathroom.

Even when my eyes adjusted, all I could make out were ghostly shapes emanating from the trees outside the windows. I picked up the phone to check its clock and was shocked to learn it was only four in the afternoon.

I fumbled for the drain mechanism and stepped out of the tepid water, thankful for the heated floors. Looking out the window, I realized *everything* was dark. The streetlights were off, and so were all the driveway lights. Every house had its blinds drawn and looked silent, as if they were in competition to see who could hide best. I didn't want to compete, so I left my blinds up, wrapped a towel around my waist, and turned the bathroom lights on.

My mother's organizational habits hadn't changed, and I had no problem finding the extra toothbrushes, her lotions, etc. I wanted to look effortlessly attractive while I acclimated to being home, so I waxed, plucked—even lasered—anything that I deemed unseemly.

"Where's my ring?!" I shouted to the mirror when I saw my naked finger while brushing my teeth.

I panicked, thinking it must have gone down the drain, but remembered I took it off. I found it on the floor and decided to put it back on my middle finger until I got it sized.

I reached for Alex's T-shirt, realizing I had nothing else to wear but the clothes I came home in. And then I remembered Mom had set up my room, what was formerly known as the guest bedroom.

Walking out of the master bedroom and into the hallway, I had to stop and orient myself. Other than the living room and kitchen, every important room lies in this hall. At the end is Marc's and Pilar's room. On the right is my mom's room and next to it the door to the basement and main closet, and on the left are the main bathroom and what is now my room.

However, instinctively I had walked out of the master and turned right toward the basement where my room had been but now was a gym and Bar's room. I stopped as I turned the doorknob, partially because I knew it wasn't my domain anymore but also because I fully intended on inspecting every inch of the place—knowing Bar would kill me if she found out—and didn't want to rush through it. Too many memories; attention must be paid.

I expected my room to be neat and the sheets to be a plain color like beige, which they were; however, on top of the bed was my comforter—the gray comforter I bought my junior year of high school. I dove on to the bed, hugging the fabric, feeling its silky texture caress my cheeks. I thought it would smell of my youth, cigarettes, and Acqua di Gio. It didn't. It smelled like fresh cotton.

Going through the dresser drawers, I found new socks, underwear, T-shirts, and tank tops—all my size, folded, and sparkling white. The closet was full too. While I was in prison, Mom had bought me clothes whenever she saw something on sale I may like. "Classic pieces that will never go out of style," she'd say. But as I perused her findings, my attention was only on the clothes I remembered.

Shirts, pants, sweaters, hoodies—all from my youth, all with a story to tell.

The crown jewel was a black leather bomber jacket. I ran my fingers over its wool collar and wool interior, the softness bringing back memories of icy nights spent at keg parties in the woods. The past crashed on me like a wave. I quickly put on fresh whites, a tank top, and baby-blue pajama pants and sprinted to the kitchen.

In the cutlery drawer, beneath the fork setting, I found four twenty-dollar bills.

Some things never change, I thought as the past engulfed me like a drug.

My longing for nostalgia filled me with a strange sense of guilt, as if I were robbing my future—Alex—of something not easily put into words. It was almost like watching the reboot of a favorite movie and not being sure which was better, the original or the remake. I thought coming home would overload my mind. I lived in a six-by-eight cell for a decade, and now I was reminded my old closet was bigger than that. Yet none of that overwhelmed me. Both places, my Mom's house and that cell, were the spaces I carved out in the world and called my own. The doormat was right, "Home Is Where You Make It."

Before I could dig deeper, headlights cut through the living room. They were as bright as searchlights, and I rushed to the door to greet Christina.

"Cole, I've missed you so much!" she said while hugging me.

Her big, heavy purse poked my ribs, and the Taco Bell bag bounced on my back.

I rested my head on her shoulder and took in her scent. She smelled like vanilla.

"I've missed you too. You have no idea," I told her.

We went into the kitchen and set the food on the island.

"It's a ghost town out there. Everything closes at six now. They barely had anything left to serve. Can you believe that—Taco Bell running out of food?" she said, genuinely shocked. "Do you have mayo?"

Her request made me smile, remembering she liked mayonnaise with her tacos—which used to disgust me until I tried it and loved it.

"Yeah, let me get it," I said, sure there must be some in the fridge.

Our conversation wasn't forced, but there was something unnatural about it, like we were trying too hard to be the people we knew and the last ten years hadn't happened. We talked about which of our friends were married, who was divorced, who had a good job, who had kids or too many kids, who was over their gay phase or just starting theirs, who got fat, who got thin, who was in rehab, and who needed to go. She told me she hated living with her parents again but had no choice after she caught her then-fiancé (who shall not be named) in bed with his cousin.

Her gaze fell to the floor, only for a second. But in that short time, I got a glimpse of the abysmal pain that had been suffocating her. It was heartrending to see, like watching a drowning person's last breath before going under. I wondered if the subtle moment was perceptible to me because of our bond or because I know pain—or both.

Before I could comment, as if she had read my mind, she said, "I'll be fine though. I've been keeping busy."

Her version of *busy* was sleeping with Simon Green who lives up the road on Northside Avenue.

"It's purely physical," she added, since Simon is ten years our junior.

Christina De La Cruz has always been a beautiful girl. At five feet five, she had the body of a salsa dancer with the grace of a ballerina. However, I could see the toll life had taken—years of heroin addiction and countless trips to rehab had left tired circles around her sharp almond-shaped, brown eyes. We were years sober now, but I'm sure she could see the same telltale markings on my face.

I didn't want to open the festering wound that was my missing family; so I talked about Alex, our past, present, and future.

"You're gonna wait for him?" she asked, more amused than believing.

"Of course I'll wait. Christina, he's the one. I can't picture a life without—"

I was interrupted by the phone ringing, and I ran to my room where I had left it so Christina wouldn't hear my conversation with parole.

"You have a collect call from Alexander Oz, an inmate—"

I pressed 1.

"Alex! I've waited all day to hear your voice. I missed your call by an hour. How are you?"

"Chicabear, you have no idea how much I miss you," he said.

Although his voice sounded breathless—hollow—Alex using my pet name was like hearing a favorite childhood lullaby. It made me feel safe.

"I watched Brian's videos, babe. I-I don't know how to take any of this shit. The news says things are getting better and not to panic, but there's a darkness they're not telling us about. There are checkpoints all around the city and Newburgh. I haven't been able to contact my family. And—shit—I haven't emailed your mom yet. I'm so sorry. I promise I will," I said.

Guilt began to creep into my heart, not for forgetting to email his parents but for leaving him in there—as if it had been up to me.

"Don't worry about that, babe. Do it when you're ready. I actually haven't been able to reach my mom either. They're starting to quarantine sections of the prison, and no one wants to work in the medical or hospice units, so I've had to do everything around here. Did you know during the Black Death, a man named Ragusa detained travelers from infected places for forty days—*quaranti giorni*—which is where the word *quarantine* comes from."

Alex's rambling put me on instant alert.

"What about Matt, isn't he helping you?" I asked.

Matt has been his one and only friend for close to six years, and they worked together in hospice, taking care of dying inmates.

"Cole, there was an accident. Matt's sick. He's infected with ACRES."

My body went rigid, fear leaving me unable to speak.

"I've never seen anything like it. Old man Danny came back from an outside medical trip, something to do with his heart. Anyway, he said he was fine and things looked normal out there. Except for the fire. He said they drove by a huge bonfire in a field. Danny didn't know what they were burning but said he smelled burned hair and thought he may have seen a body in the flames. But you remember how he is, he loves telling stories so no one took him seriously. I mean, why would people burn bodies out in the open, right? At best, they were burning mannequins, *right*?"

His pleads screamed, *"Please tell me they were mannequins, and you know because you saw it with your own eyes—even if you didn't, just lie to me."* And I almost did, but before I could speak, he continued.

"The next morning, when the gates opened for breakfast, his boyfriend, Manny, went to check on him. I don't know how Manny found the strength to walk—he's in the advance stages of AIDS."

The mention of AIDS in the same context as ACRES sounded out of place, trivial. Alex's thoughts were fractured and all over the place. He needed to get the memory out any way possible. I knew that, so I said nothing and listened.

"We all heard the scream. Danny was on top of Manny, biting his face—his *face*, Cole. Danny has always been slow and clumsy, but as soon as he saw people standing nearby, he let Manny go and lunged. He bit two people on the hand."

His voice had become monotone and distant, as if he were retelling a story told to him many years ago.

"Matt pushed Danny into his cell and closed the gate. Manny was on the floor, motionless. There was blood everywhere. I called for the CO, but he wouldn't come into the company. I told him Manny was going to die if he didn't help. 'Lock him in his cell' was all the CO said. There wasn't a lick of empathy in him, Cole. I know he was scared. Shit, I was scared too. But it's his fucking job!"

Anger oozed from his words, and I preferred it to his emotionless tone.

"We, Matt and I put on gloves and moved Manny into his cell. I had his feet, Matt his shoulders. He wasn't bleeding anymore though. I thought he was dead because his body was cold, but Matt said his forehead felt hot. And there was a smell to him, like rotting eggs. We laid him on his bed, and I left to check on Danny and the two men he attacked. It was crazy, babe. Danny was on the gate, his hands hooked like claws trying to grab me or anyone he could. His skin was a blue-gray color, and his teeth . . . he wouldn't stop biting at the bars. I looked into his eyes, and he wasn't there. He didn't look human, Cole," he said, his voice trailing off as he left the present and got lost in the past.

"Alex, what happened next?" I said, bringing him back to me.

"I heard another scream. It sounded terrible and high-pitched. I instantly knew it was Matt and got to Manny's cell as Matt was jumping out, slamming the gate shut. He was holding his left arm. It was hemorrhaging blood."

"My love, I'm so sorry."

"Manny stood at his gate. He looked just how Danny had—no, that's not quite right. Manny was rabid like Danny, but unlike him, Manny still looked human. That made it worse. I told the officer everyone was secured, and Matt and two others needed medical assistance ASAP. He said the sergeant had given orders not to let out anyone who had been exposed. I cursed at him, called him all types of bitch-ass motherfuckers. That's when Sergeant Cooper came and told me to get the people who were bitten in their cells because he couldn't do anything for us until I did that.

"I found Matt at the slop sink, washing his arm with rubbing alcohol. He knew what the bite meant. We all knew. I told him what Cooper said. He didn't fight me and locked himself in his cell. The other two weren't so easy to convince. They were scared, Cole. All they wanted was medical assistance," he said.

It sounded like a plead, as if he had to convince me or himself.

"One of them spit on me, landed a thick one on my chest. I fucking lost it. I don't know how ACRES works, I don't know how it's transmitted. I took my shirt off and ran to the slop sink. His saliva didn't make contact with my skin, but I still washed my chest with antibacterial soap. I scrubbed until my skin was raw. After, I walked up to the dude, kneed him in the stomach, and dragged him into his cell. The other guy saw this and locked in on his own. I knew it was wrong of me to put hands on him, I'm sorry. I was just so scared."

"Alex, stop. You have nothing to apologize for. You were put in an impossible position and handled it better than anyone I know."

"Thanks, babe. I needed to hear that."

"Has Matt and the other two turned yet?"

"The two have, but Matt's hanging on. He's tired but lucid," he said and began to cry.

"Babe, listen to me. You need to get out of that unit. There's nothing you can do for him."

"I can't, Cole. Sergeant Cooper wants to close down the unit and stop feeding everyone. I'm the only reason he hasn't abandoned them. And what if a cure is found? I can't leave Matt to die."

"Alex, listen! Whatever is keeping the infected on their feet is *not* life. There's nothing you or anyone can do for them."

"And what about the people who haven't been bit, Cole? Cooper won't let them out. How can I leave them to starve?"

I knew he was right, but I was in no mood for his "hard right against an easy wrong" spiel.

"Please, baby, get out of there—for me. For us. I can't lose you."

My anger gave way to fear, and I started crying.

"Chicabear, please don't cry. I can't abandon them, you know me. I won't be able to forgive myself. Trust me, the government will figure this shit out. It always does. I promise to be careful. It's the bite, I know that, and I won't let them get me. I swear it on the gods, the old and the new."

His *Game of Thrones* reference forced a smile on my face.

"Besides, I'm not alone. Jack has been helping out."

"Jack? I thought you couldn't stand him."

"Yeah, he's still a cocksucker, but he's been useful. And I'm in no position to turn down a helping hand. I promise to have him do all the high-risk shit," he said, and I could feel his smirk over the phone. "Please don't be mad at me. I need you. I love you, Cole. You're the only thing keeping me sane right now."

"And when were you sane to begin with?" I teased.

He laughed.

"This plague will end. I'll get out of here, and we'll build that beautiful life we've talked so much about. But right now, we all have a job to do, and this is mine."

His fear turned into resolve. He was sure he was doing the right thing.

I hated him for it but knew nothing would change his mind.

"You stubborn prick . . . y-you've always been a much better person than I ever could be. I know you're doing what you feel is right—you wouldn't be you if you didn't—but why does it have to be *you* helping them?"

"I'm nowhere near better than you. You're one of a kind, Cole, *you* are the reason why I'm able to be my best self. As for why it's me helping them, what can I say? I have a soft spot for broken things. Why do you think I'm obsessed with you?" His attempt at humor was annoying but welcomed. "I love you, Chicabear."

"I love you too. Please be safe. Don't take any unnecessary risks. I'll come visit you as soon as I get permission from parole and find a way to travel in all this madness. Don't worry, I'll figure something out. You're my world, Alex."

"How did I get so lucky?" he said. "And you don't worry as well. I'll leave as soon as I can get the others out. Not gonna lie, that groan the infected make is starting to drive me crazy. It's like a fucking choir from hell. Oh, almost forgot. Did you get my—"

The phone hung up. I tried calling back and remembered I couldn't. My knuckles turned white as I gripped the phone, hoping Alex would call back. When I realized he wasn't going to, I fell to the floor and cried.

Chapter 12

I had forgotten all about Christina and was startled when she hugged me from behind, wrapping her arms around my stomach and laying her head on my back.

"How much did you hear?" I asked.

"Enough to know you found the real thing."

Burying my face in her chest, I cried until her shirt was soaked in tears and snot. We didn't speak; we didn't need to. All that mattered was we weren't alone.

Once I had no more tears to shed and my insides felt hollow, as if the wind could blow me over, I said, "What's happening to the world, Chris? This plague is going to get worse before it gets better, isn't it?"

"I don't know, Cole," she said, running her fingers through my hair. "I'm scared. That's all I know."

"Have you watched Brian's videos yet?" I asked.

"No. I can't. I read the comments though. That was enough."

"No, it's not," I said and picked us up off the floor. "Come, we have to know what we're dealing with."

We walked to my brother's room and turned on his computer. I played Brian's final days for Christina, and when it finished, she looked pale, as if ready to vomit—which she did, all over the white carpet.

I got paper towels and cleaning solution from the kitchen and silently cleaned up the mess while Christina sobbed and her shell-shocked mind processed what she had seen.

"Brian's family . . . Jason, he was *so* young. They were meant to live a—" she said and began crying again.

I finished cleaning and hugged her. It was her turn to soak my clothes.

"We need to know more," I said when her tears subsided.

She nodded and wiped her face on my tank top, leaving streaks of foundation that made me cringe.

All the mainstream media outlets played the press conference with the surgeon general:

> "Is it a virus, bacteria, parasite?" asked the reporter.
>
> "We're not sure yet," said the handsome young surgeon general. "But we have been looking into the infecteds' immune system—specifically the NK cells, or natural killer cells."
>
> "Are you saying NK cells are the solution or part of the disease?"
>
> "We're looking into both."
>
> "Why are black lights being implemented during examinations?"
>
> "Once infected, the skin emits a gleam that is only detected using black lights. The higher level of infection in the system, the more a person's skin will glow."
>
> "Does that mean the infection can be transmitted through blood as well as saliva? Has ACRES mutated and become airborne as many South American nations are reporting?"
>
> "The bite is still the main source of infection, although we can't rule out other forms of transmission."
>
> "Was this a terrorist attack?"
>
> "That's a question better answered by our Department of Security."
>
> "The infection has been reported in every continent except Antarctica. It has reached pandemic proportions. Are the various world agencies working together to find a solution?"

"We are exchanging any and all findings with other nations, not only working on a cure but a possible vaccine as well. As we speak, the Russian government is conducting various studies with promising test results, which will be made public as soon as possible."

"Why isn't any information coming out of the southern states, and why have the president and vice president been secluded to an unspecified location? Is it because the government has lost all control of infection rates?"

"All branches of government are working in unison to control the situation. Our military is doing a great job of securing heavily affected areas. The executive branch is only following protocol since a terrorist attack can't be ruled out. But let me make this clear—our president has full faith in the government's ability to keep the country safe. That's all for now. Please be patient while we do our job. Follow curfew, report any cases of ACRES, and do not engage an infected person. Together we can beat this.

"One last question, sir. Please. It's being reported that the infected are dead and are actually reanimated bodies. Can you comment on this claim?"

The surgeon general, who had kept a good poker face throughout the press conference, was visibly taken aback by what should have been an absurd question. The flashing cameras distorted his face into a mixture of confusion, anger, recognition, and fear.

He walked off the podium, ignoring the question.

But as if struck by genius, he ran back to the microphone and said, "Ground squirrels. They hibernate, and a pulse is barely detected. ACRES puts the infected in a state of hibernation."

Before he could continue, guards escorted him off the stage as the press exploded in a sea of confusion.

"My dad says our government will figure it out," Christina said after watching several versions of the press conference.

Her father is a retired military engineer and staunch supporter of all things government. His faith neither surprised nor assured me. For a decade, I lived in a place where the government tries to control everything, especially the way a person thinks. I've learned to sniff out their bullshit.

"If they have it under control, how come we don't know why the South has gone dark?" I said. "I know more about ground squirrels than what's actually happening in Arizona, Texas, or Florida."

"Oh god, Cole. Your family. Have you heard from them?"

"No. I've tried calling, but it won't go through. They could be on a spaceship on their way here for all I know," I said, and we walked to the kitchen where I played her my mom's message.

"We have to do something," she said. "I don't know, warn people or—we have to warn Susan!"

Hearing Susan's name formed a lump at the back of my throat.

"How is she?" I asked, trying too hard to sound nonchalant.

I haven't talked to Susan since the night of Brooke's party. I tried reaching out eight years ago. She deleted all her social media and instructed Brian to tell me that she wanted nothing to do with me and would get a restraining order against me if I ever tried contacting her again.

"Susan's doing well. She's a cosmetic dentist—good money but work keeps her pretty busy. I guess that's a blessing though. She hasn't been the same ever since her engagement fell through and she moved back home."

"Um," I said, confused but glad for the distraction. "I thought she moved back over four years ago?"

"Yeah. She hasn't been herself since. Her ex-fiancé got a job in Buffalo and couldn't take the distance while she took care of her sick mother. The asshole broke up with her as soon as Sharon got better. I knew he was no good from the moment I met him," she said, looking herself over on the dining room mirror. "He made a stupid joke about being Susan's first. We were at a dinner party, Cole. Susan was so embarrassed."

"What a dick," I said, disgusted at a man I had never met or known anything about.

His sad excuse for a joke painted a picture in my mind of him as a cliché Long Island douchebag. However, Christina sharing that story with me also brought a smile to my face. I felt connected to Susan, as if Christina had given me a piece of history of which I would have been a part had I never gone to prison.

"Let's not waste our time on him, he's ancient history," she said. "Her eldest brother, Ben, moved upstate to Troy and opened a tattoo parlor. I heard it's doing well. Her other brother, Peter, recently moved in with Ben to help with the shop. It's like the family business now."

"Good for the O'Connells," I said.

Troy, New York, lingered on my mind, but I didn't know why.

"Chris, you should call Susan, make sure she's okay."

"I will," she said. "I'm sure she has already studied every video and news story. Have you begun to think how—and when—you're gonna reach out to her?"

Christina's tone was so easygoing, so void of any doubt Susan and I wouldn't at least *try* to reconcile, that I had to bite my lip to keep me from smiling. She was right to be confident, of course. I had thought about Susan every day while in prison: She would refuse to talk at first, curse me out, or maybe throw something at me. I would apologize for all the pain I have caused her. Susan being Susan would be stubborn, holding on to her resentment; but eventually she would burn through her anger, and the memories of the real friendship we had shared would come flooding in. We'd hug and cry, feeling the poison dissipating from our hearts.

However, instead of confessing this to Christina, I said, "Susan and I had our chance, but that time has passed. She's over it. She'll never forgive me, and I'm not going to force her."

"Susan still cares about you, in her 'I don't give a fuck' way," Christina said, meeting my gaze. "She's the one who told me you transferred from Clinton to Green Haven. She was happy—although she'll never admit it—when you majored in psychology. And she attended your father's funeral but sat at the back where no one could see her."

Her revelation shocked me. Not only had Susan kept tabs on me, but she had paid her respects. I thought she hadn't attended the funeral, and I resented her for it. My father always liked her best out of all my friends.

Hope filled my heart, but "We'll see," was all I said. I needed to revisit this new information later, when alone.

By seven thirty, hearing Alex's voice before the night ended had become a hopeless wish. Adding to my despair, I had tried countless times to call my family, but it wouldn't connect. (I had forgotten all about my parole officer.)

"Okay, it's time to go," she said, her voice suggesting what I had already guessed.

"Do you want me to follow you home?" I asked.

"Not if you can't. I don't want you to get in trouble."

"Ring the alarm. Call the authorities," I joked, remembering fond nights of having to walk her home and then walking back alone while she kept me company on the phone. "Don't worry, I think police have more pressing issues to deal with than someone driving with a suspended license."

I ran to my room and grabbed my bomber jacket. The keys to my father's truck were hanging on the hook by the door where they've always been. Getting back behind the wheel wasn't as climactic as I had envisioned. It was my first time driving since the accident, but I had never actually blamed my decision to drive that night as the reason for the tragedy.

As I pulled out of the driveway and followed Christina's taillights, all I felt was exhilaration and comfort. Driving always soothed me, and breaking the rules provided a minor high, like shoplifting or waiting until the last minute to pay a bill.

We stopped at the main gate where a young boy with bushy eyebrows and a face full of freckles sat in a booth and signaled us to lower our windows.

"I'm sorry," he said. "I can't open the gate for you."

"Excuse you?" I said, every word sounding sharp and threatening. "I'm Cole Trent, from 52 Southside. My mother is on the very board whose rules you are so intent on following. Mr. Hemburry has already explained the procedures to me, so I'm not asking you, I'm *telling* you—open the gate so I can follow my friend home. I'll be back in five."

The kid appeared to shrink in the booth, and I felt a pang of guilt. My problem wasn't with him; it wasn't his fault the world was falling apart. I looked over at Christina who had raised her window and melted into her seat.

"I-I'm sorry, Mr. Trent. What I meant was I literally can't open the gate, no one can. Everyone thought the giant wooden blocks were only there to look like a gate, but Mr. Hemburry figured out how to open and close it. However, the mechanism is old, and the chain snapped."

"Oh, okay, I'm an asshole. I'm sorry. How old are you anyway? You look a little too young to be volunteering to man the entrance," I said, attempting to pivot.

"Fourteen—almost fifteen. I'm covering for my brother. He's working the east gate 'cause, like a dumbass, he messed up and signed up for both posts. Mr. Harrison is coming at eight to relieve me."

"You guys really take this post thing seriously," I said and put the car in reverse.

By the look of Christina's flashing taillights, she had already shifted gears and had been waiting for me.

"Mr. Hemburry setup the entire system after Mr. Walker's son got sick," the fourteen-year-old said. "The Walkers tried hiding him, and the authorities had to intervene. They arrested the whole family, and no one has heard from them since."

A gust of ice hit my face, but I barely felt it. I was speechless.

Thankfully, he continued, "Mr. Trent, Bar's a good friend of mine. We're in the same grade. For weeks, all she's talked about is you coming home. I was wondering if you've heard from her. I've called, I've texted, but her phone has been off."

Meeting one of Bar's friends completed my homecoming. And seeing his worry mirror my own made me want to jump out of the car and hug him.

Fighting that urge, I said, "I haven't been able to reach her either. Don't worry, though. She's a smart girl and a fighter. Last I heard, they were on their way to the Keys. There's probably horrible cell service offshore. What's your name? I'll make sure she knows you asked about her. She'll love that."

"Eric. Eric Green," he said with a gigantic cheesy smile that screamed of puppy love. "Thank you, Mr. Trent."

"Call me Cole," I said and backed up the car.

Realizing he must be Simon's brother, I gave Christina a smirk. She pretended to ignore it and drove ahead of me.

We stopped at the center of the Pines where the four avenues meet. I hoped she would take the east route and was disappointed when she turned on to Westside Avenue. A portly man sat in the booth at the gate. He was reading a book and didn't look up when we passed him.

When we arrived at Christina's, I watched her walk in and waited until she got in her room and turned the light on to signal all was safe. I smiled, blew her a kiss, and drove off. None of this had been planned; it was all done from instinct built on decades of friendship.

I took my time driving back, detouring through side streets and enjoying every Stop sign, every bump on the road. Christina wasn't exaggerating when she said it was a ghost town. The only light came from the moon, which was crescent but luminous. I wanted to drive all over town, visit the places I used to frequent, but decided I had had enough law breaking for one day.

All things Alex engrossed me as I entered the Pines. My distress and longing for him became unendurable. Like an infected tooth, the pain overwhelmed my senses if I focused on it. So, with great effort, I guided my thoughts elsewhere—not to the happy memories Alex and I shared but instead to the darker experiences we shared. Those were the moments that solidified our bond. There's a special love that grows from seeing the shadows behind the beauty.

Chapter 13

In high school, during Holocaust Remembrance Day, regular classes were canceled and the staff would set up learning stations throughout the building. Students spent the day visiting these sites; some were purely informational and some were immersive. At the end of the day, everyone filed into the gymnasium where Holocaust survivors would share their stories with us.

Aside from the brutality they experienced, what always stayed with me was the numbness they described feeling during their darkest moment. It was an invisible, omnipresent shroud that made life colorless. They were grateful for this, though, since it dulled the sharp edges of their misery. This numbness is found in countless works written by survivors, not only of the Holocaust but any long-lived tragedy. However, no matter how vivid or detailed a description may be, nothing prepares us for what happens *after*—when the numbness is no longer necessary to dampen life.

I didn't understand how well I had adapted to the daily violence in Clinton until a few months after arriving at Green Haven. I would have paralyzing anxiety attacks before going outside for recreation, anticipating someone—*anyone*—to get into a fight or stabbed in the yard. My mind was constantly on high alert. And when nothing would occur, it were as if a sick part of me *wanted* something to happen so I could either validate my worries or, worse, so I could feel a familiarity to my new environment. I had to remind myself that life in Clinton wasn't the norm; people aren't supposed to always expect someone to get hurt.

Eventually, the anxiety attacks and feeling of impending doom became almost nonexistent. I say almost because no matter how hard I tried, how much I convinced myself I had left the violence behind, it always felt as if I were some sort of sleeper cell waiting for the right trigger word to bring me back into the fray.

It wasn't until I met Alex that I felt comfortable enough to let go of the past. He forced me to take a look within myself and question the person I was and wanted to be. For the first time since leaving Riverhead County Jail, I didn't feel as if the burden of life and the choices I had made were only mine to endure—I had found the *us* with which I belonged. Alex's patience and understanding helped me forgive myself so I could find my version of happiness. And it was his love that showed me there was a different way to be; he reminded me there was more to prison than bars and concrete.

I wasn't the only one who needed to heal though. Alex has his demons, and communicating his pain and needs wasn't his forte. We would get into big, epic, irrational fights fueled by jealousy and insecurity—which always ended with great make-up sex. But after a few months of this, I began to see the pattern.

He would have episodes of seemingly endless drive and energy, finishing all his school work, acing every exam and paper, and still found time to help me with my work. Alex would be attentive and caring, hanging on to my every word. Then without reason or warning, something—*anything*—would trigger him. We'd fight, say things we didn't mean but couldn't take back, and he'd fall into a deep depression. He described these depressive episodes like being stuck in invisible quicksand; and the more he struggled to get out, the deeper he'd sink. "It's easier to just lay in bed, watch TV, and pretend the world doesn't need me," he'd say to me.

Our last epic fight, almost two years ago, finally forced us to face the darkness within our beautiful love. It started inconspicuously enough, as all big moments do. We were still enjoying the newlyweds phase; and although I was still processing my father's death, I was well into the acceptance stage of grief.

We were at the library. I was typing the final paper for my abnormal psychology class—and dreading every second of it. Not only had I asked for an extension and was nearing my deadline, but it was my fourth draft. My teacher had rejected the previous three versions because I had "personalized the issues too much." I was writing about substance use disorders and found it difficult to take myself out of the assignment.

Alex sat next to me, brooding and idly looking over his lesson. I could tell there was something wrong. I recognized the signs—his hair was a little unkempt, his clothes a little too wrinkled, and there was the static. When Alex is in one of his moods, he electrifies the air around him. It's almost like watching over-the-air TV during a storm, the static rain distorting the picture.

I asked him what was wrong.

"Nothing. Why does something need to be wrong, Chicabear?" he said, using my pet name to give me a false sense of security.

I decided it was best to leave it alone, especially since I had a lot of work to do.

"So what is it that you're reading?" I would ask after I'd type a few paragraphs, to remind him he wasn't far from my thoughts.

"Nothing important," he'd answer.

We would repeat this dance until fifteen minutes before the library closed.

I don't know what set him off, maybe it was my asking for the time or my comment about not finishing my paper. I don't even remember his exact words. What I remember is Alex grabbing my left arm, pulling me close to him, and saying something in the vicinity of, "You really love fucking with me, don't you? Why do you care about the time, it's not like you're here anyway."

His accusation was shocking but not as shocking as the speed and strength he had grabbed me. My arm felt warm, and it throbbed under his tight grip. My skin turned red, and I knew it would bruise.

I suddenly became very aware that we weren't alone. The magic of our oasis was shattered by his brute force.

"What the fuck is your problem? Let go of me, you're hurting me," I said as I yanked my arm free, beginning to cry.

My tears were raw, ugly snot face and all—the cry of knowing he had crossed an unspeakable line and now decisions had to be made.

"Babe, I'm sorry. Please talk to me. Cole, please, just look at me. I'm sorry. I don't know what took over me," he pleaded.

His voice was cracking, his face turned red, and his eyes were watering. Seeing his pain didn't soften me—it made me angrier.

I considered hitting him, punching him in the face, thrusting my knee into his balls. But I didn't because I knew Alex would prefer me to hit him, and I was in no mood to appease him. I wanted to do all the things I've seen in movies—scream at him, call him a coward, ask if hurting me made him feel like a man—I wanted to make him feel as weak and worthless as he had made me feel. But instead, all I did was cry. So I got up and sped to the bathroom, shielding my face from anyone who may have seen me.

"Stop crying, you idiot," I said, while looking at myself in the mirror.

My arm was hot to the touch, and I squeezed it, trying to match Alex's force. I wanted it to hurt, to turn black and blue, so I could punish him by parading his shame for everyone to see.

But then, I remembered his pained face, and my steel gave way to fresh tears. Underneath my anger, I knew I didn't want to punish him; I wanted to understand him. However, it was too soon. My pain turned my heart to stone as I left the bathroom.

"I'm sorry," he repeated when I came back. "Please. I understand what *this* means, Cole. But please, just look at me."

I ignored him. I thought of taking my ring off and throw it at him as I had done in previous fights. But I didn't because this time was different. He knew it; I knew it. There will be no make-up sex.

No talk of *love* or *us*. The only question that mattered was if there would be an *us* to love.

I moved away from him and used the last ten minutes to finish my paper. (I thought it was C material at best, but I got an A.)

Three days later, we met at the school building. We were the only inmates enrolled in college at the time, so we had the room to ourselves. Alex was sitting by the back window when I entered the room. I avoided eye contact and sat at the teacher's desk at the front of the room. I set my books down in such a way that my short-sleeved shirt rode up my arm, exposing Alex's handiwork.

He walked toward me, dragging his chair, and sat across from me.

"I know I've already lost you," he began. "I can't forgive myself, so I won't ask you to."

I searched his eyes for a clue, something that would tell me he was gaming me. All I saw was genuine guilt.

"You're the best thing that has ever happened to me, and I have to live with knowing I've hurt you," he continued. "I'm a broken man, I know this—"

He stopped, unsure whether he should say the rest.

Seconds that felt like minutes passed as Alex pushed through his uneasiness. I said nothing; he wasn't going to get any help from me.

Taking a deep breath, he said, "Look, babe, there's nothing I can say that will make you change your mind. I love you. You deserve better."

I remained silent, pretending to mull over his words. I wasn't deliberating anything. I knew what I wanted—him, all of him. But I needed to understand him; no, I needed Alex to understand himself.

"Why?" I asked.

"Why what?" he said, startled by my break of silence.

"Why did you get so angry?"

"I don't know, Cole. What can I say? I'm a fuckup."

"That's not an answer, Alex. You say I deserve better, so why can't you be the better I deserve?"

Hearing his words repeated back to him always annoyed him. I didn't care; I welcomed it.

"I don't fucking know, Cole. I've dealt with this my entire life. My mom would shower me with love and affection and then throw me through a wall if I'd spill milk on the floor. My dad would take me to baseball games, play catch with me, and then disappear into his dark moods and drink himself to sleep. My brother and sister were constantly getting into fights, the slightest diss would set them off. That's all I know—drink and feel better or fight. I'm sober now and trying to get my shit together, so none of that is an option for me anymore. I don't know how to deal with this . . . this curse," he said, disgust showing all over his face.

"You know what my father calls it?" he continued. "'Oz the Great and Powerful Temper'—like it's a fucking inevitable family inheritance. It's easy for him to joke about—my parents have been on antidepressants and going to therapy for years. They've gotten their shit pretty much under control. Now my mom's the sweetest lady you could ever meet. Where the fuck were these pills when I was growing up?"

"Wait," I said, "your parents are prescribed mood stabilizers? You do realize the apple doesn't fall far from the tree."

He nodded, but it wasn't necessary. It was a rhetorical question.

"Why didn't you tell me this before, Alex?"

"Because I'm not good with this shit, Cole. I'm not used to talking about feelings or sharing what's inside. Do you know I lie awake at night wondering what's going to happen when you go home? I know I see the parole board a year after your release, but it's not a guarantee that they'll let me go. I'm scared. I'm scared you're gonna realize I'm a piece of shit from a trailer park in the middle of Bumblefuck, New York, and leave me."

His emotions had an echo, vibrating the air between us.

I took his hand and looked deep into the oceans of his eyes. For the first time, I was seeing Alex in all his glory and flaws. And I knew that I have never, and will never, see a face as beautiful as his.

I wrapped my arms around his neck and kissed as if we hadn't seen each other in years. The sex was great too.

As we zipped up and made sure we were presentable, I heard music coming from the window. It was a song by Pink, "You punched a hole in the wall and I framed it. I wish I could feel things like you." I smiled, knowing Alex didn't need fixing. His episodes are as much a part of him as his kindness and love. He has been given a different way to experience life. Alex feels the bad more keenly, but he also gets to feel the good as strongly. That's nothing to want to change, only admire.

We had more arguments, of course. Therapy and pharmaceuticals weren't options for us, rejecting the Department of Corrections' one-size-fits-all approach to mental health. Instead, we learned to read our moods and ride each other's waves.

Sometimes this complacency became trite—boring, even. We hungered for the passion of our unadulterated whims. However, we knew our limits, the danger behind wild abandon. We weren't going to allow anyone or anything—including ourselves—to destroy the *us* we had built.

I parked the car adjacent to the mailbox. As I picked through junk mail and magazines, the music blasting from Mr. Hemburry's house distracted me. All his lights were off and all the curtains drawn. But before I could investigate further, my focus was stolen by the small Manila envelope addressed to me—from Alex.

Running into the kitchen, I threw the rest of the mail on the dining room table and ripped open Alex's mail. His thoughtfulness brought me to tears. In the envelope, there was a yellow rose made of tissue paper. When I was little, my mom would always tell me, "Boys like to give girls flowers. A smart girl finds ways to let boys know which flowers she likes. If she doesn't, she can expect a lifetime of filler flowers." I've made it my business to let guys know I love yellow roses. Alex remembered.

Attached to the rose was a note:

Hey Beautiful,

I don't know what you must be feeling, but what I do know is that you're smart, free-spirited, kind, humble, and always yourself. Oh, and you're model material. You outshine the world and are capable of handling anything life throws your way.

Even though we come from different backgrounds, our hearts and minds are as one. We are always on the same page, and we always feel each other's love, especially when we're separated.

Our love is exceptional, where one is weak, the other is strong.

It's been a while since I could rely on someone. I trust you with my life, babe. Ups and downs, our love will never fade.

This time apart will be nothing but a small footnote in our story.

Love always & forever ever

His words coursed through my body, a wildfire spreading from the pit of my stomach to the tips of my fingers. I held his letter close to my heart, as if it carried life itself, when the phone rang.

Chapter 14

"Cole! Baby, I've been so worried about you," Mom said, tears choking her words.

"Mommy," I began but choked on tears of my own.

We cried until my eyes felt heavy and burned. My pain gave way to awareness, remembering how unreliable phone service had become.

"I've tried calling all day. What happened? Where are you? Are you guys still at Mr. Tomson's? Is everyone okay? Why aren't the phones working?" I bombarded her.

"Everyone is fine. I'm sorry, baby. Just—everything has been surreal," she said, and I could almost hear her teeth grinding as she decided where to begin. "You remember I mentioned the Seven Mile Bridge? They blew it up! And not just where it connects to the mainland, but everywhere it connects to a key. We lost power and water for several hours, but the island has its own water power plant and desalinization structure. Phone and internet service never returned though."

I was lightheaded with relief as air rushed into my lungs. It were as if I had been holding my breath since I last spoke to her. Now I could breathe again.

"Wait, how are you calling me?" I said, composing myself.

My mom steeled herself too and said, "There's a naval station a few islands nearby. They provided us with supplies when we arrived. Later, they returned and dropped off a satellite phone. The first thing

I did was call you, but the charger broke. Marco and Janet are trying to fix it, 'til then, we have to use it economically."

I sensed she instantly regretted using the word *economically*; it was probably something the others had been jabbering about as they decided who to call. But before I could speak, she continued.

"The mansion is huge and so beautiful—a Greek revival with the Atlantic as its backyard. There's another home on the island, a family of five. They're really nice, and two of their kids are Barbara's age. It's an Eden. Avocado trees and coconut palms dot the land. There are orange groves and tomato gardens. Mr. Tomson keeps chickens, and I'm sure we can fish the ocean. The only thing missing is you. God, you're all alone. I'm so sorry," she said and began to cry again.

I was out of tears. My family was alive and thriving. The weight of the world had been lifted off my shoulders, and now I could focus on me.

"Mommy, stop crying, please. I'm happy you guys aren't marooned on an island. I'll be okay, I swear. I'm a survivor. You want to do something for me? Stay safe. Don't drop your guard, just wait the infection out. It should eventually burn itself out. We'll see each other soon enough. Who knows? Maybe I'll learn how to drive a boat and meet you there," I said, making Mom laugh.

Her laugh is contagious—a mix of wonderment and mischievousness with a hint of wicked witch. And as her laugh warmed my body, I wished I could bottle it. After my father died, I found myself saving pieces of him (his scratchy laugh, the scent of his aftershave and how he'd always nick his birthmark with the razor, and, of course, all his shopworn sayings). But as my memory of him became more and more distant, my keepsakes began to distort. Now I find ways to save pieces of the people I love—a recording, a letter, a picture or video—all the most mundane, everyday things a person wouldn't think to miss until a loved one is truly gone.

"Oh my god, Cole, Mr. Tomson's mansion is called Villa La Tortura! I think the entire east wing is a sex dungeon! Barbara's not allowed on that side of the property."

We laughed, and as I fumbled with the phone, hoping it had a record function, she said, "Oh, let me tell you about our close call. The infected were everywhere as we left Biscayne. Two army trucks escorted us to the bridge. They were running over the infected. Sometimes they even went out of their way to do it. It was—I can't even describe it. I have no words for it. Barbara was horrified as well. She lowered her window and stuck her head out to vomit. One of those things lunged at her. Thankfully Pilar was able to pull her back in time. Barbara was crying but unharmed. Pilar's okay too. It tried biting off a chunk of her arm, but its teeth only grazed her."

Her last words affected me as if I had been hooked up to an IV filled with arctic water.

"Mother, where's Pilar?"

"Um, I don't know. I think she's upstairs resting. Why?" she asked, but her uneven tone told me she had begun putting the pieces together.

"It's the bite. You have to find her now!" My urgency startled her, and I could hear her running into the house.

"Please, don't engage her," I said as she yelled for Pilar, Marc, and Barbara.

"She's in her room. Her door is locked." I could hear her rapping on the door and fiddling with the doorknob. "Pilar, sweetheart, please answer me. Please, are you okay?" she pleaded, desperation giving way to terror. "Pil—"

"Laura, sorry, I didn't hear you," I heard Pilar say as she opened the door. "I passed out. I don't feel so good."

Her voice sounded weak and distant.

Mom helped her back to bed, closing the door behind them.

"Who's on the phone?" Pilar asked.

"Cole. You want to talk to him? I'll be right back, I have to find Marc," Laura said, handing Pilar the phone.

"Pilar?" I said. "How are you feeling? What do you feel?"

"Cole, it feels like antifreeze coursing through my veins. It's the fucking bite," she said, breaking into a dry cough.

"So you know what's happening then?"

"Yeah, I figured it out. That thing barely nipped me, and it hasn't stopped bleeding yet. My body is so cold, but my head is hot. I feel it burning up my brain cells, destroying everything that makes me, *me*. I can't let it use me to hurt my family," she said.

Her voice had sounded weak, confused at first; but now it sounded sure—resolved.

"Pilar, what are you saying?" I asked, already knowing the answer.

"I've seen what this sickness does to people. I know the ravenous death that follows. This island—it's real. Our family is safe, they can make it work here. But not with me," she said, tears accentuating her words. "I know your mom will be back any minute with your brother. I'm not sure they'll allow me to do what must be done. And I wouldn't want them to live with the burden of such a decision. Cole, I have to do it now while I'm still me. I have to get to the beach. Blood could carry the infection. Make sure they check under my pillow, okay? There are letters for everyone."

"I will."

"Do you think Barbara will forgive me? I didn't want to leave her without a mother," she said and began sobbing.

"Mom, what's wrong? Who are you talking with?" asked a tiny unmistakable voice.

"Barbara, I'm sorry. I'm just tired and stressed," Pilar said, sucking back her tears.

Come on, I thought, *This is your chance to do it right—to say goodbye.*

"I love you so much. You know I'd never want to hurt you," she began. "I know you're scared—we all are—but I need you to be strong. Life is going to get really hard and ugly. You're going to find yourself having to make impossible decisions. Please don't let that change you for the worse. Don't become someone you don't want to be. This thing that's happening to the world will end one day. You just make sure you're on the right side of history, okay?"

"Why are you telling me this?" Bar said.

"Just needed to say it. Here, you want to talk to your uncle? I have to go get something from downstairs," she said, and I heard the bed creak as she stood.

Lowering her voice, Pilar said, "Cole, I'm sorry we weren't able to see you home. I love you. And whatever you do, stay alive. Take care of our family. Don't forget, you're a fighter. Survive."

I wanted to scream, cry, tell Bar what her mother was about to do, and put an end to this madness. But I didn't. Instead, I played the part.

"Cuteness!" I said as soon as Pilar handed her the phone. "How are you? I miss you so much. You know, I met one of your friends. Eric Green? He was asking about you."

I tried to sound cheerful, but I probably sounded as if I were speaking through a straw.

"Eric asked about me? That's nice, but how did you meet him? Did he come over to the house looking for his—" she said and was interrupted when Marc and Mom rushed into the room.

"Where is she, Barbara? Where's your mother?" Marc asked, his voice frantic.

"I-I don't know. She said she needed to get something. Why? What's wrong, Dad."

Fear saturated Bar's words—a fear she would need to learn to live with.

Marc ran out of the room, screaming Pilar's name. My mom sat next to Bar and cried.

"Co-Co, what's going on. What did my mom tell you?"

The terror in her voice almost knocked me to the ground.

"She said check under her pillow. Everything you need to know is there," I said and wondered if she'll ever forgive me.

I heard the ruffling of sheets and the unforgettable sound of a gunshot. Its roar blasted my senses and ushered the end of Bar's childhood.

Startled, she dropped the phone. I tried calling back, but it wouldn't go through.

I threw myself on the cold kitchen tile and cried, beating my fist into the floor. Rage overtook me, and I began trashing the kitchen—pots, cutlery, food everywhere. There was a gold-plated spaceship on the counter. I hurled it across the room, realizing it was Bar's science fair trophy as it crashed through the window over the sink.

I ran to the broken window and searched for it, but it was too dark to see anything. Then coming from Mr. Hemburry's house, I heard the song that, ever since I was seven years old, plays on repeat in my mind whenever I go through a major life moment—"Landslide." Except, Mr. Hemburry wasn't blasting the original version; it was a male group I didn't recognize. But the lyrics were unmistakable: "So take this love, take it down. Oh, if you climb a mountain and you turn around. If you see my reflection in the snow-covered hills, well, the landslide will bring you down."

The song followed me as I crawled to the dining room table. I made sure the phone's volume was on high and rested my head on the rug. Exhaustion, guilt, and pain lulled me into a dreamless slumber.

Chapter 15

The sun's rays warmed my face, pulling me out of my sleep. For an instant, I had no idea where I was. I panicked, expecting a CO to knock on my bars and ask me if I want chow. Grabbing on to the table's black metal leg, I ran my other hand over the rough rug, and recognition began creeping back.

There were no missed calls on the phone's memory. I remembered my parole interview but quickly dismissed it as a low-priority problem. I crawled out from under the table and walked to the sliding glass door, scanning the deck and backyard for Bar's science trophy.

It was on the bushes encircling the pool. Mr. Hemburry's musical soiree had ended. The sky was a bright blue, the sun engulfed the scenery in white light. Any other time, it would have been considered a lovely October morning; however, due to circumstances, it didn't look beautiful—it looked sterile.

The cleaning process began slow, starting with duct-taping the broken window and picking up glass shards. Luckily, the TV remote was unharmed. I was hoping to learn of some new life-saving development. But every channel was playing either reruns or movies, and the news channels were replaying old interviews. I tried searching the TV menu, but TBA appeared on every time slot. So I began channel surfing the old way, one channel at a time.

I almost settled on the original king of ASMR, Bob Ross, but decided on *Sex and the City* instead. Carrie Bradshaw's voice has always soothed me. So I listened to her make fun of scrunchies and have a life-altering revelation over a Post-it, as I scrubbed Taco Bell off the walls and escaped the world for a little while.

The morning went fast. I had done a good job of running away from the truth, but as noon approached and I finished cleaning the kitchen, reality made its unwelcomed return.

Staring at the phone, willing it to ring, I felt the dreamlike tentacles of madness attempting to snare my mind. I called Christina, but it went straight to voice mail, and I wasn't ready to call her house and talk to her parents. None of my family's numbers went through, which was actually a bit of a relief.

What would I tell Bar? I thought. *"Your mom loved you very much, but she was infected and didn't want to hurt or burden anyone with her death"?*

I knew all this and decided to talk about Eric Green instead.

Who I wanted—needed—to talk with was Alex. And he was the only person I couldn't even *try* to call. Having to wait by the phone for a proof of life frustrated and sickened me, literally. I ran to the bathroom and vomited hot bile.

As I sat on the bathroom floor, recovering my breath, I remembered the blue nylon fanny pack with its two doses of Naloxone. I wondered if it was anything like Suboxone, the orange drug used to treat opioid addiction. However, if used without taking opiates, it creates the very same high it's trying to combat.

Breaking sobriety saddened me, but reality suffocated me. I wanted to escape. I rinsed my mouth and walked to the liquor cabinet. Mom's favorite wines have been removed, but I knew the strong spirits remained. My mouth watered in anticipation, but when I entered the living room, I was surrounded by the faces of my family. I needed to stay in reality for them. For me.

From the doorway, I saw Alex's yellow rose atop the dining room table, and it fired me up better than any vodka ever could. So I decided to do what Alex would have done—work out. I changed into a new tank top and light-fabric pajama pants, choosing to go sans underwear and socks; they'd only get in the way.

I grabbed the phone and headed to the basement, my domain, once upon a time.

Chapter 16

"How things have changed," I said as I turned on the lights of the almost unrecognizable basement.

The laundry room, bathroom, and my old room—which is now Bar's—remained. The kitchenette and living room have been knocked down to create a state-of-the-art gym and sauna. The walls are adorned with floor-to-ceiling mirrors, and a large area on the back corner has been made into a boxing ring, all Marc's doing. I guess Mom wasn't the only one who made impulse purchases after Dad's death.

I tried opening Bar's door to see the changes she's made to my old kingdom, but it was locked. The "Do Not Enter" sign on the door angered me for some reason.

"We'll see about that," I said and made a mental note to look for the house keys.

The gym and the entire house are equipped with surround-sound controlled by the home's mainframe, which is accessed by the touchscreens in every room. It took a few minutes to figure out the settings, and when I got the hang of it, I found the large music library. Every family member has his and her own music file, including me. My brother had transferred my extensive music collection from my old computer into the house's mainframe.

"Thank you, Marc," I said, tipping my imaginary hat to him.

I was tempted to go through everyone's music collection and the folder labeled "New Music" but decided against it. I was about to push my body to its limits. I needed a surefire playlist.

Maybe next time, I told myself.

So I mostly picked songs from my file, borrowing a few songs from other family members, and composed the theme of the next forty-five minutes:

1. Notorious B.I.G. ft. Eminem—"Dead Wrong"
2. Kanye West—"Spaceship"
3. Shakira ft. Alejandro Sanz—"La Tortura"
4. Madonna—"Hung Up"
5. Christina Aguilera—"Fighter"
6. Linkin Park—"Numb"
7. Matt Maeson—"Cringe"
8. Twenty One Pilots—"Heavydirtysoul"
9. Switchfoot—"Meant to Live"
10. Moby ft. Gwen Stefani—"South Side"
11. Muse—"Madness"
12. Staind—"It's Been Awhile"
13. Righteous Brothers—"Unchained Melody"

"Dead Wrong" began blasting over the speakers as I entered the boxing ring. I performed Sun Salutation to warm up. (I've been doing yoga since I was sixteen when my mom introduced me to it after horseback riding wreaked havoc on my thighs.) And as the tempo increased, I got lost in the moment.

Alex taught me how to work out—train. Yoga aside, I had relied on youth and genetics to keep everything tight. But as my thirties neared, I realized one universal truth: no matter how genetically gifted one is, in the end, gravity always wins.

And although violence was everywhere in prison (it's the nature of the beast), I had never had to resort to fighting—physically, that is. A fighter I was not but decided when in Rome.

"Come on, Alex," I begged. "Teach me how to fight."

We were the only ones in the gym's weight room. He volunteered to clean the gym once a week. And four months into our relationship, *his* chores had become *ours*.

"Why do you want to fight, babe?" he said while spraying cleaner on the windows. "You have me, I'll hurt anyone who fucks with you."

"That's not the point. I want to learn to defend myself, and you're the best fighter I know," I explained. "You *know* what happened to me in Clinton. I don't ever want to feel that defenseless again."

I knew bringing up a failed rape attempt from three years earlier was a low move, but I needed him to take me seriously.

"Wait, is someone fucking with you? Yo, don't lie to me, are you okay?" he said, dropping the cleaning bottle and rushing toward me.

"Relax, I'm fine," I said, gently laying my hand on his chest and looking him in the eye. "I'm just serious about this, Alex. I want to be able to protect myself no matter what happens. And, babe, I'm getting fat—marriage is making me lazy. It'll be a good way to work out. Two birds one stone, you know?"

His body relaxed, and a smile touched his lips.

"You're nowhere near fat," he said. "I don't know, Cole. I love that you're not violent, I don't want to change that. Besides, you're already smart, calculating, manipulative, and ambitious. You're dangerous in your own right. Imagine if you also knew how to fight."

"You flatter me, Mr. Oz," I joked, unsure of how much he had meant in jest. "So teach me how to fight and help make me *more* dangerous."

I rubbed my hand over the front of his shorts, making sure he was at full attention.

He smiled, shaking his head, and I knew I had convinced him.

"Fine. We'll sign up for the boxing class so we can train alone," he said. "But you gotta take this shit seriously, okay?"

I nodded, looking like an eager student, and pulled out his dick through the leg of his shorts. I got on my knees and showed him how grateful I was.

We began training a week later.

"Have you ever heard of Krav Maga?" he asked.

"Is it that thing douche lords who've watched too many Jack Reacher movies think they can learn," I joked.

"Be serious," he reproached. "*Krav* means 'combat' and *Maga* means 'contact' in Hebrew. It's derived from boxing, wrestling, aikido, judo, and karate, with realistic fight training. I'm going to teach you certain aspects of this—the parts that are ideal for combat in small spaces, that is."

"How did you learn Krav Maga?" I asked, skeptical and fascinated at the same time.

"When I first came upstate, I was bunked with an older man named Doran. He was from Israel and had been part of Israel's counterterror army—or so the story was. He rarely spoke, and I never asked if the rumors were true," he began, his eyes unfocusing and going back in time. "One day, the COs searched our cell and threw our property everywhere. I was picking up papers off the floor when Doran came back from program. He must have thought I wrecked the place or that I was going through his shit because when the cell door opened, he rushed me. Now, I'm no small guy and Doran *was* like five six, a buck thirty—if that. I was just going to push him back, but this motherfucker spun under my reach, got behind me, kicked in my knee, and got me on the floor. I rushed him time and time again, and he always knocked me down using my own weight to unbalance me."

"So did he fuck you up?" I asked, enthralled in his story and practically drooling.

"Nah, he never attacked me. I finally stopped rushin' him and said 'Teach me.' Doran said something in Hebrew and smiled. We trained for three years. Brutal lessons—broken bones and torn ligaments. And even then, I knew I was only getting the watered-down version of Krav Maga."

"Hold on, you are not breaking my bones!" I protested. "I just want to learn to defend myself."

"We're not taking it that far, babe," he said. "I'm going to teach you to handle yourself in close quarters and against a larger opponent."

He trained me for the next two years. At first, I found the concept of using my body to cause someone else physical pain much easier in theory than in practice. I would cringe whenever my fist made contact with Alex and cowered when his fist would return the gesture.

"Have you ever been in a fight?" he asked.

"I've never even been punched," I confessed. "My brother used to torture me by locking me in closets, but he drew the line at violence."

"Okay then," he said. "We need to get you past the fear of pain. And the only way to get over the fear of something is by learning about it and collecting enough safe memories to dampen the fear. I call it logic and triumph."

We made a game of sneaking up on each other and landing a punch, a game which I quickly got the hang of.

"Shit your feet are quiet," he said, rubbing his arm where I had punched him. "You're like a little bear—a Chicabear."

And thus a pet name was born.

The black mat was sleek with my sweat. The music's tempo slowed down, cueing my workout's cool down, and I began Sun Salutation.

Midpose, the phone rang as the Righteous Brothers sang, "Lonely rivers sigh, I'll be coming home, wait for me."

Chapter 17

"Excuse me, Mr. Trent? This is Simon Green from up front. You have a visitor, but I don't see anything in the logbook."

Endorphins had me feeling peppy, and I was tickled to be talking to Christina's young paramour, who was eight the last time I saw him. I wanted to tell him that Mr. Trent was my father or my brother; however, I was the only Trent in the house—the king of the castle.

"Who's the visitor, Simon?"

"Uh, a Mr. Singh. Faaahsal Singh," he said, butchering Fessy's name. "Should I let him in?"

My heart skipped a beat. It was bittersweet—I was happy to hear from Fessy but knew his unexpected return could only mean bad news.

"Yes, let him in, Simon. The gate's still broken, right? Can you please direct Faysal to the East entrance and call that gate to let him through."

"Of course. No problem, Mr. Trent," he said, and I almost told him to drop the Mr. Trent shit. "Excuse me, sir, have you seen Mr. Hemburry? He was supposed to relieve Mr. Harrison this morning, but he never showed up. I've called, but all his phones are off. I don't mean to impose on you. I just know Mr. Hemburry is your neighbor."

Hearing that John Hemburry had missed his shift made my neurons fire in all directions, as if my brain were trying to complete a jigsaw puzzle in the shortest amount of time.

He said his wife was sick, I thought, *the loud music last night, his absence—*

"Excuse me, Mr. Trent, are you still there?" Simon said, preventing me from completing the dark puzzle.

"Yeah. Sorry, um, I haven't seen him, but I think he's busy with the twins since his wife is sick," I said, the final word carrying the weight of the world. "Don't worry about the front gate, it's not even like it works. Go home, be with your family. I'll stop by Mr. Hemburry's house and tell him you couldn't wait, okay?"

"Thank you. I really appreciate that, Mr. Trent—"

"Call me Cole. Mr. Trent is my brother," I interrupted, unable to help myself.

Simon laughed, sounding every bit the handsome young man Christina had described.

"Okay, mister—Cole. Please let Mr. Hemburry know I'll be back for my shift tomorrow morning. Thank you again. I'll send Mr. Singh over right away."

I hung up and ran upstairs. I wanted to shower but knew there wasn't enough time. So I lathered up with one of my mom's many lotions, changed into a fresh pajama bottom and tank top, making sure to put on underwear and socks, and tied my hair in a messy bun.

Instead of waiting by the front door for Fessy, I put on my bomber jacket and heavy steel-toe boots and headed outside. The sun was blinding, and I considered running back inside to put on sunglasses but was distracted by Mr. Hemburry's ominous home.

His curtains were drawn, and I couldn't spot a single bird on or near his house.

I started walking toward it, but the foreboding was so thick, it felt as if I were being repelled by an invisible force, when a black Land Rover pulled into my driveway and parked.

Fessy, wearing a brown trench coat he wasn't wearing yesterday, stepped out of the SUV. I ran to greet him and stopped a few feet away, noticing the right side of his coat was caked with dried blood. Instinctively I pulled back and covered my mouth.

"No, it's not mine," he said dryly, as if he were reading a to-do list. "It had blood on it when I put it on."

There were dark circles around his eyes and a detachment to his demeanor.

"Fessy," I said, extending my arms to hug him. "What happened to you?"

"I—"

His words choked in his throat as he fell into my arms and cried.

It didn't feel safe to show such vulnerability out in the open. So as he cried, I supported him on my shoulders and led him into my house.

"It was the Day of Judgment, Armageddon, Ragnarök— everything rolled into one," Fessy said once his tears had dried.

We were sitting at the dining room table, and he was holding a glass of water that had yet to touch his lips.

"I made it as far as Westbury on the Northern Parkway. There were cops everywhere directing traffic and people on foot. All of a sudden, the cars on the opposite side—the lanes heading away from Queens—began crashing into each other. They were trying to escape something we couldn't see . . . yet we all knew what it was."

His voice sounded sandy, and he finally took a sip of water.

"People grabbed whatever they could out of their cars and began running."

He stopped, took another sip of water, and remained silent while his shell-shocked brain processed what he was going to say. And I wasn't sure if I wanted to hear it.

"The cars on the outer lanes broke away in all directions—over sidewalks, through trees, anywhere they could fit. I was in the inner lane and closed in by other cars, so I ditched my ride and ran to the nearest exit ramp. There was a girl standing in the middle of a grassy knoll. She looked to be around ten, although it was hard to tell because of the blood. She was covered in it. People were driving all around her. A man in a suit rushed toward her. He picked her up, and when he turned to run back, the girl bit into his neck. They stumbled down the hill and a police truck ran over them. A woman screamed, and then we were in hell."

Fessy exhaled as if he had been holding his breath the entire time.

"Women and children were being tackled by those things," Fessy continued. "People were screaming and shoving each other to the ground. The people who had locked themselves in cars were surrounded by the infected. It's that groan they make . . . that's how they communicate—one groans, then another, and another. Alerting each other to—I don't know—victims? Food?"

A glaze fell over his eyes, and he became stuck in his memory.

"Fessy," I said, attempting to bring him back to me, "how did you get away?"

"Um, there was a man. His name is—*was*—Caden. He's who I got this coat from. I couldn't move, Cole. I couldn't stop watching the carnage around me. Caden ran up to me, shook me, and told me we needed to go. He led me into the woods, away from everything and everyone. I followed him in silence. My brain was on autopilot, unable to process what I had witnessed. I'd be dead if it hadn't been for him," he said, tears running down his face.

He wiped them away, knowing he must do justice to this part of his story.

"He led me to a small park and handed me a juice box. I told him I wasn't thirsty, but he insisted. He asked where I was heading. I told him Newburgh, and he said it would be impossible to get there. He had come from that direction and said Queens and Brooklyn were overrun with the infected. He asked if I had somewhere else I could go, somewhere in Nassau or Suffolk. That's when I remembered your address."

"Thank god," I interjected.

Fessy smiled and continued, "He was heading to Ronkonkoma and said it was next to Smithtown. And like that, we were partners in all this."

"What happened to him?" I asked.

His eyes told me something horrible had happened to Caden—something that had changed Fessy forever.

"Caden knew all the side roads, so we avoided civilization and traveled all night on foot. As we crossed a school parking lot, a car flashed its headlights. It was a Honda, but the two men in it wore soldier's uniforms. But they didn't look right. Their eyes were bloodshot, and their uniforms had blood splatter," he said, hate and disgust beginning to sharpen his words.

"The driver said we were breaking the law by being out past curfew, which made the passenger snicker. Caden explained what we had been through. He pleaded for their help. The driver pulled out a gun and shot Caden," Fessy sobbed, his tears smacking on the floor as he showed me where the bullet had exited Caden's coat.

"They howled as they sped away. I pulled him behind a tree and held his hand until he passed away. They killed him . . . for no fucking reason. I was freezing, so I took his coat and looked for the nearest police station."

"I'm so sorry," I said, unable to make eye contact with him. "I can't imagine . . ."

"I found a station. The streets were empty and the building looked empty, but I could sense them watching me as I banged on the door. Can you believe that? Caden was killed in cold blood, and there was *no one* to exact justice. So I walked into the car dealership across the street, found the keys to the Rover, and drove off. If they can't be bothered with murder, they can go fuck themselves over stealing a car. I also went back for Caden's body, but it was gone."

He stood at the sliding glass door and looked at the sky. When he turned to face me, he had the same faraway look he had had yesterday at the gas station.

"Cole, there's no going back to normal from this. It's the end, period. I don't know how this sickness came to be, but it doesn't matter—there won't be anything left after it. And it's heading straight for us."

"It's not the end, don't say that. We're here, aren't we? We have lives to live, people to love. If we start this 'it's the end' bullshit, we'll be as good as dead," I said with more anger and frustration than I had intended. "What happened to you is horrible. What happened to my family is horrible. But I'll be damned if I'm defeated before putting up a fight."

I felt hot tears forming, and I willed them to stop.

Not yet, I told myself.

Fessy looked at me with an odd expression, as if he couldn't decide if he wanted to cry or smile, and said, "What happened to your family?"

I told him about Pilar's fate and Alex's situation. And once I finished, my tears were allowed to flow. We had a good cry and heard a noise coming from the sliding glass door, startling us.

We jumped in unison, falling over each other, expecting to see one of the infected crawling on the deck and trying to break through the glass. Instead, we saw a fat gray squirrel holding an acorn as it stared at us. We broke out in unfathomable, stomach-hurting laughter. And in that moment, I knew—we'll endure or die trying.

"Okay. We need food, water, and whatever other supplies we can get," I said. "If power fails, there's a portable generator and fuel tanks in the shed, but I don't know how long we'll need to hunker down. So I'm thinking we focus on canned foods and anything with a long shelf life. I don't know how much cash there's in the house. Do you think credit cards still work?"

"I don't know about credit cards, but I have a boatload of cash in the Rover. Found it when I was looking for keys," he said. His mischievous smile was reassuring. "But where are we going to get food? Everything is closed."

"Are you up for more breaking and entering?" I asked, returning his smile.

"Let's do it, but I gotta use your phone first," he said, and it reminded me that I couldn't leave the house.

Fessy dialed his number and walked into the living room. He returned a few minutes later. His eyes were a little red, but his demeanor appeared positive.

"They're okay," he said. "They've barricaded themselves in the upstairs apartment, and my brother's protecting them."

"Good. But I have bad news. I can't go and break the law with you. The phone is my only connection to Alex and my family."

"I understand," Fessy said, nodding. "I'll get the supplies, just tell me where to go."

I gave him directions to the nearby 7-Eleven and supermarket and made sure he changed into Marc's clothes before leaving. As I watched him drive away, I picked up the phone and called Christina's house, not caring if her parents answered.

Thankfully, they didn't, and I told Christina everything that had transpired since we last saw each other.

"I'm scared," she said after a long silence.

"Yeah, me too," I said.

I wanted to comfort her, tell her everything was going to be okay, but I chose not to. She needed to be scared. Fear puts life in perspective.

"My dad is boarding up the downstairs and moving all our supplies upstairs. I'm pretty sure he's ready to block off the staircase and force us to come in and out of the house through the window!" she said, feigning amusement, but I detected the high-pitched sound of terror.

"That's really smart of him," I began. "If anyone is ready to get through this shit, it's your father. Remember when our dads went camping upstate? For years they told the story about the bear that stole their food and they had to live off the land for three days."

We laughed, remembering the fond memory and drawing strength and hope from it.

"Do you think your parents will ever forgive me?" I asked, emboldened by nostalgia.

"Of course, Cole. You're family. It's just . . . you know how militant my parents are. They never understood the drugs. They blamed you for my addiction, and I never let them believe otherwise. I'm sorry, it was just easier to have them blame you than me," she said, her confession not at all shocking.

"You have nothing to be sorry about. I understand. I probably would've done the same thing," I said, feeling years of guilt dissipating between us.

"You know what?" she began. "I don't want to be alone right now. I'm coming over, and I'm telling my parents exactly where I'm going. I'll see you soon, okay?"

She hung up before I was able to answer.

I tried calling my family and had no luck, so I ran around the house, picking things up, making sure everything was clean. I don't know why—habit, I suppose.

And then the phone rang.

"You have a collect call from—"

One, one, one, one! I thought, mashing my phone.

"Babe? Listen, I can't talk for long. I love you. I'm sorry, I was—"

Alex's call dropped before I was able to say a word. And for the umpteenth time since yesterday, I fell on my knees and cried.

Chapter 18

There has to be a limit to how many tears we're allotted for any given situation. I was ready for the floodgates to open, but after the first tears flowed, they stopped—no more.

Ice coursed through my veins, and clarity liberated my mind. I knew what had to be done—get Alex. All I needed to do was figure out how.

Pacing in the living room, I dissected Alex's words, *"I'm. Sorry. I. Was."*

Between each word I heard was the unmistakable groans of the infected in the background. And that knowledge tortured and frightened me.

I called the prison, but as suspected, no one answered. Looking out the window, I felt my steely resolve give way to desperate insanity, when Fessy and Christina drove up at the same time. I considered greeting them outside but decided to let them introduce themselves. Christina looked stunning, dressed in her finest, and her makeup looked fresh and natural.

Why is she so well dressed? I wondered. *Did she expect us to go out on the town? Habit, I guess.*

By the big, goofy smile on Fessy's face, I could tell he liked what he saw.

I opened the door and said, "I see you've met each other."

"Yeah," Christina said, leading Fessy by the arm. "And you didn't tell me how handsome he is."

Fessy grinned from cheek to cheek, and his face was as red as a rose. In that moment, I was happy, glad to see after everything that was happening to the world, we could still find sweet distractions.

"That was quick, Fessy," I said, eyeing the boxes in the Rover. "What did you find for us?"

"The supermarket had been depleted, but the 7-Eleven was untouched. The front door was locked. I was about to move on when I spotted the back door, and can you believe it was open?" he said and flashed a smile made for a bank commercial. "I got as much as I could, but think we should make more trips before someone else finds the trove."

"You're right. But I think you should take my father's pickup so you could fill the entire bed," I said and turned to Christina. "Chris, maybe you can follow Fessy in a separate car, and we'll take the whole store."

"Nope," she answered. "Sorry, but I'm not made for looting. Why don't *you* go with Faysal and *I'll* relax at the house."

"Because I have to wait by the phone," I protested. "What if Alex or my family calls?"

I wanted to tell her about Alex's call but decided not to. I didn't want to make the moment any heavier than it needed to be, knowing *something* would eventually do that anyway.

"I'll answer and pretend to be you," she joked. "Don't worry, I'll take down notes, record the call—whatever you need me to do. You can take my phone, just in case."

Alex and Christina speaking for the first time intrigued me, and it would be nice to go "shopping" for the things I like.

"Fine. But if Alex calls, you *must* have him tell you *everything*. Tell him about Queens and Brooklyn being overtaken. I'll be back soon, so whoever calls, tell them to call right back, okay?"

"Ditto," she answered, unlocking her phone and handing it to me.

Fessy had unloaded the boxes during my exchange with Christina. I quickly scoured my room and found my old sunglasses collection. With no time for a fashion show, I put on my Burberry aviators and headed out in Dad's truck. Driving without a license, breaking and entering, looting—I was really tempting the fates of parole.

I followed Fessy to 7-Eleven and noticed there was no one manning the gate at the end of Eastside. It was left wide open. When we entered the parking lot, I backed up the truck's bed up to the door, parked, and began our "five-finger discount" shopping spree.

He dealt with the heavy stuff—water, sodas, boxes, canned food. After grabbing the essentials (first-aid kits, medicines, hygiene supplies, lighters, coffee, tea, powdered milk), I focused on my favorite snacks. I grabbed all the candy, gum, mints, and chocolates I could find, spending extra time in the pastry–cereal aisle.

"I thought you quit," he said, watching me throw cartons of cigarettes in the bed.

"I did. But, Fessy, we don't know how long we're gonna be locked indoors or what shit we're gonna have to live through. I rather be prepared. It is perfectly okay to have a cigarette when the world is devouring itself."

As he laughed, a silver van crashed through the front of the store. It sounded like a bomb.

All the windows shattered, creating a blizzard of glass, inside the store. The noised stunned me, and I heard a beep humming in my ear as I ran inside to help—assuming the driver must have lost control and crashed.

The man in the van appeared to be fine as he attempted to kick open his jammed door. When he saw me walking toward him, he smiled so widely I could see his gums.

He stuck his hand out the window and pointed a gun at me.

"This is all you people's fault!" he shouted and fired.

Fessy tackled me from behind, covering my body with his. The bullet blasted a hole in the ceiling—nowhere near us. All the gunshot accomplished was hurt my ears and make me angry. I've met real killers; I've lived with them. I wasn't afraid of them then, and I sure as hell wasn't going to be terrorized by some fuck with a gun and no aim.

I crawled toward a metal rod on the floor, when Fessy grabbed my wrist.

"We have to go—now!" he said, snapping me back to my senses.

We ran and jumped into our cars. As I drove away, I heard wild gunshots and that crazy fuck laughing—a taunting, insane laugh, like a clown laughing while burning alive. Without discussing it, Fessy and I decided not to tell Christina about the guy in the van.

The three of us unloaded the loot and stored it in the basement. My mom's affinity for open spaces, large windows, and sliding glass doors made it impossible to defend the upstairs against a horde of whatever was to come.

Even though Christina told me no one had called, I obsessively checked the phone. I saw Alex's last call, and my body began trembling. It felt strange, as if my mind had split in two and were fighting for control. On one side was the crying mess who's one bad news away from giving up, and on the other side was the resilient fighter ready to do whatever to survive. I took a deep breath and chose to be the latter, banishing all thoughts of a missing family and faraway love.

"Okay, we have music and liquor. Let's make a party out of fortifying the house," I said and took drink orders: gin for Fessy, brandy for Christina, and vodka for me.

Drinking alone during the apocalypse is sad and irresponsible; drinking with others during the apocalypse is cathartic, and, well, it's still irresponsible—but context.

I handed them their shots and said a toast, "To living."

"To living," they said, although their timing was off and the distortion made it sound as if they said, "To *the* living."

Christina and Fessy operated the house's controls, making sure the music was heard in every room, and created a playlist—peppered with a few of my choices. Manual labor is not as fun without some

Britney. We divided the tasks among us, took another shot, and went to work. In the garage,

I filled up every empty bottle, bucket, and container with water. But after filling up the millionth bucket, the task became grinding. It reminded me too much of prison, of being at the mercy of others. If we needed to clean up and we missed shower time or an officer denied us a shower for whatever reason, our only option was to fill up a bucket with—hopefully—warm water and wash up. It's called a "birdbath"; I hated it.

Christina walked into the garage and asked if I could help her board up the basement windows. I jumped at the offer.

The three of us worked well together and finished before sundown. Downstairs was secured, and Fessy had even managed to move the small generator from the shed to the basement with the rest of our supplies. (Bar's room was completely ignored.) Since it was impossible to effectively barricade all the sliding glass doors and windows upstairs, Christina (inspired by my work on the kitchen window) duct-taped the glass like people do before a hurricane and covered them with thick blankets which we nailed to the wall. Where possible, we moved furniture in front of a glass door for added security. The sofas were moved to the outside of the hallway, creating a fortress around the entrance and making a fast retreat to the basement possible.

"Chris, it's gonna be curfew soon. Do you want one of us to follow you home?" I said, instantly regretting the alcohol.

None of us had even considered that someone would have had to drive when we decided to do shots.

"Not me," Fessy said. "Nope. Sorry. Too drunk."

"Oh shit," I said, feeling a buzz of my own.

"To be honest," she said, "I was hoping to stay over. I don't want to sleep alone tonight."

"Nobody does, but isn't your dad going to have a seizure if you don't come home? I'm surprised he hasn't shown up in a tank to get you."

"Brother is covering for me. I was waiting until after curfew to call home. You know Dad isn't gonna want to break the law," she said, and we laughed at her father's innate need to abide by the rules—no matter the circumstances.

"Come sit with us, Faysal," she said. "It's bonding time. Let's play 'Never Have I Ever.'"

Fessy grabbed a few snacks from the kitchen. I grabbed the three bottles and handed Christina three shot glasses. The three of us made ourselves comfortable in our cushion-made fortress.

While playing "Never Have I Ever," the light began to flicker—not often enough to alarm us but often enough for awareness to creep in. The blankets and boards covering the windows made us feel as if we were in a secluded cave, safe. The music had been turned off as soon as the sun had gone down. The outside world was kept at bay. We could've been surrounded by the infected, and we wouldn't have noticed.

I knew we were being irresponsible, stupid, reckless—all of it. But for that hour or two, we played, laughed, joked, bonded—lived—and forgot our miseries. In my opinion, when life is misery, a temporary escape is worth calculated risks.

It's not all about survival; it's also about saving a life worth living.

Chapter 19

"Never have I ever been pregnant or gotten someone pregnant," Christina said, smirking.

She and I looked around, giggling, expecting no one to have to drink. Fessy's head was down, staring a hole through his shot glass. He drank, never making eye contact with us.

Fessy had never mentioned having a kid. I didn't know where that story led but felt it was nowhere pleasant.

"Chris, it's almost eight," I said before she had a chance to comment on Fessy's revelation. "You should call home."

"Yeah, you're right. Pass me the phone. I gotta pee too," she said and walked to the bathroom, locking the door behind her.

"I am fucking drunk, and I want a cigarette," I said, retrieving a carton from the basement and standing at my room's doorway so I wouldn't flood our makeshift fortress with smoke.

Smoking my cigarette, I took a good look at Fessy. He was wasted, slumped against the door to the master bedroom, and nestled in blankets and pillows. We had made sure the shots had been filled less than a quarter way as to not get too drunk, but I remembered Fessy is only twenty years old.

"Come on, Fessy. Time to call it a night," I said and put out my cigarette inside a soda can.

Supporting him on my shoulders, I walked him to Marc's room and laid Fessy on the bed.

"Faysal," I said, looking him in the eye, "how are we gonna get to Newburgh?"

"Huh? What are you talking about?" he said, sounding completely sober.

"I need to get Alex. I can't leave him in there," I said and turned the light on. "You must want to make it back to your family, well, so do I. Mine's in Florida, but Alex is family too."

"He's in prison. They're not just gonna let him out because people are getting sick."

"Get real. This is more than a sickness, and you know it. You've *seen* it. I'm not even sure there will be a government to keep him in—you know what, that doesn't matter. I'll worry about that. You just think of how we're gonna get there. Without passing Queens, or Brooklyn, or Nassau, or any highway."

"What . . . about . . . a . . . boat . . ." he said as he closed his eyes, the alcohol forcing sleep upon him.

I took off his shoes and moved him on his side.

He woke up and said, "I didn't drop out of seminary because Dad got sick. That's just the excuse I tell everyone. I got a girl pregnant."

He laid a hand on my shoulder, and his eyes were misty.

"Haleigh—beautiful Irish Catholic girl from Ohio. We had been dating on and off for a few months when she told me she had had an abortion. I couldn't even look at her. She couldn't tell me she was pregnant but could tell me she had killed our child?"

"I'm sorry, Fessy. That's a fucked situation, for everyone involved."

"You know what's really fucked? She tried talking to me, sought comfort from me. She needed a friend, but I avoided her. I blamed her—hated her. But now, I realize I hated myself. Deep inside, I knew I didn't feel hurt or betrayed that she terminated the pregnancy. I felt relieved," he confessed, sobbing and wrapping his arms around me. "What kind of man does that to a woman?"

"It's all right, get it all out," I said while rubbing his back. "We all do fucked-up shit, things we're not proud of—especially during challenging times."

"But isn't that when we're supposed to try to do our best?" he asked; his tears had stopped.

"We're supposed to, but life doesn't come with a manual. Sometimes, life gets *really* difficult, and we're faced with impossible decisions. And it doesn't matter which decision we make. What counts is who we are after those big moments. That's when we find out who we really are," I said, knowing I was beginning to get away from Fessy's confession and jumping into my own struggles.

Luckily, the alcohol took hold again, and he fell asleep. I dimmed the lights and left the door slightly ajar.

"My dad's fine with me sleeping over. He actually sounded pleased I was doing something normal. He said I better make sure I'm home first thing in the morning. Where's Faysal?" Christina said, wrapping herself in the blankets on the floor.

"I tucked him in bed. He was wasted. Question, if I wanted to get to a boat, what would be the easiest way?"

"A boat? Um, I don't know. The Smithtown Marina, I guess. Why?"

"Do you think the keys to the boats would be lying around somewhere nearby?" I asked, ignoring her question.

"Maybe? Oh! Private boats—Nissequogue is full of them. You may be able to rent one or you can borrow Brooke Leeman's boat. You remember her, right?"

How could I forget? I said to myself.

"The Leemans have been gone since September. But again, why?"

"I don't know. I haven't formulated it all yet—"

"You want to go after Alex, don't you?" she interjected.

"I do. He's family. Green Haven is near the Hudson river, which is also near Fessy's home. The world is falling apart, Chris, and I think we need to start asking ourselves what's important. For me, the answer is love."

By her expression, I could tell she didn't want to support my crazy plan but understood why I had to do it.

"Do you or Faysal even know how to drive a boat?"

"I don't, but Fessy might."

"Susan!" she exclaimed. "She knows everything there is to know about Mr. Leeman's boat. She's been taking boating lessons on it for a year."

"Why? Are Susan and Mr. Leeman friends?"

"No, of course not. He's like eighty years old. Frank, Brooke's brother—Susan has been taking lessons with him, *for* him? I think they're dating. She won't admit it though. You know how private she can be, and I'm guessing she's ashamed of dating someone younger. I don't know why, Frank's a babe."

I laughed, remembering how overly self-conscious Susan could be.

"That's stupid, Frank's only like four years younger than us."

"Let's call her," she said. "We need to check up on her."

"No, let's not. I doubt she wants to hear from me."

"Who cares?" Chris responded as she dialed Susan's number and put the phone on speaker.

It went to voice mail after six rings.

"Susan, it's Christina aaand Cole!" she said, shoving the phone in my face.

I waved her off.

"We miss you and wanted to make sure you're okay. We're at Cole's— oh, and Cole's friend, Faysal, is here too. You have to meet him, he's adorable. Call us back, okay. We love you, don't *we*, Cole?"

I don't know if I was emboldened by nostalgia or the alcohol, but I said, "We do love you, Susan. I miss you so much, even if you hate me!"

"See, that wasn't so hard," Christina said, hanging up the phone. "I wonder if she's even home. Maybe they went to her brother's in Troy."

Troy—there was that name again, and it hit me.

"That's where the Erie Canal begins!" I shouted, startling Christina. "Sorry. Troy—I've heard it before from Alex. Apparently the Erie Canal was the pride and joy of Western New York, connecting the entire area from the Hudson River to Lake Erie."

The doorbell rang, making us jump.

"Oh, shit, sorry. I forgot to tell you I invited Simon. You don't mind, right?" she said as she climbed over the sofas to let Simon in.

"Hi, mister—Cole," he said, taking in the sight of our lair. "Christina told me you guys made some alterations, but this is incredible. I couldn't even tell any lights were on from outside."

"I know, right?" I said. "We built the adult version of a kid's fort. Who wouldn't love that?"

"Cole, did you get in touch with Mr. Hemburry?" Simon said.

I wondered if he and Christina had played some sort of perverted version of Simon Says in the bedroom? I would've.

"Yeah I did," I lied, remembering what I had chosen to forget.

Like a winter's chill, I felt it in my bones: Nothing good awaited behind Mr. Hemburry's door.

Tomorrow we'll find out, I convinced myself. *Tomorrow everything will change.*

Instead, I said, "He says not to worry about the post, Simon."

"Okay, good., I'll see him in the morning when I relieve him," he said. "Do you mind if I sleep over? I figured since the front gate is just down the street from here."

"Christina, do I mind?" I teased.

"Not at all," she answered.

We hung out for an hour, talking and not drinking much but eating chocolates instead. Christina and Simon retired to the master bedroom, taking a bottle of brandy with them. I cleaned up the hallway and took a long hot shower. I tried putting the puzzle together while the water washed over me. It was all connected: Susan, Fessy, Mr. Leeman's boat, the Hudson River, Newburgh, Troy, Erie Canal, Green Haven—Alex.

I fell asleep in my new bedroom. All the lights were on, every bedroom door slightly ajar.

We slept well that night, the weight of the incoming change lulled our senses.

I'm not sure if the others were as aware of this change as I was. I think, on a primal level, they were—like a wake of buzzards circling a dying animal.

Chapter 20

"Stop, guys. There's enough food for everyone," I scold Alex and Jack who are sitting at the end of the long mahogany dining table.

"But, babe, Laura made it only for me. He's the dick who's doing too much," Alex protests, wrestling the pumpkin pie away from Jack.

"Fuck this shit, I'm leaving. I know where there's a better party anyway," Jack says, throwing his napkin on the floor and disappearing into the background.

"Who invited him? He is the rudest person I have ever met. How was I to know he also liked pumpkin pie?" Mom says. "Please, Cole, keep your questionable acquaintances out of family events. Anyway, where's your brother? His food is going to get cold."

"That's not my friend. Alex invited him. He was helping him at the hospital or something. I invited Christina, Susan, and . . . where's Faysal?"

"He's passed out on the sofa. I don't think he handles his liquor very well," Christina says while holding Simon's hand.

She turns and continues whispering into Susan's ear who's wearing blue surgery scrubs. Her hair has chunky blonde highlights, and her face is expressionless.

"What about me! Someone please tell me there's more food," Liz says, wearing her blue-and-white Smithtown High School cheerleading uniform.

There's a light around her, a radiant aura that illuminates the room. She sits next to Susan, and my three childhood friends hug and cry. I walk toward them when a heavy hand on my shoulder stops me.

"Not yet, son. We all have a job to do," Dad says and hands me a carving knife. "Make sure Mr. Hemburry gets a drumstick. Oh, here's your brother!"

Marc and Bar run into Jeffrey's arms, and the same light that encircles Liz engulfs them. Tears run down my face, landing on the turkey I'm meticulously attempting to carve into equal servings.

"Take a break from that," Mom says, taking my hand and guiding me toward my embracing family. "Your father is here. Everything is going to be all right now."

I stop and run to Alex. He's staring at the pumpkin pie on his lap.

"Come meet my father," I say, taking his hand.

But he won't move, and his hand is as cold as a slab of freezer-burned meat.

Without picking up his head, Alex says, "She's coming."

Pilar approaches the table, dragging her left foot which bends in an unnatural angle. She's wearing a white dress, maybe a wedding dress? It's impossible to tell because of the torn and dirty fabric. Her long, black hair is matted, and her skin is the color of gravel.

As she staggers toward us, she devours the light and warmth in the room—the only light unaffected is the one radiating from Dad who stands in front of Mom, Marc, and Bar. Pilar doesn't frighten me though—she saddens me. It's not her fault death has become her.

She opens her toothless mouth, and blood pours onto the front of her ragged dress.

In a deep, ancient voice not her own, she says, "Go, now! It's coming. *Run!*"

Her voice shakes the ground, plunging the world into darkness and turning the room into a freezer. As the world fades, I see my breath and my father's face.

"Cole, remember to do your job," he says. "Don't forget, get your ducks in a row. I love you. Now, wake up!"

The pillow was cold and wet. My eyes felt heavy with salt from my tears. Rubbing the sleep off my face—and banishing my dream from consciousness—I sat up and allowed my eyes to adjust to the dark. Small rays of light escaping from the blanket-covered window let me know it was daytime.

My house was frigid. With my comforter wrapped around me, I shuffled to the touchscreen on the wall. It was off, and realization punched me in the gut—all the lights were on when I went to sleep. I dropped my comforter and ran to the phone. It still worked, being battery operated, but there was no dial tone. Complete radio silence.

I walked to check on Fessy, but his loud snoring told me he was okay before I got anywhere near Marc's room. Christina was asleep on my mom's bed, alone. I figured Simon had left to start his shift up front, which reminded me of John Hemburry.

Fear can be paralyzing, forcing our minds to shut down and reboot. "Fight or flight" is how the hypothalamus reacts to fear—preparing the body for action or inaction. I couldn't stop to think about what I had to do; if I did, I would have found a reason not to go, and then another, and another.

I changed into my going-home clothes plus my bomber jacket, brushed my teeth, washed my face with cold water, and tied up my hair in a ponytail. I pulled my hair back so tightly, it gave me an instant facelift.

The white sunlight was blinding, so I put on my aviators. Walking past the willow tree, I realized I would need something to protect myself with. I couldn't show up at Mr. Hemburry's door holding an obvious weapon.

Should I wake up Fessy and Christina and bring them with me? I wondered.

Instead, I walked to the shed and picked up a small spade shovel.

"This shovel? Oh, I'm digging up a hole in the yard. Hey, John, is your power out?" I said, rehearsing a plausible story.

I was crossing my driveway when the odor hit me. It was the stench of burning rancid meat, like earthworms cooking over asphalt on a hot summer day. I heard a scream and hid behind the Rover.

The woman ran up the street, chased by a heard of ten or twelve infected. My brain should have registered the infected for what they were—a crowd of sick humans. But it didn't; I couldn't.

The herd moved as if it suffered from rigor mortis, slow and stiff. Five infected leading the herd wore civilian clothes; some had missing limbs, all had gaping wounds, and the blood dripping off their clothes was still fresh enough to mark their shambling steps. The rest were a mix of bodies wearing hospital scrubs and bodies so badly burned as to make their gender indistinguishable.

The woman tripped over her pink pompom slippers, and her jaw hit the pavement.

I wanted to scream, get their attention so she could get away, but my body had disconnected from my brain. I didn't even breathe.

She wiped blood from her mouth and got back on her feet. An infected lunged; she swerved, leaving it holding her pink robe in its claws. The woman ran to the house across mine and banged on the door, but no one answered. With the herd a yard away, she gave up on the door and ran to the backyard. I watched her disappear from sight, taking the herd with her.

I don't know how long I hid behind the car. Hours? Minutes? All I remember thinking was, *The Infection has arrived.*

Sirens were heard in the distance, and a faraway explosion shook the ground. I ran to the front door when it spotted me.

The lone lumbering body looked to be a young girl in a running suit, but I couldn't be certain due to half its body being scorched. Its leg bent inward, causing it to move raptor-like. And its head rested on its shoulder. While staggering up the driveway, it moaned; however, it was only able to make a choked gargle—like a drowning animal—because its throat had been ripped open.

I froze.

But as it neared, I heard Alex's voice in my head, *"Push through the fear, Chicabear. We deal with fear by learning about it. And how do we overcome it?"*

"Logic and triumph," I said and shifted into action.

I led it to my backyard. The stink of sulfur and burned hair overpowered every other smell. There was no humanity in its face, only a vacant hunger. It snapped its jaws as it clumsily lunged at me.

I pivoted under its hooked arms and swept it off its feet. When it hit the ground, I dug the shovel in its knee and severed its leg. It didn't flinch, wince, or in any way acknowledge pain. The wound didn't even bleed. I severed its other leg, and all I accomplished was force it to drag itself on the ground. It was relentless, never taking its eyes off me as it tried to sink its teeth in me.

Chapter 21

"What the fuck are you doing?!" Fessy yelled, standing on the deck.

He wore the same gray sweatsuit he slept in; and his face was filled with judgment, disgust, and fear. I was embarrassed, felt guilty, as if caught committing an unspeakable act.

I pushed those feelings aside and said, "This is what the world looks like now. You need to face it, Faysal. This is the enemy—this is what death looks like, and we need to understand our enemy."

I finished by planting the shovel in the creature's back, piercing its spinal cord to keep it in place.

"Are you fucking crazy? We need to go now! Christina thinks you've lost your mind. She's locked herself in the bathroom, scared witless."

"Go where? You've seen it. You *know* there's no getting away from it. We fight or we die. It's that simple," I said and extended the shovel to Fessy. "And I don't know about you, but I prefer to know what I'm fighting."

Fessy looked back, nodded to Christina, walked toward me, and then said, "How do we fight it?"

With its spine broken, it writhed on the ground and snapped its teeth. We severed its arms, punctured its lungs and heart—nothing. It never registered anything was being done to it.

"I don't think it's alive," Fessy said. "Whatever this sickness is, they're not human anymore."

I took the shovel from Fessy and pushed it through the reanimated corpse's brain. It stopped moving.

"Do you know how to drive a boat?" I asked.

"Huh? A boat? Yeah, sorta. My father used to take me fishing. Why?"

"Because we need to get the fuck off this island, and I know where there's a lot of boats. Get all the supplies you can from the basement to my dad's pickup—"

"We should take the Rover," Fessy interjected.

"Okay, sure. Load it up and then get Christina and tell her what you've seen. Tell her it's time to go. Please, be careful. Those things are everywhere. I'll be right back."

"Where're you going?"

"We need guns, and I know where to find them," I said, walking to Mr. Hemburry's house.

Shovel in hand, I ignored the front door and walked to the back. The laundry room carried a faint smell of metal, and there were blood splatters on the floor and bloodied towels in the hamper. I banged the shovel on the washing machine and shouted, "Come and get it!"

No response. The house was as silent as a tomb.

I held the shovel in front of me, its spade ready to strike, and made my way through the house, opening the blinds as I moved along. The metallic scent became thicker the closer I got to the kitchen, like sucking on a penny.

The blinds in the kitchen weren't shut, and the early-morning sun washed the room in pale light, which made the pool of coagulated blood on the floor appear a livid scarlet. On the small, round wooden table were guns of various sizes and boxes upon boxes of ammunition. Sitting at the table was John Hemburry, his back to me and his body slumped forward. Even though I couldn't see his face, I could see the bullet hole on his right temple.

I stood behind him, stupefied, memories playing in my mind as if I were watching a home movie.

I'm eight—Mr. Hemburry assures me the Roman candle is perfectly safe as he lights the wick. Time slows down. *Will it blow up in my hands? Will it shoot backward and burn me? What if it burns someone else? What if it fizzles and disappoints?* Then *boom*! Lights. Colors. Joy.

I'm sixteen—John's eldest, Braelyn, finds the bottle of vodka I had hidden in the hedges between our houses. Mr. Hemburry calls me over and asks if the bottle is mine. I don't want to lie to him, but I also don't want to incriminate myself, so I just stare at the ground. I expect him to accuse me and tell my parents. Instead, he talks to me about the dangers of underage drinking and promises to keep an eye on me. He kept the bottle.

I'm eighteen—a few days before Brooke's graduation party. John's wife, Jessie, has gone back to work after maternity leave. He asks if I could watch the twins while he takes a quick nap. The twins are beautiful and already very different from each other. Arissa has curly, brown hair like her mother and Gianna has her father's strawberry-blonde hair. They're sleeping as the musical mobile spins above them. It has four pictures—Jessie, Braelyn, Arissa, and Gianna. John is in every picture.

I began thinking of ways to move his body so I could give him a proper burial when I saw the small bitemarks on his arms. The kitchen seemed to implode and every shadow became an omen of impending death. I took the gun from John's hand and aimed it indiscriminately. It was a small handgun with a silencer attached, and it weighed as much as a large wrench. On its side, it read "Beretta 9mm."

My only shooting practice were paintball fights with friends and the one time I shot Brian's BB gun when we were twelve. I held the Beretta as I had seen in movies—sideways kill shot. Aiming at a picture frame on the wall, I squeezed the trigger. The gun jerked, completely missing the target and hitting the opposite wall.

Realizing the kill shot was a Hollywood invention, I held the gun with my right hand and used my left hand to support its weight. I aimed again, centering the picture frame within the V-shaped sight, and pulled the trigger. Bullseye. I shot a few more rounds until the magazine was empty. The mechanism was confusing, but I eventually got the hang of popping the magazine in and releasing the slide.

The magazine in the Beretta carried fifteen rounds. I aimed and fired at every picture frame and decoration I could see. The power the gun provided was intoxicating. I felt anger and pain leave my body through each bullet I shot, until all that remained were empty tears.

I found a groceries tote and filled it with two more identical guns and as many boxes of ammunition as it could hold. I knew I couldn't give John a funeral. I knew I needed to get out of his house and never look back, but I couldn't. I needed to know what had happened to his family.

Gun aimed, I followed the blood droplets upstairs.

Jessie's body lay on the floor in the doorway to the master bedroom. The top of her skull was missing, pieces of it splattered on the walls and ceiling. By the lack of blood, I guessed Jessie had already turned when she was shot.

The door to the twins' room was closed, and on it, written in black permanent marker, it read,

PLEASE SHOW MY GIRLS MERCY. DO WHAT I
COULDN'T. I'M SORRY, BRAE. DADDY LOVES YOU. ALWAYS.

There was faint scratching coming from behind the door.

My mind screamed *run*, but I ignored my fear, turned the doorknob, and pressed all my weight against the door.

"This is for you, John," I said and shoved the door.

A small body flew backward, falling next to its bed. The stench of sulfur burned my eyes, and it pushed me back into the hallway. Arissa—or what used to be Arissa—was hogtied to her—*its*—bed, and a shirt was duct-taped to its mouth. The thing that once was Gianna got back on its feet and lumbered toward me. Its mouth was also duct-taped, but instead of arms, it had bloodless sinew stumps. Its arms were still tied to the bed.

I kicked it back down and pushed down the gorge dilating my throat. I had to finish it for Mr. Hemburry—for Braelyn. Stepping on the Gianna-thing, I put a bullet through its head. Then I turned and showed Arissa's corpse the same mercy.

"Our Father in heaven, hallowed be thy name . . . thy kingdom come," I said as I wiped my tears and walked downstairs.

I heard a woman's scream.

Christina's! my mind raced.

I grabbed the tote and ran outside.

Chapter 22

"Fessy, look out!" I yelled and dropped the tote.

Christina cowered on the front steps as Fessy used a rake to push back a zombie. However, he hadn't seen the kid-sized monster shuffling toward him. When he heard my warning, he turned in time for it to miss his leg, and he kicked it down the short hill. It grunted and got back up. The corpse was recently turned, still resembling a human, and thus more agile. I aimed my 9mm at its head and fired, finally striking it down on the eighth shot.

People ran in every direction, followed by the infected. With so much movement, the creatures had abandoned herd mentality, and each was attacking its closest victim.

"Cole, we must go," Fessy said, grabbing me by the shoulders.

The world was spinning around me, and it felt as if I were sinking into the earth.

"Look at me. Everything is loaded. Christina insists on taking her car so we'll follow her home."

"Go start the car. You don't know the way to Nissequogue, so I'll drive," I said, snapping out of my stupor. "I'll get Christina."

I ran past her, who looked to be borderline comatose, and went into the kitchen.

I wrote my family's number on a piece of paper and grabbed a few wallet-sized pictures of Alex and my family out of the Manila envelope.

I looked at the copy of *Pet Sematary* and thought, *You were right, Mr. King. Sometimes dead is better.*

"Christina, we don't have time for this. Snap out of it, we gotta go," I said, eliciting no reaction from her.

She just wept.

"Fuck this," I said and slapped her.

"What the hell! That hurt," she said, kneeing me in the groin and missing by a millimeter. "Wait, we have to get Simon. He's at the front gate."

"Are you sure he's not home?"

"I'm sure!"

"Okay, we'll follow you then leave through Northside."

She ran to her car, and before following behind, I took a deep breath and one last look at my home.

Hope to be back one day, I told myself.

I picked up the tote, passing it to Fessy as I got in the driver's seat, and closed the door.

"What's this?" he asked.

"Survival," I said and placed my gun on the dashboard. "There's one for you in the bag. It comes with a silencer."

As I pulled out of my driveway, a man banged on the window.

"Let me in, please!" he implored.

I ignored him and focused on Christina's taillights, hoping no one would plead with her in this manner since I wasn't sure she'd have the heart to ignore it.

It was less than a thirty-second drive, but in that short time, I saw a woman locked in her car surrounded by corpses, a garage blaze which seemed to attract the zombies—mindlessly walking into the flames. Countless people on the side of the road were being torn apart and devoured by reanimated dead.

This is what one of the circles of hell must look like, I thought.

Nearing the gate, there were thick skid marks veering right, to an ambulance that had flipped on its roof and was tangled in the pines. The driver was impaled through the shattered windshield. It wasn't trying to break free, not really. It writhed in place and clawed at the air. Distracted by the horror, I didn't see Christina step on her brakes, and I tapped her bumper. Her car jerked forward and rammed into the booth.

Simon's corpse pawed at the window; its face was repulsive. His upper lip had been ripped off, taking with it the front part of his nose.

The impact loosened the booth's glass, and the Simon-thing toppled over Christina's hood.

I reversed the Rover to give her room to flee and honked the horn.

No response.

"Damn it, she's mind-fucked," I said, putting the car in Park.

I grabbed my gun and turned to Fessy. "We can't stay here. I'll jump in her car, you follow us."

I ran to her door, taking a mental count of the corpses lurching toward us (three). Christina was crying and pointing at Simon as it scratched at the windshield, trying to break through. I put my gun to its forehead and fired.

"I know, Chris," I said when I opened her door. "But it wasn't him anymore."

"Simon," she said, sobbing.

"It's fucked, I know, but—"

I heard its moan, crouched, and mule-kicked it.

The creature, wearing a bloodied sleeping gown, hooked on to my boot and dragged me down with it. Its dead weight felt like being tied down to cinderblocks. When I landed on the street from beneath the car, I spotted the other zombie nearing us. The creature gnawed at my heel; I kicked it in the face, caving in its nose, and shook my boot free.

"Move, now!" I yelled and shoved Christina to the passenger seat.

She hadn't put the car in Park, so as soon as she let go of the brake, the car rolled forward.

135

Without missing a beat, I jumped in her seat—which was tight and uncomfortable—and stepped on the gas, making sure to sideswipe the nearing zombie.

I made a wide U-turn and expected Fessy to follow. He didn't. The Rover's door was open, and he was nowhere in sight.

I can't do all this on my own, I thought as panic swept over me.

Suddenly, Fessy appeared from a driveway. At first, I thought he was holding a backpack close to his chest but qucikly realized it was a small child.

The boy wore cowboy pajamas and clung to Fessy's chest as if attached by an invisible baby carrier.

I don't know what my expression must have been; Fessy shook his head, got in the Rover, and made a U-turn.

Over the rearview mirror, I watched him swerve to the left and ram the zombie I had kicked in the face.

The horrors around us began snapping Christina out of her daze.

As far as we could see, Northside Avenue was impassable, jammed with frantic bodies. How many of them were living or undead was impossible to tell. I felt an ache in my heart for Eric Green as we turned onto Westside.

The streets outside of the Pines were even worse. Police cars sped aimlessly, running over people and zombies. A fire truck zoomed past us, corpses clinging to its sides.

"How are people ever going to come back from this?" Christina said when I turned on to a side road and the world quieted down. "Was Faysal carrying a kid?"

"Yes," I answered matter-of-factly, unable to process Fessy's actions.

"What about the kids' parents?"

I had no answer.

"There are so many fires. This town is going to burn," I said, hoping the implication would sink in and alert her to the danger her family faced. Mr. De La Cruz would protect his home, no matter what. But his stubbornness could be the end of them.

Will Christina realize that? I wondered.

"I think those . . . people are attracted to fire," she said; her voice sounded hollow.

"They're not people anymore."

"Of course they're people, Cole," she protested, her empty words suddenly carrying a shade of condescension.

"No, Christina, they're not. People don't walk around with their throats or hearts missing—"

"Just, stop," she interrupted. "I can't bear this anymore."

The drive to Christina's was oddly calm; it were as if the Infection moved like a tsunami and had yet to reach this suburb. The only signs of the incoming chaos were the dark smoke trails in the sky and the faraway sirens.

I pulled up just as her dad and brother were getting in their van.

"Get Faysal and come in the house, please," she said and ran out of the car to embrace her family.

They waved me over and walked toward a ladder on the side of the house.

Fessy parked on the curb.

I turned the car off and walked to the Rover, trying to figure out what I was going to say.

"So what do you want to do about him?" I said, sitting in the passenger side. "His parents are going to worry about him."

The boy rested his head on Fessy's chest. He sucked his thumb and, with his other hand, grabbed on to Fessy's sweatshirt. I've always been bad at guessing kids' ages; he could've been anywhere between five and nine years old.

"His parents are dead, Cole."

"He told you that?"

"No, he hasn't said a word since I found him. I know his parents are gone because that's who I saved him from. He was hiding behind the hedges on his porch. His mother was hanging out the window, clawing and snapping at him."

The boy opened his eyes at the mention of his mother. His green eyes were wide and blank.

"I couldn't leave him, I'm sorry."

"You have nothing to be sorry about," I said, meeting the boy's gaze.

His freckled, traumatized face dug a dagger through my heart.

"We can't take him with us though. His family may be looking for him. We should leave him with Christina's family."

"Leave him here?" Fessy exclaimed, causing the boy to tighten his grip. "You saw the fires—it's only a matter of time 'til this town is leveled."

"I know," I said, unable to argue his logic. "He still shouldn't leave Smithtown, and I know you agree with me. I'm gonna go in and find out their plans. Bring the boy inside when you're ready. The entrance is through a ladder at the side of the house. If you see any infected, blast the horn and get ready to go."

Scaling the roof brought back memories of youth and sneaking out of Christina's house to go to a party or to smoke a cigarette. I wondered what I would tell my teen self.

What's the one thread I could pull to fix everything without obliterating the life—the love—I've come to know? I pondered.

Christina's brother, Edmund, called over to me from the window. As I entered what used to be Christina's room and was now an office, I was in awe of all the weapons hanging on the walls—swords, daggers, staffs, etc.—of all different shapes and sizes.

"Yeah, I'm a bit of a collector," Edmund said, noticing the amusement on my face. "They're all authentic, all battle ready."

"These weapons are beautiful, Eddy. It must've cost you a fortune."

"You don't even want to know," he began. "Listen, I don't know if I'll see you again, so I want to thank you for bringing Christina back safe—"

"No need to thank me," I interjected. "I know it has been a long time, but when you're in prison, it's like the outside world stops. Even though life went on for you guys, a big part of me is exactly where I left off. You're all family, and family protects each other."

"You didn't just save her—you showed her what the world really looks like now. She's with my parents, sobbing and raving about walking corpses, but at least she knows what we're facing. The shock will wear off, and she'll be stronger from it. You know she doesn't deal well with earth-shattering moments. That's why she didn't visit you. Often—okay, never."

I stopped fiddling with his weapons and locked eyes with him.

"You were her world, and losing you destroyed her reality," Eddy said. "She knew your world was shattered as well—you were the one actually living it—so she didn't want to burden you with her pain and resentment. But, man, she never stopped remembering you. None of us did."

Edmund's revelation, as heavy as it was, made me feel as if I could float. I cried and hugged him; and for this brief respite, they were tears of joy.

"She told me where you're going, and I want to help. Pick a weapon. Guns are good and all, especially ones with silencers," he said, pointing at the 9mm sticking out of my coat pocket. "But nothing beats edged weapons when you're surrounded by those things."

"You've had practice, Eddy?"

"Yeah, took a few down this morning when I tried to get Christina before my parents woke up."

I nodded.

"So what do you recommend?" I said, scanning my options. "I want something compact and sharp enough to easily pierce a skull— but not threatening enough as to make people nervous around me."

"I know the perfect weapon," he said, rummaging through his closet.

He placed a wooden chest on the desk and opened it, revealing a pair of beautiful, elegant blades.

"Are those daggers?" I said. "Oh, wait, sais, right?"

"The plural of *sai* is *sai*," he corrected.

"That's confusing, and it hits the ear wrong. Are you sure? I could've sworn I heard the Ninja Turtles call them sais."

"It's sai. Look it up. They're sixteen inches long from end to point and weigh roughly five pounds each. They're made of a superlight, superstrong alloy. You can hold them by the handle like regular daggers or, preferably, you can lay your palm on the hilt. Do you know what I mean?"

"No, I must have been absent that day in ninja school," I joked and picked up the sai.

The leather handle provided a firm grip. I switched to the position Edmund had suggested. The hilt cradled smoothly in my palm, and the thin, cylindrical center prong was perfectly balanced between my middle and ring finger—albeit, the weight on my wrist took some getting used to.

"That's' perfect, Cole. The two prongs curving outward will protect your hands from snapping jaws. And I have a ton of different holsters you can choose from."

I picked a black leather holster that wrapped across my chest and around my waist, giving me the option to keep the sai hidden on my back or visible on my waist. The buckle was a silver snake medallion that ate its own tail when clasped. He also gave me a holder for my gun and ammunition, which attached to my sai holster. Everything stayed concealed under my bomber jacket. I took a gun holster for Fessy and thanked Edmund for all he had done.

"Don't mention it," he said.

The sai were hidden on my back. I was practicing sheathing and unsheathing them when Christina and her parents walked into the room.

"Cole, thank—" she said and was interrupted by the blaring horn.

I ran to the window and watched Fessy making a U-turn over the lawn as a large herd staggered toward us.

"I have to go," I said and began climbing out the window.

Halfway out, I paused and looked at the faces of the De La Cruz family. I was thinking of some cliché goodbye, something in the ballpark of "It's not goodbye—it's I'll see you later," when I remembered sleepless nights spent reminiscing not the things said but left unsaid, the spaces between the silences. And although that in itself is a cliché, it is nonetheless true. Take it from someone who was stripped of everything he knew: as we near the twilight of our lives, we regret the things we didn't do most of all.

"Christina, I'm sorry for never putting that Rihanna song on a mix for you. It's funny the things that haunt us at night. You were it— you were everything. You taught me what friendship really means."

"Mr. and Mrs. De La Cruz, I'm sorry"—Fessy's frantic honking filled me with dread—"you guys helped make me an adult. Sorry it took me so long to get it. Eddy, you already know, *survive*. I love you all," I said and turned away before they could respond.

"Wait!" Christina yelled as I ran down the roof. "What about the boy? You can't take him with you."

The herd was too close for Fessy to bring him in the house; he had to come with us.

"Susan—her house is on the way to Brooke's! Please, Cole, check on her. She's one of us."

And just like that, I was part of the *us* again, the one Brian had made me feel I didn't belong to anymore all those years ago.

I nodded and jumped down the ladder. The herd was still yards away, but the noise had attracted several stragglers. A bloated, pale corpse wearing blue jeans and nothing else staggered out of the spruce trees and grabbed me by the arm. It pulled me in so clumsily that I was able to push it down with my shoulder, but I tripped over my feet and fell.

Before it could get up and lunge, a bullet pushed its skull back. Edmund stood on the roof, holding a rifle. He knocked down two other zombies, clearing a path for me.

"Go!" I yelled, jumping into the car and startling the boy.

As we drove away, Fessy pressed the horn, and I stood out the sunroof screaming at the lumbering mass of corpses. We were trying to lead the herd away from Christina's house, but I knew eventually there will be another herd and another.

I looked back one last time before turning the corner. Eddy was back in the house, and the curtains were drawn—all except for the last window on the left. Christina stood there, her hand on the glass.

Chapter 23

"So let me get this right, we're *not* driving to the marina because your friend Brooke Leeman has a boat?" Fessy said while maneuvering through empty, forgotten side streets.

The main roads were death traps, jammed with traffic, people, and infected. The chaos would have devoured us had we not cut through parks, yards, school fields, and bike paths. However, as soon as a new path was forged, the infected would mindlessly follow. There was no going back to Christina's—no going back, period.

"Yes, but we have to stop by Susan's first because Christina asked me to check on her, and Susan has a lot of practice driving Mr. Leeman's boat. Her brothers live in Troy, so maybe she and her family will want to join us. If not, we can, at least—*you know*," I said and pointed at the drowsy child resting on Fessy's chest.

The boy still hadn't said a word; he just sucked his thumb and the occasional head scratch.

Fessy was glad I had left it unsaid. He knew the kid's family would be looking for him and we shouldn't take him away from his home.

"And this is the Susan you grew up with," he said, changing the subject and mood, "but haven't talked to in a decade because she hates you?"

"She doesn't hate me, per se. It's complicated." I was taken aback by his choice of words but could hardly blame him since I was the one who had told him that. "Fessy, Susan and I used to pop each other's pimples. That kind of love doesn't just disappear."

"Ugh, that's fucking disgusting," Fessy said, grimacing.

"No, that's real friendship."

He smiled, and the outside world looked calm, normal. The temporary respite was nice.

"Have you figured how you're gonna get Alex out?"

"There was this rumor in prison that if the country is overtaken, the COs would be ordered to shoot every inmate and abandon the prison. I doubt the shooting part is true, but I'm banking on the COs abandoning their posts to be with their families. If not, I'll grab the first person I see, hold a gun to his or her head, and demand they free Alex," I said, surprised at my certainty.

I've never held a person hostage, yet I knew I'd have no problem doing it for Alex.

"You're insane," Fessy said, with a hint of humor in his tone but zero judgment.

He knew *crazy* had gotten us this far.

"Make the next right, it'll be the corner house on my side," I said.

There were two zombies clawing at Susan's door—an overweight man wearing boxers and a red flannel shirt, the left side of his face was a mangled mess of torn flesh; and a woman in her twenties or thirties wearing black yoga pants and a bloodied gray sweatshirt.

"Park on the curb," I directed and called out to the creatures by tapping my gun on the door.

The corpses groaned and staggered toward the SUV. I aimed and tried shooting them in the head. I kept missing but finally struck one down on the fifth shot.

The other zombie, the woman, neared the Rover; and Fessy panicked. I unsheathed my sai and stepped out of the car. Using the door as a shield, I thrusted my weapon through the creature's temple. It instantly went limp and fell.

"Sorry if that was too close," I said.

Fessy's and the boy's eyes were wide and darted wildly from me to the body on the ground.

"I'll stay in the car, in case more come," Fessy said.

I ran to the door and hesitated before knocking. End of the world or not, Susan had been the authoritarian in our group, and I had always had a healthy amount of fear toward her—like a child toward a parent.

We're not children anymore, I reminded myself as I banged on the door.

No answer.

My brain began suspecting the worst, *Maybe I'm too late.* The door of the beige Cape Cod–style home was locked so I walked to the backyard but was stopped by something that hadn't been there ten years ago, a tall wooden fence. It encircled the sides of the house, enclosing the driveway and large shed—what I remembered as Mr. O'Connell's domain.

Unable to find the entrance, I began climbing over the air-conditioning unit when a section of the fence swung open and I stared into the barrel of a shotgun.

Susan's likeness as an eighteen-year-old, the image I had conserved, was trying to consolidate with the twenty-eight-year-old woman standing in front of me. It took a few seconds for my mind and eyes to find agreement, but once they did, I saw the beautiful woman she had grown into. She wore blue jeans and a navy hoodie. The thin eyebrows of our past have been replaced by thicker, longer brows which follow the arch of her round eyes, and the artificial orange-tan hue of our youth has given way to her natural fair skin tone. Some things never change though—the fingers wrapped around the trigger still sported a French manicure, and her breasts were still double Ds, which were getting in the way of the weapon aimed at my head.

"Why the fuck are you trying to break into my house?"

"Break in? I'm here to save you, Susan," I said, unsure if she had recognized me or not. "It's me, Cole. Christina asked me to check on you."

Recognition came over her, although I couldn't tell if she acknowledged me or Christina's request. Her eyes filled with anger and resentment but with a tinge of relief and appreciation.

"I don't need your help. Leave!" she barked, not lowering her weapon.

"Have you seen what's going on out here?" I said, ignoring her anger and shotgun. "It's chaos, and it's heading toward you. You and your family need to get out of town. The infected are relentless and move as a herd. They'll overrun this place."

"I know how they move, Cole. I had it under control until you came and made all that noise."

Her accusation pissed me off.

Yes, Susan, this is all my *fault.*

"Please, listen to me. I get it, I'm a piece of shit, I don't deserve to be in the presence of the righteous Susan O'Connell. But a herd is coming! Don't you want to be with your brothers? We're heading that way. Come with us. I'm sure your parents want to see their sons."

She lowered her weapon, held it like a bat, and shoved the butt of the shotgun into my stomach.

"Don't talk about my family! You don't know shit!"

I moved in time, and it only grazed my side.

"You know what, Susan. Fuck off!" I was done feeling guilty, perpetually asking forgiveness for something *I* had lived through. "Liz was my friend too. All I wanted to do that night was party, make up with you, and make a memory with Brian. But life had other plans, and I'm paying my debt. There's nothing shitty you can say to me that I haven't said to myself a thousand times already, so give it up. You're not gonna hurt my feelings. Now, get your shit together because death is coming our way. My friend Faysal and I are planning on finding a boat and head to the Hudson River. You're either in or you're out, do whatever the fuck you want. But do *something*. I love you, and I care too much to watch you perish."

My emotions vibrated the space between us. I thought she was going to try to hit me again. Instead, she put the shotgun down, covered her face in both hands, and began wailing.

"I'm all alone, Cole. I don't know what to do," she cried and fell into my arms.

"Susan, where's your family?" I said, knowing her emotions weren't due to our reunion.

"Oh, god . . . I can't."

Susan's father had been bitten four days earlier during a fishing trip with a few of his friends. Her mom, Sharon, was taking care of him as his health deteriorated. It had been a tiny bite—a scratch, really. Mr. O'Connell was a strong man of about six feet three, and it took two days for him to succumb to the infection. Sharon died much sooner.

"He stayed in his shed. He didn't want to bring the sickness into the house," Susan said while we stood in her kitchen.

Fessy was parked in the driveway, in case we had to make a swift escape.

"We were supposed to report him to the authorities, but we didn't want to get separated from him," she explained as if she needed to make me understand. "We knew it was illegal, but we had heard horror stories of infected loved ones taken to hospitals and never seen again."

"I would've done the same, Susan," I assured her.

She nodded, took a deep breath, and continued.

"Dad was unconscious so I left Mom alone with him only for a couple of minutes while I ran to the house to make us coffee. I was walking back to the shed when she screamed and ran out holding her bleeding shoulder."

Susan drifted into her memory.

I laid a hand on her arm and said, "Where are your parents?"

"Mom left the door open, and Dad stumbled outside. By the time I realized he was gone, I saw a crowd forming a few streets down. A man said an infected was found and shot in the head. I wanted to claim his body, tell them the man they had shot was my father, but I couldn't! They would've come for Mom next! And . . . I figured they were going to identify him anyway, but they never came!"

She was frantic, sobbing, and practically ripping out her hair.

"It's okay. You did what you had to do to protect Sharon," I consoled, holding her in my arms and running my hand through her hair.

Remembering Sharon had been infected, I calmly looked Susan in the eye and asked, "Where's your mom?"

"She fell to the floor and cried hysterically, covering her mouth with her hand. I wanted to comfort her, but the danger was too great."

"Where is she?" I demanded.

"In the basement, the room at the end of the hall. She turned hours after being bitten."

"Okay, we have to go. But we can't leave her for someone to find. She can hurt people."

"What are you saying, Cole?"

I didn't want to say it; I didn't want to think it. But what other option was there?

"Susan, you've seen what happens. I know you've watched Brian's videos. The infected aren't alive—they don't even feel pain."

"That's crazy. There's no pathogen that can bring the dead back. Mom's in there, and a cure *will* be found!"

"There's no cure! There's not even a government to find a cure!" I yelled with more frustration than intended.

Our argument had brought back everything I had experienced since waking up and how it was all heading straight for us. I understood Susan's medical background would make it hard for her to believe the dead could walk; however, I also knew Susan well enough to know she had already put the puzzle together. She knew what we were dealing with—she just didn't want to accept it.

"There's no help coming, only death. You know what needs to be done."

She exhaled and said, "I know . . . but I can't do it. But neither can I leave her here, trapped in that room for someone to find. What if my brothers find her or my aunts?"

"I'll do it. She deserves a proper burial," I said, almost in a whisper.

"No. No, I can't. You can't," she pleaded.

"Susan, enough! It has to be done, and we don't have a lot of time. We'll go to Brooke's and get you to your brothers. Now, go pack. Essentials only," I directed her and saw something click in her brain.

It were as if she had finally accepted my words or her brain had shut off and allowed someone else to take the wheel.

She got up and walked to her room. I opened the door to the basement and walked down the dark steps.

The stairs led into a small laundry room, and ahead was a narrow hallway with three doors. I ignored the doors to my right and left and walked up to the one at the end. A hoarse, monotonous groan came from inside the room, and the basement reeked of sulfur, as if Susan had made hundreds of egg-salad sandwiches and left them to rot.

I reached for my gun and remembered my sai. With my right, I held the sai by placing my palm on the hilt; and with my left, I gripped the other one by the handle so I could turn the doorknob. Stupidly, I didn't notice the door opened out, and the thing that used to be Sharon O'Connell rushed me into the tight hallway and I dropped my left sai.

Using all my strength, I pushed the zombie back into the room, and it flew backward over the bed. I wanted to attack, put my weapon through its brain and watch it deflate, but I couldn't. I froze—watching Mrs. O'Connell stumble toward me. I searched the reanimated corpse's face for any sign of the beautiful woman she had once been, looked into her eyes for a shadow of recognition.

"Cole!" Susan yelled.

The creature closed the distance between us in remarkable time. It hooked on to my bomber jacket and pushed me to the floor. I grabbed it by the throat and held its snapping jaws away from me. The cramped space didn't allow me to lift my right arm and drive my sai through its temple, so I continuously punctured its body in hopes of weakening it—but to no avail.

Panic rose within me, and I felt my end nearing. There was an odd serenity though. The finality of it dulled my screaming nerves.

Susan shouted from behind, but I didn't hear her voice. I heard the voices of my mother, brother, and niece. I heard Christina, Fessy, and, most of all, I heard Alex. They were all telling me to fight, to keep going, *we all have a job to do.*

I pushed its head up as far as I could and drove my sai up through its neck into its brain. The lifeless body went limp and fell on me like a pile of wet clothes. Exhausted, I pushed it aside and rested my back on the wall.

That was the closest I had gotten to death, but that wasn't what scared me; it was how easy it had felt to give up. I almost welcomed it. I also realized my defenses had dropped because, for a few seconds, I stopped seeing the zombie as an *it* and saw it for what it used to be—a *she.* I couldn't make that mistake again.

We wrapped Sharon in a white sheet and picked a spot in the garden. There was no time for a burial and the ground was frozen; so we covered the body with sand, fertilizer, soil—whatever we could find. Susan brought flowers from her living room and placed them at the head of the grave.

"I'll leave you to say goodbye," I said and walked to the Rover.

"We've spent too much time here, Cole. We gotta go," Fessy warned as I stood outside the driver-side door.

The boy still clung to him, still sucking his thumb.

He looked a little pale, and I wondered how his traumatized mind was processing everything.

"Susan's coming. There's a fire station and town hall on the way, maybe we can drop him off there," I said, mouthing the last part so the boy wouldn't know.

Fessy didn't respond, but his scowl said it all. The boy had become part of our group, and leaving him behind didn't sit well with me either.

"Let's go. I'm driving, I know the safest routes," Susan said, wiping her tears and handing me her pink backpack to store in the back.

Fessy didn't argue, he opened the door and got out.

"Faysal, Susan. Susan, Faysal," I introduced them and began moving our supplies to make room in the car.

They exchanged greetings, and her eyes fell on the boy glued to Fessy.

"And what's your name, buddy?" Susan asked.

Her voice was sweet and motherly. She was always great with kids.

The boy didn't answer, but he did smile—the first one since we met him.

I jumped in the passenger seat, and Susan adjusted her seat.

"We have to drive by the fire station," I said, nodding toward the boy to help her understand.

She nodded and pulled out of the driveway. I expected her to take one last look at her home, but she didn't.

The sounds of sirens hummed in the air. And if we closed our eyes and concentrated, we could hear faraway screams and grunts. As we drove out of her street, I saw movement behind many curtains.

They're watching us, I thought.

We weren't as alone as we felt.

I read somewhere that humans can sync up their brains, sort of like a computer network to amplify our thoughts and make the impossible possible. Maybe that's the power behind prayer or why miracles are more abundant during the holiday season. Right now, as the world burned, maybe everyone alive was focused on the same thing—surviving. And thus spreading the will to survive among each other.

I hope so. We all need something to believe in—something to help us fight.

Chapter 24

The town hall burned as corpses flocked to the flames. We didn't reach the fire station—we didn't need to. The entire area was lost. There was no order or rhythm to the inferno; it was dizzying. Stray bullets flew everywhere. Seas of bodies, living and undead, crashed in all directions.

A man wearing head-to-toe camouflage stood in the middle of the road. His face was distorted into a ghoulish grimace as he aimed his rifle at the crowd and fired. Susan said he was shooting at the infected, but I didn't think so. I saw him fire at cars and people. The only infected he shot were the ones that got too close for comfort. An ambulance barreled past us and pushed our vehicle toward the man. Susan veered right to avoid hitting him and rammed straight into a herd of zombies.

Their dead weight threatened to topple us over. She shifted into Reverse and floored it, leading us down a hill. I thought we would get stuck in a ditch, but it actually led to an old horse trail. I didn't know if it was luck or she had meant to guide us there; I chose to believe the latter. We crossed a stable and came out on a street leading to Nissequogue—and also past Liz Anderson's home.

"They don't live there anymore," Susan said.

"When did they move?" I asked, embarrassed of what she must have seen in my face.

"They moved to California a few years ago. I'm surprised no one told you or more like I'm surprised you never asked about them."

Her words ricocheted in my mind—my soul.

The road was narrow, and only woods surrounded us. It was the perfect time to open up and tell her my truth—tell her how all these years I had been too embarrassed and guilt ridden to even speak Liz's name, tell her how I believed the pain I had caused was too great and thought it best to disappear from the world so the Andersons wouldn't be punished by having to hear my name. I even wanted to tell her how long ago I had learned that although we can't choose the tragedies that befall us, we can choose how we allow those tragedies to affect us; and I had decided to use my pain, not become a victim to it. And out of the ruins of my past had grown a beautiful love and future.

Of course, I didn't say any of that. And as I grew more and more quiet, almost to the point of implosion, all I could think was the spaces between the silences.

Learn to take your own advice, asshole, I scolded myself. *Saying anything would be better than sitting here watching the trees pass by. Shit, even quoting Adele's "Hello" would even be more helpful.*

"How did you guys meet?" Fessy asked, breaking my soliloquy.

I wasn't sure if he asked out of the need to escape the awkwardness growing in the car or because he actually wanted to know. Either way, I was thankful.

"Liz's sandwiches," Susan said, a half smile touching the corner of her lips.

Fessy looked confused, so I elaborated.

"It was freshman year. Liz's mom used to make her extravagant deli-sized sandwiches for lunch. Susan and I were in constant competition over with whom Liz shared her sandwich. That day, Liz didn't feel like sharing, so she told Susan I had taken the sandwich so she couldn't get it—"

"So I grabbed my lacrosse stick and chased him around the cafeteria, finally cornering him by the boy's locker room," Susan interjected.

This was our shared story.

"We locked eyes and realized how ridiculous we were being. We laughed so hard, it hurt and became instant friends," I finished and beamed at Susan.

She smiled back, and our bond warmed the cabin.

"You Smithtowners have the weirdest stories," Fessy said, snickering. "What kind of boat are we taking, Susan?"

"It's a million-dollar *yacht*."

I didn't like her emphasis on the word *yacht*. It made the journey sound leisurely—it was everything but.

"A Jeanneau 58-footer, 79'4" mast height, 150 horsepower Volvo Penta D3-150 engine."

"Wow, impressive," Fessy said.

It was unclear if he was in awe of Susan's knowledge or the boat itself.

"It has a *gargantuan* dinghy garage, lounging space galore, owner's cabin forward with a set of double cabins with plenty of natural light and ventilation, state-of- the-art navigation, and generators and a pair of alternators feeding battery banks. Enough power to travel around the world," Susan boasted in words I knew weren't hers.

She memorized Frank's ostentatious specifications verbatim, I thought. *She must really like him.*

"Okay, Capt. Phillips," I said. "No need to sell us on it—we're sold."

Fessy chuckled and Susan sneered.

We turned onto Brooke's street, and the forest opened up to mansions sitting atop rolling hills. The infection appeared to have left the area untouched.

"I'm sorry about, *you know*," Fessy said, gesturing to the sleeping boy on his lap. "I swear he'll be my responsibility. I won't burden you guys."

"There's no need to apologize," Susan said. "You saved him, that's commendable. We'll find his family. And if you guys can't take him, I'll take him to my brother's."

"Yeah, he's one of us now. I think all that searching for a place to drop him off was a way to cover our asses in case his family accused us of kidnapping," I joked. "We'll make it work. What kind of people would we be if we couldn't find it in us to help a child?"

Fessy smiled—we were family now.

At the front gate, Susan entered the house code.

"No fucking way," I said, watching her enter the numbers 2-3-2-5-1-1-2.

"Yeah, Brooke adopted it too. We all did. I think it's on the list of most common passwords though," Susan said, smirking, Liz's memory still a presence between us.

She parked between the main and guesthouse. Mr. Leeman's beautiful, sleek white boat was in full view past the pool and tennis court.

"Wait, that's not the same boat Brian and I hooked up in."

"Of course not. This one is new, same make though. And he kept the name."

"What's it called?" Fessy asked.

"*Lady Lazarus*," Susan said, allowing the irony to sink in.

"You can't be serious," Fessy said, deadpanned. "I guess he's a fan of the Bible."

"Or Sylvia Plath. 'Dying is an art. Like everything else, I do it exceptionally well,'" I said, quoting the boat's namesake poem.

I stepped out of the car and opened the door for Fessy.

"Here, pass me the kid so you can help Susan load up our supplies."

The boy was pale and looked ready to vomit. When I held him, he felt cold; but when I touched his forehead, it was hot.

"What's wrong? Cole, what happened?" Fessy asked, seeing the alarm on my face.

Susan heard the panic in his voice and rushed to our side. I stood the boy on the driveway. He was weak, and his knees buckled.

He steadied himself, and for the first time since meeting him, he stopped sucking on his thumb. A tiny drop of blood formed on the tip of his thumb as he extended his hand toward us.

"Mommy bit my finger," he said—his first words all day.

Chapter 25

His name is Timothy, and he's six years old. Timothy's mother attacked him, pushed him through the window, and he cut his finger on a rusted nail. He's lucky that's all she did. His life was still in danger though. Not only was his hand badly infected, but constantly sucking on his thumb had prevented the wound from clotting and he had lost a lot of blood. It was touch and go. Susan used all her medical knowledge to save him; all the while Fessy couldn't stop blaming himself for not noticing the symptoms sooner. Thankfully, Tim's fever broke. He's an orphan now, but there's strength within him. I see fire behind his emerald eyes.

Tim is going to have to find a new normal—all the ones who survive will have to. However, Timothy is proof that life perseveres. He's proof that the light within us can shine during the darkest of time.

That's how the story should have been; that's the story I wish I could tell.

We never learned his name or age; he fell unconscious before we could even think to ask. Perhaps asking that should have been a priority, but we couldn't see past our own pain. I did name him though. Everyone deserves a name before dying. Timothy.

Sensing the change in us, Tim began crying, and Fessy picked him up. Susan led us to the main house. Her spare key worked, but when she entered the code to shut off the alarm, it wouldn't work.

"Shit," she murmured while frantically punching in different codes, although she could have been yelling.

The alarm whined as loud as a fire truck's siren; it was maddening. It stopped after a few minutes, and a very polite woman's voice notified us that the police have been alerted.

We panicked, looking at each other as if to say, "Should we run?"

But then reality set in—somewhere out there, a light is flashing at a police station, alerting to a possible breaking and entering, and it's being drowned out by the end of the world. Without saying a word, Susan left to the guesthouse—Frank's apartment. Tim was infected, and she didn't want any part of the decision-making process.

"Come on, let's put the boy in bed," I said, leading Fessy upstairs.

Brooke moved out of her parents' home when we graduated high school. So I was surprised at what I saw when we walked into her old room—everything was exactly as I remembered. Her room was a time capsule. The walls and furniture were still shades of lavender, the bedding still crisp and white. The pictures on her dresser and desk were all the same as well. There were no pictures documenting her college years. Even her cosmetics and perfumes appeared to be the same. J'adore Dior and Calvin Klein One bookended this eerie museum of our childhood.

"He's asleep," Fessy said, laying Tim down on Brooke's bed.

Putting my hand on Fessy's shoulder, I said, "Let him rest. It won't be long now."

He didn't turn to face me, but I could hear his labored breathing. I could feel his body fighting the tears that were sure to come.

"I'll do it, Cole," Fessy said, sounding as if he were trying to hold down his vomit. "When the time comes, I'll do it."

I should have said okay, left him to do what had to be done, and gone to help Susan load up *Lady Lazarus*. However, something told me this experience would damage Fessy in ways from which he might never recover. I didn't think the task would have been any easier on me, but I wanted to spare Fessy from it. I had already done it for Susan; I knew I could carry the burden.

"Go find Susan and help her get the boat ready," I said. "I'll stay with the boy."

"No, I brought him. He's my responsibility."

"Faysal, look at me," I directed and made sure to hold his gaze. "This isn't your fault. We all wanted to save him and be heroes. I got it. Now say goodbye and then go find Susan."

The same brain click I had seen in Susan I saw in Fessy. He nodded, and I walked to the other end of the room to give him privacy. I didn't want to hear his goodbye; I didn't want to be there. And as long as I faced Brooke's dresser, it felt as if I weren't actually there. I was ten years in the past, and I remembered what I had wondered while on Christina's roof—*What the hell would I tell my past self?*

This question created an existential dilemma. I could save everyone mountains of pain. However, doing so would annihilate not only who I am today—someone who knows how to survive—but also my relationship with Alex. Every mistake, every choice has led me to him. To change anything would mean to kill what I love most.

But I must, *right?* Liz lost her life. That type of sacrifice shouldn't be worth any future.

ALTHOUGH . . . GOD, I WISH SHE WOULD'VE WORN HER DAMN SEATBELT—

"I'm done," Fessy said, forcing me to abandon the impossible paradox my mind was traveling down.

That's what we become as we get older—a series of paradoxes.

Fessy walked out of the room, not making eye contact with me, and I sat next to Timothy on the bed. He looked like he was dreaming. I listened to his breathing and waited.

And waited and waited.

Tim didn't succumb to the infection as fast as I thought he would. Somehow, Brooke's home still had electricity, so I walked to the desk and picked up her lamp. It had a switch to change the light; I put on the black light and held it up to Tim. His body—even his hair—radiated an effulgent ultraviolet glow, which intensified the closer it got to his hand where the contagion had entered his bloodstream. I saw my reflection on the dresser's mirror and I too appeared to be glowing, not nearly as bright as Tim but enough to cause concern. Especially my teeth. It looked as if I had recently used whitening strips.

Shaking off my confusion, I attributed the gleam to the beauty products I had used in my mom's bathroom and turned the lamp off. From the window, I watched Fessy and Susan loading up the boat. They exchanged a few smiles and even a laugh or two. Resentment rose from within me, and I tasted metal from accidentally biting my tongue. I knew it was illogical of me to feel that way. The entire journey had been my idea, from bringing them together to staying with Tim. It was envy I felt, not resentment.

Envy—because they haven't had time to see what adapting to this new world will cost them. They haven't even considered that it'll have a price. They soon will, but for now, however short, they believe they can still be the same once this is over. I knew better.

There's no leaving prison behind, no shedding the hard outer shell I had built. I thought I could jump back into my old life as if nothing had happened, but I was only playing pretend. This was who I am—a person who's able to turn certain feelings off and do what must be done to survive. Although prison sharpened this ability, it didn't create it. My drive went beyond the will to survive, from a more primal place, more selfish. I guess it's always been with me; I've always seen life as a battle I needed to win.

While waiting all those hours, I watched as the number of infected along the gate's perimeter slowly but steadily rose. And as the sun set, the clank of the metal gate crashing on the stone driveway echoed in all directions.

Tim hadn't turned yet. His breathing was shallow, his skin had a bluish tint, and the smell of sulfur no stronger than a fart. He was still alive. It was a matter of seconds until the infected lumbered up the house. I thought about leaving Timothy in Brooke's room, lock the doors, and hope no one finds him.

"Please forgive me," I whispered as I pointed my gun to his forehead and pulled the trigger.

I chose the living over the dying.

Shooting the infected was always the same—a bloodless wound and their bodies dropping like rag dolls. This was different; I *saw* Tim flinch. And he bled; his wound bled.

Vomit burned my throat when I heard Fessy screaming as he raced into the house. Pushing my disgust aside, I wrapped Tim in a sheet and carried him downstairs.

The stench of the undead was thick in the air, and their hellish chorus drowned out all other sounds. Fessy reached for Tim's body, but I stopped him. I didn't want him to see Tim. I didn't want him to see my shame. Perhaps, if only I saw it and only I knew the truth, I could bury the memory deep down and pretend it never happened.

We didn't have time to bury him; we just laid him down on a flower bed. I grabbed Fessy's arm and pulled him toward the dock— avoiding his eyes.

There were corpses everywhere, their number and dead weight destroying the structures around us. It were as if the whole town had come to bid us farewell.

Fessy and I got on *Lady Lazarus*, drew up the bridge, and took in the chaos. The Rover was barely visible over the sea of dead. Zombies filled every space, tainted every scene in the horizon. And they came for us.

Susan roared the engine to life, and we moved farther and farther from land. I tried envisioning Brooke's home as I had seen it the night of the party. I wanted to imagine the infected were people again, a mingling crowd. But I couldn't. All there was to see was the walking dead.

The three of us left a piece of ourselves on land. Would we get it back?

Could we get it back?

Part II

ADAPT

And all the woe that moved him so
That he gave that bitter cry,
And the wild regrets, and the bloody sweats,
None knew so well as I:
For he who lives more lives than one
More deaths than one must die.

—Oscar Wilde, "The Ballad of Reading Gaol"

Chapter 26

My soul feels heavy, dirty. I don't want to tell this story anymore. I don't want to be the person who does what must be done—I don't even want to know what has to be done.

I was wrong, thinking prison and pain had taught me how to endure. I don't know why I felt more prepared than the others to adapt to the pain in this world; it's not like I own the patent on pain. I thought I was evolving into who I needed to be—who I *wanted* to be—but I hadn't even begun. Can I still call myself a good person? What makes a good person? How many wrong turns does it take for a good person to not be able to recognize himself or herself?

My heart tells me it desires for the world to right itself, go back to how it used to be. However, doesn't my entire plan rely on the assumption that the world must burn down? How else could I get Alex out of a state prison with thirty-foot walls? So what I *really* desire is for the world to burn just long enough for me to get what I want. *Then* things can go back to normal.

This way of thinking is sad. Believing anyone can control this hell is as idiotic as changing the past while still holding on to Alex. So I suppose that makes me a sad idiot.

Chapter 27

Susan and Fessy have shared navigating duties. None of us have said much to each other. We haven't been able to play pretend. Silence has become the fourth passenger on this boat. It began last night when we left Nissequogue.

We sailed off Short Beach into the Long Island Sound, but we weren't alone. It were as if the entire North Shore had taken to the water. We anchored and watched the island burn. The flames were as tall as buildings occupied by the undead, illuminating the island as far as the eye could see. The dead's moans washed over all of us like a tidal wave from hell. The fire appeared close enough to touch, but it provided zero warmth. The earth was an inferno, but the air was ice like the infection—a fever that froze the body.

The next day I woke to land being a tiny speck in the background, but boats littered the area. The Coast Guard had corralled everyone into a makeshift floating community. I'm not sure why we didn't just leave, perhaps our brains were still wired to follow authority.

Some of the ships around us had become nothing more than floating coffins and death traps. The worst were the sounds of children and babies crying. We tried helping—once.

Susan was navigating, following the wails, but it sounded as if they were coming from all directions. We heard a grunt and then heard when the zombie found the crying child first. We got as far away as we could from other ships after that.

I don't deal well with awkward silences, so I decided to push our unwelcomed fourth passenger overboard.

Susan navigated as Fessy searched all radio channels for any survivors, or news, or anything.

"How's the search coming, found anyone yet?" I asked Fessy.

"There's something. I—wait—almost got it," he responded as he fumbled with the radio.

All I heard was static, and then the clean-cut voice of a man boomed over the speakers.

"'If the Spirit of God, who raised Jesus from death, lives in you, then he who raised Christ from death will also give life to your mortal bodies by the presence of His Spirit in you'—Romans 8:11, ladies and gentlemen. This is the truth from God himself."

"What is he saying, Fessy?" I asked, but he didn't answer.

His attention was completely on the man preaching over the radio.

"When the body is buried, it is mortal. When raised, it will be immortal. When buried, it is a physical body. When raised, it will be a spiritual body. We shall not all die, but when the last trumpet sounds, we shall all be changed in an instant, as quickly as the blinking of an eye. For when the trumpet sounds, the dead will be raised, never to die again. For what is mortal must be changed into what is immortal. What will die must change into what cannot die . . ."

The signal was lost, and static returned.

"That was crazy. Was he really just telling us to get infected?" I asked.

Fessy wouldn't stop fidgeting with the radio. He wouldn't say a word.

After several minutes of radio static that grated my nerves, he finally said, "He's not crazy. He's quoting Corinthians."

"Wait, I thought Corinthians was all about 'Love is patient and kind, it is not jealous or conceited or proud'?"

He looked at me with a raised eyebrow, surprised I knew the Bible.

"What? Alex—and every wedding ceremony—likes Corinthians."

He smiled, the first I've seen since leaving Brooke's, and said, "Don't you see what he's doing? He knows people lean on religion during moments of crisis. He's preying on people's hopes and beliefs—warping them into his own madness. We have to stop him, Cole."

"Fessy, how would we even find him? We're nearing the city, he could be broadcasting from anywhere—"

"It's a weak signal," he interjected. "But I think this equipment can pinpoint the origin."

"Okay, fine. Say we find him, and then what?" I said. "Put up posters and banners with our own ideology to discredit his beliefs? The world is going to devour itself before it gets better. The only thing we can do is survive and be there when the dust settles."

Fessy shook his head and went back to fiddling with the radio. He didn't want to hear it, and I supposed it wasn't such a bad thing for Fessy to have a side mission to keep himself occupied.

—⁓—

The sun set, and darkness fell on us like a wool blanket.

Fessy navigated the boat during nighttime. We had to move slow due to the drifting ships that had turned from floating coffins to icebergs threatening to sink our ship. The digital map announced we were to reach New York City by dawn.

I knew no one would be able to sleep; the anticipation was worse than drinking a gallon of coffee. Susan and I hadn't talked much since our ride in the Rover, so I thought we were overdue for a heart-to-heart.

I entered the bright central cabin—"Stateroom Forward," Susan had called it but never explained what *forward* meant. Figuring it was boat talk, I added *forward* to everything: dinghy *forward*, bathroom *forward*, radio *forward*. It was Fessy who told me I was using *forward* wrong, but he didn't elaborate.

Past the two double cabins was the large owner's cabin (*forward*), which, went unsaid, would be Susan's quarters. She's our captain. I put my ear to the door and heard nothing. I knocked, my knuckles barely touching the mahogany panel. It swung open. Susan's eyes were swollen and red but wide awake.

Chapter 28

"What's wrong? What happened?" Her voice was a mixture of terror and dread.

It was painful, like hearing a child crying for her mother on the first day of preschool.

"Everything's okay. Fessy's manning the boat. He's a natural, a real Captain Nemo. He's a bit too obsessed with tracking down that weird preacher though. Anyway, I just wanted to check on you, see how you're feeling."

"How do you *think* I'm feeling?"

Her tone was full of venom.

I felt stupid and hated, like I was wrong for asking her or not knowing the answer.

She walked back to the queen-sized bed but left the door open behind her.

"I know everything is shit," I said, entering her cabin and taking in the interior, which was extravagant in a ridiculous James Bond sort of way—everything was white leather, mahogany, and gold accents.

I sat on the edge of the leather booth, my tailbone barely touching the seat.

"This is uncharted territory, Susan. Every decision is going to be new. It's impossible not to feel lost—unsure if we made the right choice or not."

"You know what to do," she said—or more like accused. "You're the reason we're here. You don't seem affected by *any* of it."

Her words felt like the slap of a mother; I felt dirty and bare. Not because of her tone, but because I had wondered the same thing. I felt pain, and I felt fear, but I also felt ready or knew what it took to become ready. It were as if I had been preparing for this world my whole life, and now everyone else was catching up.

The first time I had noticed this desire to be ready was in Mr. Hemburry's home, but I didn't see the full picture until Susan's. At first, it was hard to discern, like trying to catch a glimpse of a hummingbird's flapping wings. I had shown the Hemburry twins mercy and helped Braelyn if she ever came back home. Then I had shown Sharon the same mercy, helping Susan in the process. However, there was a darker reasoning that connected both events—I needed practice using my weapons.

"You don't think I'm affected?" I said, almost yelling. "Do you think this is the homecoming I had envisioned? I don't know if my family is alive or dead, if Alex is safe or trapped. These are supposed to be happy days. I'm supposed to be worrying if Alex will get paroled next year, if his family will accept me—if I'll fit in with people or constantly be reminded that I'm not one of you anymore. Shit, I rather be doing *anything* than what I've had to do since I came home. I'm tired of doing the things *others* can't."

I expected Susan to slap me and kick me out of her cabin; but instead, she sat across from me, looked me in the eye, and said, "I know. I'm sorry. I just . . . I don't understand this world. It's cold and cruel. I can't see what we're fighting for. All I see are the faces of the people we've lost. My mom—it wasn't fair to burden you with . . . but I couldn't—"

"Stop, Susan," I interrupted and sat beside her on the bed, laying my hand on her shoulder. "If we begin breaking down what's fair or unfair, a tiny violin will be playing for us. I did what needed to be done—that's all. This world hasn't even begun to chew us up and spit us out. Figure out who you want to see again, make them your mission, and put the rest aside for now. We'll mourn the loses later when we're done. The people you love—that's your fuel. Use it, draw strength from it, but don't get lost in it. Do you know I haven't allowed myself to think of Alex since I set out with Fessy?"

"Why—how? You're doing all this for him."

"I can't think about him because he's home—he's everything—but I'm afraid of who I could become if I let that drive me. See, love anchors us to the world. Love is the flame that keeps us going when we don't think we can anymore. But if left unchecked, that fire can consume us. The fear and pain of losing that love can cloud our judgment and make us do some terrible things to protect it."

I paused, realizing I was getting away from my initial point and getting lost in my misgivings about bringing us on a dangerous journey to rescue a faraway love.

I expected Susan to say something, ask anything, but she remained silent. There was an innocence to her face, like a child waiting to be told a story. And there was also pain behind her eyes, a pain which mirrored my own. I turned from her gaze; it was too real, too present.

I focused on the small cabin window, to the dark sea or perhaps beyond. And I told her a story. One from my past.

Chapter 29

Brian's last visit in Riverhead County Jail was the first time I became aware I was part of a new *us*; however, that was only the prelude to a new chapter in my story. My journey began in Clinton Correctional Facility, a.k.a. the Colosseum.

As we passed through Clinton's gate, the man shackled to my right turned to me and said, "Don't worry, if we end up in the same block, I'll make sure you're good, kid."

I had avoided looking his way for most of the eight-hour ride. He was in his forties, and tattoos covered most of his face. His earrings and gauges had been removed, making his sagging earlobes look like what old cheese smells like.

Trying my best not to offend, I smiled politely and said nothing.

Tattoo Face got the hint I didn't want to talk and went back to fiddling with his shackles, but not before sharing his last gem, "Just stay away from the three *G*s—gambling, gangs, and gays."

I thrived during my first year of incarceration in county jail because my overwhelming guilt and desire to be punished made it easy to accept, and I welcomed whatever hardship befell me. I also survived out of shear naivete, breaking up fights between gang members and voicing my opinions because no one ever told me I shouldn't. I didn't even consider that there could be grave consequences. However, none of that applied in Clinton. Violence was woven into the fabric of daily life.

After a year of drowning in guilt, I craved a semblance of the world I had left behind. Not ready to process everything that had led me here, I began my time in Clinton by clinging to what was familiar—the "true love conquers all" mentality indoctrinated by Disney films during my childhood and the comfort of a man.

This part of my story is tricky to tell. I believe we learn a lot about ourselves from the people we date, love, and lose. Alex doesn't agree. He's a firm believer that lovers from the past are just that— the past. After a while, I began to see things his way. However, the lessons I learned from those men cannot be ignored. A single person didn't teach me what love is; that's only in the movies. And this isn't just a story of Alex and I or of my present and future. It's a story of everything, and that includes the truth. So I will replace names with single letters, in hopes those men become one interchangeable entity.

My early Clinton years are marked by one bad relationship after the other. There were rebounds after Brian, and most don't even deserve a mention—just forgettable bodies in my attempt to feel. But then there was X.

He was charming and ridiculously good looking. I ignored his flirting at first. X was going through a messy divorce, and I thought encouraging his advances would be predatory; it's bad form. But he was persistent, lavishing me with gifts and flattery. He had me before the ink on his divorce papers had dried.

A couple of weeks into our courtship, I learned X was in a gang. Homosexuality is forbidden in gangs; if caught engaging in any sexual activity with another man, gang members pay a hefty price—a price always paid in blood. The first time we met, he had told me he was a "businessman" and part of an "organization." I didn't know *organization* was another word for *gang*. I mean, they had fundraisers where they sold art supplies! I thought he was part of a prison company—CEO, maybe?

His business was bringing heroin into the prison—a lot of it. I knew he wasn't Mr. Right, but he was so damn beautiful. And the power from being with him was intoxicating. If someone so much as looked at me wrong, all I had to do was tell X, and it would be taken care of.

We were a walking contradiction. Our relationship was forbidden, yet we were. His friends showered me with attention as a way to court favor from him. They tolerated our relationship because X made them a lot of money. He was *useful*—until he wasn't.

X's gang split into two factions. A power struggle ensued. During this time, his heroin connection was arrested, consequently putting an end to X's reign.

He was stabbed on a Thursday night. I went to breakfast Friday morning expecting to see him. Instead, I was greeted with the stares of every person in the mess hall. That's how I found out what had happened to him.

Since I knew all about their dealings, X's gang labeled me a security risk. And their next move was to vote among themselves to decide whether to get rid of me or not. With my head on the chopping block and unsure of what to do, I acted clueless about everything and was all smiles and nervous chuckles—torn between mourning a horrifying end to a relationship and self-preservation. All I knew was that I didn't want to meet the same fate as X, so I shut off my feelings and planned an exit strategy.

X's tenacious, albeit reckless, pursue of his desires taught me an important lesson: In a harsh world, you're measured by how useful you are—everything else is secondary.

Using that knowledge, I made myself useful by buying as much of his gang's drugs as possible since I was sure they wouldn't want to get rid of their number 1 customer. Although I was trying to turn off my feelings, I couldn't escape the abysmal guilt. I blamed myself for X's downfall; our love and desire had caused his pain, and I couldn't wrap my head around that.

My plan had been to find different ways to unload the product I was purchasing so I could use the money to buy more. But I ended up unloading the drugs right up my nose. A couple of weeks later,

I was called for a urinalysis to test me for drug use. I tested positive and got 120 days in solitary confinement—which I welcomed.

I needed to detox, mourn, and heal; it was also a graceful way—in prison logic—to remove myself from the equation. Four months in the SHU (Special Housing Unit, a.k.a. "the hole") was long enough for me to become yesterday's news and press Reset on my journey.

My do-over came in the form of more bad decisions, more bad experiences, more bad relationships. I can count at least three times—that I know of—when there was a price over my head because of some stalker or ex-boyfriend who felt wronged by me.

So I played the game. When I was challenged, all I needed to do was ask myself what or whom could I use to win. Life became cheap. Everything had a price, especially love. Dating became an emotional transaction, a question of how much of my heart was I willing to barter so I could be somebody's "mine." And if the numbers didn't favor me, well, it was nice meeting you. Next.

I didn't recognize how far I was from the person I had been until a few months before leaving Clinton. It felt as if everyone was in love or getting on with their lives. Brian's son, Jason, was born. Christina was in a serious relationship. And everyone I grew up with was either getting an amazing job or engaged. Prison aside, I was losing at the game of life. That's when I met Y.

"Damn," he said as I moved into downward-facing dog.

I looked up to see who said it. Y stood at my cell door. He was holding a drawing pad and dropped it on the floor when our eyes met.

"Sorry. I—uh . . ." he stammered, clearly embarrassed by his outburst.

Smiling, I reached through the bars to pick up his pad. He reached for it at the same time, and our hands touched. There was a static shock, which hurt and made a loud crackle, and we jerked back.

We laughed, and he regained his confidence.

"I wasn't perving out on you or anything," he said. "Just surprised to see a fellow yogi, especially in prison. My mom owns a yoga studio in Queens. I've been doing it my whole life."

Friendship came easy to us. We'd talk for hours at a time; he was a great listener. Y was smart, funny, kind, and a talented artist. He enjoyed drawing manga and could tell a full story and teach a moral in seconds through his art. His dark eyes, chiseled bone structure, and eight-pack abs didn't hurt the attraction either. Y loved ruffling his fingers through my hair during sex.

I think we fell in love, but I never got the chance to find out. Y had demons, as we all do. He died of a heroin overdose. Drug dealers had just begun lacing it with fentanyl, and no one knew better.

His name was Yien. He deserves a name.

Although there were rivers of tears, I wasn't mourning; that came later. I was angry—it fueled me. I hated him for making me care and then leaving me. I hated the people who had sold him the drugs. I hated the world for breathing and continuing as if nothing had happened. And I hated myself for feeling *anything*.

Two months after losing Yien, I met Z.

My canine tooth went through my chin. I got back up, picked up my shower items, and walked out.

"You fucked up," I said, meeting my would-be attacker's stare.

"What are you gonna do, get a boyfriend to beat me up?" he said, smirking but with a wince of pain in his gestures.

I ran to the mirror when I was back in my cell. My adrenaline raged as I assessed the damage, and I began to cry. I wasn't crying because of what he had attempted to do to me or the bleeding wound on my chin. I didn't know why I was crying. I didn't want to cry; it was involuntary.

I composed myself, looked into the mirror, and said, "Don't be a victim."

My neighbor, Z, was a sizable man. He was the silent type, but I could tell he liked me, always laughing at everything I said and never missing a chance to do small favors for me. So I told Z everything that had happened in the shower, making sure to emphasize the deplorable details with tears and deep sighs.

I was in the shower room, drying off. The water had been steaming hot, filling the small space with a pleasant mist. I put on my green bathrobe and collected my shower items.

He was standing at the entrance, naked, in a Superman pose— chest pumped out and fists on his hip. Although I didn't know his name, I had seen him around and knew him as a low-level drug dealer. We had met four years earlier on the white Ford van. I had suspected Tattoo Face's speech about staying away from the three Gs had been a front because of the way he would stare at me in the yard. However, anyone who has been the recipient of the unwanted stares of a man knows the "I want to fuck you" look is *very* similar to the "I want to kill you" look. And I had never cared enough to investigate which look he meant. Tattoo Face had been irrelevant, until that moment.

"What are you doing. Get out!" I whispered as to not attract attention.

"Just touch it, please. I'm just really horny," he panted while stroking his erect penis.

He walked slowly toward me and inched me to the back of the room.

I tried poking him in the eye, but he held my wrist down hard enough to leave a bruise that I nursed for weeks after. He was overpowering me, so I stopped struggling and allowed him to get close—close enough to smell his breath. It smelled of coffee and stale cigarettes. When I felt his body relax, I kneed his balls as hard as I could. In his pain, he pushed me toward the door. As I made my way out of the room, the strap on my sandal snapped, and I fell on the tiled floor.

Riled up, Z offered to punch Tattoo Face in the mouth, and I thanked him, assuring him I would make it worth his trouble.

The next day, he walked up to my would-be rapist and kept his word. Except, it didn't go as I had envisioned it. Z was savage, stomping his face until all that remained was a misshapen, bloody mess that used to be covered in tattoos.

I had been giddy with excitement the night before, believing Tattoo Face was going to get what he deserved. But what I had set in motion wasn't justice; it was vengeance. It made me sick—sick at the monster I had unleashed. And most of all, I was disgusted with myself. After Yien died, all that rancor consumed me. Pain and hate had fueled me, and the attempted rape had been the excuse it needed to lash out.

Two weeks after Tattoo Face was sent to the hospital and Z was sentenced to a year in the SHU for nearly killing him, I was transferred to Green Haven. I didn't know what it would take for me to process everything I had endured—decompress the past five years—but I was sure of one thing.

Life can't be cheap.

Chapter 30

"I-I'm sorry you had to go through all that," Susan said, holding my hand.

Unwilling to burden the moment with my shame, I didn't tell her that the incident had led me down a six-month-long drug binge. And I didn't tell her that I call him Z because I never learned his name. The man spilled blood for me, and I couldn't be bothered to know his name—that's the fucked-up person I had become.

"Don't cry for me Argentina," I said, hoping to inject a little humor and levity. "Yeah, life was tough, but all those hardships not only taught me how to survive but that I *could* survive. And it wasn't all bad. I partied, I loved, and I learned. I lived. When I got to Green Haven, I focused on myself, learned sign language, finished my studies, and began planning a future with Alex—"

I stopped as tears began to blur my vision. I didn't want to cry—*not yet*.

"I lost myself in my quest, to find my 'happily ever after,' I said. "Not only did I cost those who cared about me pain, but I hurt anyone who got in my way. That's why I take my love for Alex and bury it deep down. I allow it to keep me warm at night, but I refuse to let it make me do anything I can't look at myself in the mirror after."

Like what I did to Timothy, I thought and was about to say it.

"Cole, do you remember eight years ago, you reached out to me and—"

"You erased your social media and threatened to get a restraining order against me, even though I was in the SHU, and just needed to talk with someone who knew me before prison? Yes, I remember."

"Okay, I deserve that," she said, standing up and looking around the cabin. "I did that because I called the prison, and they told me you were locked up because you failed a drug test. I was so disappointed and angry. I thought you hadn't learned anything and would never change. I'm sorry, I never could've guessed what you were going through."

"Don't worry, Susan. Just knowing you cared enough to inquire about me means everything to me. Besides, who could blame you for feeling that way? I was such a fuck-up. All I went through was my own fucking doing. You want to hear something crazy, though," I said, shifting my weight on the bed and suddenly feeling as if the air in the cabin was sucked out. "I . . . I don't regret where I ended up—I regret how I got there.

"Yeah it was prison, and yeah I experienced and witnessed a lot of fucked up shit, but I love the things I've learned. God, Susan, I love the life I envision with Alex. And I'm not sure I'd be able to appreciate everything I have, had I not known what it is to lose everything. Trust me, I know how fucked up that sounds.

"There's not a day I don't think about Liz, about how much her family was affected. But I can't deny how *blessed* I feel. Even now, as the world dies, I feel like I'm still winning because I found what most people spend their whole lives searching for."

I had stood up and moved all over the cabin as I shared my truth with Susan. She sat at the bed, rummaging through her backpack while I spoke. She stopped as soon as I mentioned Liz and was now silent. Unable to read her, I decided I had to finish what I started. I took a deep breath and continued.

"It was involuntary at first. Every night I'd have this dream where I'd go back to the night of Brooke's party, and each time I would change a small detail—take my cigarettes with me so I wouldn't come back to my car, Danny and Liz wouldn't get into a fight, the man wouldn't be on the road, a different song would play on the radio, etc. Point is, I'd change something, and Liz would be alive. Then the dreams stopped, but I continued the habit, changing one detail and imagining what would happen. It was torture, really, forcing myself to relive the worst moment in my life over and over again.

"But when I met Alex and we fell in love, I stopped playing what-if and just lived in my reality. It wasn't until the world fell apart that I began obsessing over that night again. And now, I'm starting to think I'm a fucked-up person because I moved on! I had figured since I was living the punishment, why continue to punish myself? But I've been a selfish asshole, living my life, looking for my happy ending when my—*our*—best friend died; for me to get here. I live and Liz doesn't."

I was trembling and sobbing. I couldn't see her expression through my stinging eyes, and I was unsure she had followed my outburst. Suddenly, she wrapped her arms around my shoulders, and we cried on each other. I don't know how much of our crying had to do with Liz or the horrors we had lived through since the dead walked. I suppose it doesn't matter—pain is pain.

"You're not fucked up," she said when our tears had subsided. "After everything you've been through, you still feel the pain. You still care and haven't forgotten what it's taken for you to get here. You can't change the past, Cole. All you can do is honor it by helping the future. Besides, the love you and Alex share is a much-needed beacon in all this darkness. Thinking of love as something we need to keep and protect makes this chaos seem less—I don't know—hopeless."

We smiled, invigorated by our heart-to-heart.

"Are you hungry? I haven't eaten in days. Want to share this?" she said, pulling out a cookie from her backpack and grinning.

"I can't believe you still eat black-and-white cookies," I said, nostalgia enveloping my senses in velvet.

It was Susan's turn to make the world feel a bit more manageable, especially since the last thing I ate were chocolates, with Christina and Simon, before hope became something to be rationed and traded.

She split the cookie in half, sharing equal amounts of vanilla and chocolate since we both preferred the white side. *Some things never change—we like what we like.*

"Sharing these with Christina was so much easier because she always preferred the chocolate side," I said, taking a bite.

Christina's presence was palpable in that moment. The too-present pain between Susan and I was welcomed now, filling the agonizing Christina-shaped void.

"Do you think she's okay?" she said. "You saw what I saw. It looked as if the entire island was on fire."

"I know, I've wondered the same thing. But I choose to believe she's okay. Besides, you know her dad is tough. I wouldn't be surprised if he has commandeered a tank and has found a way to teach zombies to take orders."

"Okay, that's absurd," she said, shaking her head, "but oddly comforting and touching."

"As oddly touching as Susan O'Connell and Frank Leeman dating?" I teased, seeing my opening and seizing it.

"Ugh, what did Christina tell you?" Susan's face turned as red as a beet.

"Not much, just that you've been taking lessons with him . . . on his boat . . . alone . . . in the middle of the ocean. But I was sure you guys were dating—or, at least, sleeping together—when I heard you describe the boat. I can recognize a woman remembering mundane facts to impress a guy anywhere."

"That is so simpleminded of you," Susan huffed. "Of course there's *no way* a woman can enjoy boating and engineering without wanting to impress a man."

"Please, save me the 'I am woman, hear me roar' spiel. I know you well enough to know no one can force you into doing something you don't want to do. What I'm talking about is 'gargantuan dinghy garage' and 'lounging space galore'—Really, Susan?" I said, laughing and finishing my cookie.

Susan laughed too. I saw her walls drop and for the first time in who knows how long she let another person in. "I know he's young—and Brooke's brother—but he's really mature. He gets me, Cole."

I lay on the bed and propped myself up on my elbows, resting my head on the palm of my hands, slumber-party style, and gave Susan my undivided attention.

"After losing Liz and you, I don't know, I had no taste for relationships. I threw myself into my studies and pursuing a career," Susan said, lying beside me.

She pulled out a bag of Twizzlers, took a handful, and passed me the rest.

"I didn't lose my virginity until I was twenty-four, to Ian Milbrook, a guy I met working at a dentist office," Susan continued. "He always said and did the right things. He actually orchestrated a flash mob at the Port Jefferson pier to ask me to marry him."

"Aww, Susan, that's so romantic," I lied.

I'm not big on over-the-top, internet-ready proposals. I appreciate intimacy, call me old-fashioned.

"We planned for a short engagement. He had a lucrative job offer in Buffalo, so we wanted to marry before we moved. It wasn't a problem, you know I've planned my wedding since we were kids. It was supposed to be a large but intimate ceremony. But then Mom got sick—cancer. I couldn't just leave her, Cole," Susan said.

Her voice was full of pain and resentment. I knew those emotions weren't aimed at me, so I said nothing and continued listening.

"Ian said that he understood, that he has waited his entire life to meet someone like me, and that he'd wait as long as it took to call himself my husband. What's a year or two when you're planning a lifetime. We did the long-distance thing. It was torture, but it was love. Then, a year and a half after her prognosis, my mom's cancer went into remission. After the doctor's visit, I got in my car and drove the nine hours to Buffalo. I didn't call him—I wanted to surprise him. He wasn't at his apartment, so I drove around town. I spotted him outside a restaurant on Main Street, kissing a pretty blonde girl."

"That asshole!" I yelled, beating my fists on the bed.

"There was no dramatic breakup, I was determined not to be the typical scorned fiancée. Told everyone the distance was too much, sent him back the engagement ring, and moved in with my parents—to take care of them, of course."

"You should've keyed his car," I said, wielding a Twizzler like a knife. "Fuck taking the high road—who decided the high road was so great anyway? I guess you, Christina, and I have more in common than we knew. The three of us were really getting fucked by life."

"Yeah, we were," she said, smirking. "I was a mess for years, thinking I'll never love like that again—the first love always feels like the last—so I threw myself into my career. Started rubbing elbows with some of the best cosmetic dentists on Long Island. And guess what they all had in common? A love for boobs and boats. It was Brooke's idea for me to take lessons with Frank. And, I don't know, we became a thing."

She smiled, and I knew I had found Susan's fire to help her keep going.

"Do you know where he's at?"

"No. They left suddenly. He said his father didn't give them a reason . . . just that they needed to leave. Frank figured it was for a funeral."

"Susan, what if his dad knew something was coming? I mean, wealthy people live in a different world than us, right? What if this sickness was an experiment gone wrong? The funders of such projects—the uber rich—would have an early-alert system so they don't get stuck with us common folk."

I watched as the gears in Susan's mind churned. It was clear she hadn't considered this scenario.

"So if his dad knew something was coming," she said, "he would've taken his family to safety, which means Frank's out there—somewhere but safe. Alive."

Tears fell from her eyes, but they weren't sad, stealing the life from the room. It was the opposite: Her tears filled the cabin with hope.

"Exactly. Frank's probably in the North Pole, hanging out with the royal family," I joked; her hope was intoxicating.

She laughed and pulled out her phone.

"I keep expecting it to ring," she said, poking at the screen. "You wanna look at pictures?"

As we scrolled through years of pictures—years of history I had missed out—the cabin began to get lighter and lighter. We were drinking our third cup of coffee when Fessy's voice boomed over the speakers.

"Uh, Cole, Susan, you guys need to see this."

Chapter 31

The sky was a brilliant blaze of amber and purple, a majestic image that I'm sure inspired a score of "America the Beautiful" anthems. However, our entrance into the East River was anything but glorious.

All the land around us smoldered. The bridges had been destroyed, which against the blazing sky made the scene look like a postapocalyptic postcard. And screams drifted in the salty breeze, seemingly chasing the scent of scorched earth. They were the screams of survivors fighting for their lives, people mourning their loses, and the walking dead groaning with insatiable hunger.

"This area is called Hell's Gate," Susan said. "It gets its name from the dangerous currents and whirlpools. I'll take over now, Faysal."

"Nah, I got it," Fessy replied. "I need the practice. Look, there's Rikers Island!"

Rikers is a gigantic prison, a city within a city. Two large buildings burned, another building had a "No Survivors" sign hanging from its side. And on the roof of a large inmate housing complex, there were people holding machine guns. They didn't look like officers though. They looked restless and wild.

Roosevelt Island was ahead, and we encountered our first navigational decision.

"We can cut through Harlem River, shortening our trip by about twenty miles," Fessy said. "Or we can stay the course and take the West Channel, following the East River to the Hudson."

"It's a no-brainer then—we take the Harlem," I said.

"Wait," Susan said. "The Harlem River is relatively shallow, and it cuts through densely populated areas. Do we really want to risk getting stuck just to shave off some miles?"

It sounded like a suggestion, but it wasn't—it was captain's orders.

Fessy nodded and stayed the course.

I hated seeing the Brooklyn and Williamsburg Bridges lying in ruins. I used to take the Williamsburg into the city all the time to avoid tolls.

The water was crowded with boats. Thankfully, they all appeared to have been boarded by the living—no floating coffins in sight. The infected littered the shores; I watched one after the other trudge toward the vessels and fall into the water and not resurface.

I guess they don't float, I surmised.

But among the destruction, there were pockets of light. Liberty Island was covered with tents as humanity clung to life.

Good. Keep holding on, I thought. *This sickness can't be the end of us. Where there's life, there's hope.*

Loud blasts snapped me out of my daydream about humanity's hopes. Recognizing the noise had been gunshots from a very big gun, I dove into the central cabin.

Susan and Fessy yelled something that I couldn't make out because the shots had been close enough to rupture an eardrum.

But where are they coming from? I panicked.

We were passing under another ruined bridge—the George Washington, I believe—when over the hum in my ear, I heard the laughs of what seemed to be children.

There were about four or five kids sitting on a boardwalk on the bridge. Their little legs dangled over the edge as they pointed machine guns at us.

So much for humanity, I scoffed.

They fired indiscriminately until the groans of the dead could be heard over the laughs of the devil children. The imps scurried into the bridge's undercarriage.

"Are you okay?" yelled Susan as she grabbed my arm.

"Yeah, I think so. Are you guys okay?" I said, patting myself down to make sure I was intact.

My only injury was the killer headache emanating from my ear.

"Those bastards busted our power and fuel tanks," Fessy shouted from the cockpit. "I don't know how long we have until we're dead in the water."

"The dinghy!" Susan said. "We can use it to keep going until we find a safe place to make land."

"Great idea," said Fessy. "Get the dinghy ready, I'll steer *Lady Lazarus* away."

Susan ran below deck, and I stood at the railing, watching the shore and holding my pulsating ear. I hated that Fessy used the boat's name. I hated the irony in its name. And I hated those fucking kids.

I packed the following in my backpack:

- quart-sized water bottle
- water-purifying straw
- lighter
- various candies, chocolates, mints, gum, protein bars, beef jerky
- hair ties, comb, bandana
- travel-sized toothpaste, toothbrush, dry-on shampoo, body lotion
- ibuprofen
- tweezers
- cigarettes

We spread the ammunition among the three of us due to its weight

I finished packing the black backpack I had found aboard and wondered if leaving our ride was as depressive to Susan and Fessy as it was to me. It wasn't fear that depressed—fear was ever present, an inevitability of this new world. What filled me with dread was that at sea, we were in our own bubble; everything and anything was possible. But on land, the real test begins: we find out what our plans are worth, what we're really made of. I wasn't ready to leave our gargantuan reprieve.

Putting on my sai holster, I noticed something ominous about its clasp—a serpent perpetually devouring itself. I could take it as a sign of infinity or an omen of our desires and goals consuming us. My heart leaned toward the former interpretation, but I felt the latter's pull as I tucked my 9mm Berretta into the side strap.

I brushed my teeth, pulled my hair into a high ponytail, and lathered green-tea-and-cotton-scented lotion on my skin. The James Bond–esque ship boasted a small washer and dryer so my clothes smelled like fresh cotton as well. Looking myself over on the mirror, I posed and practiced the look I'd give Alex when I saw him again. It felt as if I were preparing to go on a date, not a dangerous death-filled mission. I knew I was being foolish, but I didn't care. We all need to play pretend sometimes.

I applied Burt's Bees lip balm as if it were lipstick. I kissed Alex's and my family's pictures, I kissed my gold ring, I blew the mirror a kiss, and I said "Here we go."

Fessy had set anchor in the middle of the Hudson near West Point in Orange County. The power was gone, and the ship had begun taking in water. We sat near the dinghy and examined the map sprawled out on the floor.

"Okay, we're fifteen miles from Newburgh. There's a small marina a mile upriver. It's on the opposite shore of Stormville, but it's our best shot at finding a suitable ride," explained Fessy, using the butt of his gun to point at the map.

I looked at Susan and spotted the outline of her gun under her gray bubble coat. She insisted on taking her shotgun, but thankfully,

I convinced her to take the third Berretta with silencer. Not only would it make sharing ammo easier, but who wants to travel carrying a shotgun?

It was surreal knowing the three of us were armed. It felt pretend, as if we were acting in a movie or playing a game.

"What if the place is overrun?" Susan asked, breaking the illusion of being in a movie (Perhaps adding to it? I couldn't be sure since the lines governing reality were blurring.)

"I've marked other possible options in case the place turns out to be a dead end."

I was glad for his consideration. The dinghy was able to get us to Newburgh, but Troy was farther away. We had no intention to leave Susan on her own, but if we couldn't convince her to come with us, the least we could do was give her the best chance at survival by finding a vessel that would accommodate her journey.

"We're nowhere near understanding these creatures, but massive trauma to the brain seems to do the job," Susan said while we made a final supplies check. "The cranium is at its thinnest through the eye sockets and temples."

She handed Fessy a Ranger combat knife made of black stainless steel, which used to belong to her father, and said, "Don't bother stabbing the cadavers through the frontal lobe—forehead and top of the head—the bone is too thick. Severing the cerebellum should work too. It plays a major role in controlling movement."

She finished her anatomy lesson by pinpointing the brain stem using the back of her head as the model.

We boarded the dinghy and unceremoniously drove away from *Lady Lazarus*—glad for it to be the last time I'd say that name.

Chapter 32

The marina and all shore landings were a bust. There were no boats to be found and the roar of the motor attracted an army of corpses anywhere we came close to land. Susan turned off the engine and we rowed to a wooded bank. Fessy had the map and compass. He said he knew the area; he was our captain now.

I understood why there were so many fires; the infected are attracted to it, ignoring all other movement unless a person comes within biting distance. Unfortunately, not everyone was able to take fire-safety lessons. Whole buildings were reduced to ashes.

We avoided streets, but metal coffins were everywhere. People left their infected loved ones locked in cars. Some of these had signs like "I'm Sorry" and "Leave Mommy Alone! She's Sick!" Those were the worst. I'd picture a child writing it, trying to understand the incomprehensible; and it would remind me of Timothy—of what I had done.

It haunted me—torn between feeling justified and inhuman. I knew there had been no saving Tim; had I not done what I had done, he might have killed whoever found him.

However, as soon as that logic would lift the blame off me, I would feel guilty for beginning to forgive myself. Although, to be honest, that turmoil in itself gave me comfort. Killing someone, sick or not, should never be easy—the moment it becomes easy is when we know we've lost ourselves.

"It's in us all! No one gets away—you die, you come back!" the man yelled as he weaved through littered sidewalks.

We were crossing through a park, so we hid in a playhouse.

The man's face was covered in grime, and he appeared to be wearing twenty layers of mix-matched clothing. His vociferous ranting was jubilant. He was almost skipping as hordes of corpses followed him, pouring out of every shadow—a Pied Piper bewitching his flock.

"We have to get away from here. Follow me," Fessy said and led the way.

There was a kind of manic determination in his voice and gestures. I knew a lot about manic episodes, and I worried.

"Susan," I said, when Fessy was several yards ahead of us, "do you notice anything different about Fessy?"

Zombies were everywhere, but while they focused on Fessy, they didn't pay much attention to Susan and me.

"What do you mean *different*? He's taking charge, Cole."

"Yeah, but it's as if he knows exactly where to go. This isn't the Hudson Valley. What are the odds he knows the inner workings of a random small town? It's like he's sure of something. I'm just not sure what that—"

A shambling corpse, a man in a tattered blue suit, pounced on Susan. I released my sai and drove one through the back of its skull. Its dead weight was heavier than I had anticipated, and it dragged me to the ground with it.

Their hungry groans engulfed us.

Susan grabbed my jacket's collar and pulled me through our rapidly closing pathway. As my feet gained traction, a zombie wearing a bloodied sundress lunged at my legs. I moved to kick it in the face, but before my boot made contact with its snapping jaws, the hungry corpse flew backward. The zombie on my left fell to the ground like a rag doll, then the zombie on my right fell, and another, and another.

Fessy stood at the end of an alley, aiming and shooting. He cleared a path for us and deflected the horde's attention off us and on to himself, causing the herd to bottleneck into a narrow path. Susan and I followed through an adjacent alleyway and met him around back.

"Thank you," I said, hugging him.

"You would've done the same," he said, and the three of us made our way through obscure backyards and littered alleys; the dead were always a few yards behind us.

I felt guilty for ever questioning Fessy's intentions and decided my doubts must have stemmed from putting my life in the hands of a twenty-year-old.

"It's getting dark," Susan said, panting. "We need to find a place for the night."

Fessy led us into a tight pathway between two identical brownstone apartment buildings. A herd awaited us at the end of the trail. We tried turning back, but the dead had already begun to file in behind us.

"Fuck!" I shouted and unholstered my gun.

Susan did the same, and we scanned the wall of corpses for any weak spots through which we could escape. There were none.

"If you don't have a clear headshot, do two body shots and then aim for the head," Susan instructed.

My brain began firing off different scenarios in which we didn't die, when Fessy yelled, "This way!"

He jumped, stepping on the wall for added height, and grasped on to the railing of the iron emergency escape staircase. His weight wasn't enough to release it from its rusty hinges, so Susan and I grabbed his legs and pulled.

The ladder came crashing down, knocking us on the pavement. The dead were almost upon us. Susan climbed first, then me, and Fessy was last. Susan and I shot several zombies who came close to grabbing him.

I pulled the ladder back up and out of the corpses' reach, although I doubted it was necessary. I don't think zombies keep any of their motor skills from their humans days, and they haven't done anything to prove me wrong.

We chose the attic apartment, and thankfully, it was empty. It was a small studio, not big enough for a family to live in comfortably but plenty of room for two Long Islanders and a seminary dropout.

While Susan and Fessy secured the place, I looked out the window and realized my senses were adapting to our environment. They were becoming keen to the slightest stir. A few days ago, I would have looked out and thought nothing but death was out there. Now, I saw the gentle ruffling of curtains. The effort the living put into hiding their movements was miles away from the clumsy, careless movement of the dead. There was life all around us.

"There's a small marina west from here. We'll visit it tomorrow," Fessy said as he served us dinner of beef jerky and juice boxes.

We ate it with gusto.

"I've brought dessert," Susan said as she rummaged through her backpack.

She pulled out a box of mixed chocolates and handed it to me.

It was Halloween themed, and the candies were shaped like ghosts and bats.

"Watch out, Fessy," I said, holding up the tin box so he could see it. "Susan is the worst with these. When we were young, she used to scratch the bottom of each chocolate to find the ones she liked and then put the rest back in the box."

The three of us broke into snorting laughter.

"You guys are disgusting," Fessy said in a tone that carried no judgment but was full of appreciation instead. "Popped each other's pimples, fingered each other's food—are you going to tell me you shared chewing gum as well?"

"I didn't," Susan said, pointing at me.

I cringed, remembering the look on my biology teacher's face when she saw me and Brooke sharing gum.

"I love Halloween," I said, trying to change the subject.

However, remembering All Hallows' Eve made me incredibly sad. It was like saying goodbye to my childhood all over again.

"How will anyone be able to dress up as monsters and ask for tricks or treats when we've all seen real monsters—or perhaps became the monsters ourselves. What holidays are gonna survive?"

While we mulled over this question, I chose three chocolates and passed the box to Susan. I kept the top where it detailed the different flavors—the mystery would be fun.

"Christmas has to survive, right?" Susan said.

"I don't know if *any* of the holidays with religious overtones can survive," Fessy answered.

The asperity in his voice sounded neither deliberate nor unsure.

"Thanksgiving will survive. It'll evolve into a new version of itself, but it'll gain worldwide recognition. Who can be more thankful than the ones who survive this shit?"

As if on cue, Fessy's words were punctuated by the flashing streetlights. The sudden blaze was as shocking as it was blinding. It lasted a second or two, but in that short time, the world looked alive again. Neon signs lit up, and shadow figures appeared behind apartment windows, giving us a taste of days gone by.

"The garden grows more than the gardener sows," I mumbled after the shock and adrenaline rush subsided.

The flashing lights reminded me that just as the three of us were on a mission, there were thousands—millions—of other survivors on their own mission, people with enough know-how to operate a power grid and who knows what else. Everything from the old world lay around for anyone to find: power sources, machinery, medication, and gear and weapons from machine guns to nuclear bombs.

Who will fare better post apocalypse? Doctors? Scientist? Builders? Or better yet, who will rise to unite all these valuable skills? Civilization pressed the Reset button on itself, and it was anyone's world for the taking.

I wanted to pursue this subject further; however, I was too exhausted to dive into all that.

Instead, I asked the *other* haunting question, "What do you guys think happened to the world?"

"I don't know," Fessy said as Susan passed him the box of chocolates. "Maybe a terrorist attack gone awry or a military experiment that escaped."

"Or maybe it's an ancient pathogen from a time before humans," Susan added.

"Like, dinosaurs?" I said.

"Perhaps. Or something from *before* that. Humans are only an eye blink in the earth's history—if that. We see this world as ours, but it belonged to other creatures for much longer than it has been our home. Do you know that fewer than one-tenth of one percent of all animal species have survived in a fossilized state?"

"I did not, Susan," I said, feeling a shiver course down my spine. "But I have often wondered what walked this earth before the time of before. Like all those tales of monsters and magic—where there's smoke, there's fire. Some people believe our thoughts are power, and if we sync up our brains, anything is possible. What if those creatures—the things that called earth their home for far longer than we have—disappeared because we, as a collective, stopped believing in them? Like we took their power or something. And this plague is their parting shot or their way of evening out the score."

"Maybe it is the Rapture," Fessy said, smirking, which I didn't know to take as sarcasm or utter belief. "Funny—every generation always thinks they're the last, that they're seeing the beginning of the end. I suppose someone had to be right."

Fessy's distressing—but accurate—statement was a total mood killer.

Sensing this, he shook his head and added, "All I know is you guys are some of the best people I've ever met. I can't think of better company to face the end with."

Although he still ended on a downer, Fessy's sincerity was heartfelt. No words were needed to acknowledge that the sentiment was reciprocal—our smiles said it for us.

"Ugh, licorice. Who eats licorice chocolate?" Fessy grimaced as he forced himself to finish the candy.

We laughed and settled in for the night. I don't know if we believed the infection was an ancient disease found in fossils or brought upon us by an extinct race of fairy-tale creatures following the scorched-earth approach. It didn't matter what we believed; it was just a way for our traumatized brains to process the impossible.

Alex likes black licorice jelly beans. I don't know why, but he does. He also likes the orange and cherry ones. I don't like those flavors. Curiously, he doesn't like the bubblegum, grape, and coconut ones-—my favorite. Do I need more proof that we're perfect for each other? He's the lyrics to my song.

Chapter 33

"I need your help," Alex says, closing his social psychology textbook.

"I'm not cleaning any more rooms for you," I warn him.

"Nah, it's not that. Do you know Rob? Short deaf guy, blond hair, square-shaped head, still in his teens?"

"Yes, I know Rob. I interpreted for him in orientation. What about him?"

"He came to the library the other day looking for an ASL Bible. We didn't have one, so I asked how else I could help him. His signing was too fast for me to comprehend so we switched to writing back and forth. He comes from a very religious Catholic family. Can you believe no one in his family knows sign language? He's forced to read lips and write notes, but he hasn't been able to understand any services because—"

"He has no one to interpret for him, and you'd like me to do it," I interject. "Alex, I love that you have faith and read the Bible and go to church every Sunday. It's endearing. But I grew up going to church and felt ostracized because of who I am. And don't get me started on what happened when I asked a priest how the Bible explains dinosaurs. Sorry, but I'm not looking to relive all that. And interpreting in religious settings is a whole different ball game. I'm not that good."

"Those were shitty people using religion to justify their own beliefs and insecurities. Besides, this isn't about religion—it's about helping. Church is the only connection he has to his family. You're an amazing interpreter. I know you can do it. Here, I'll say something and you sign it. 'Love never gives up and its faith, hope, and patience never fail'—Corinthians 13:7."

"L-O-V-E give up never. L-O-V-E list—first of list, faith; second of list, hope; third of list, patience, fail never," I sign. "And I think Corinthians is fingerspelled."

"See—I knew you'd be great!" he says, wrapping his arms around my waist and kissing me.

And with that, I had a new interpreting job every Sunday.

I awoke in the unfurnished living room and savored the remnants of my dream—or more like my dream of a memory. It was bittersweet being reminded of Alex's kindness, the same kindness that may have gotten him trapped on a company full of hungry corpses.

Shaking those thoughts away, I walked to the bathroom. The water in the apartment—and probably the entire state—was off. I had half a mind to use our drinking water to wash up but used the water-purifying straw to extract water from the toilet's tank instead.

Brushing my teeth, I looked out the window. The sky was an odd shade of gray, almost green, like a bruise. And the clouds rolled as if they were in a hurry to end the day.

Good, we must be nearing Stormville, I thought, trying to will it into existence, and realized I had no idea where we were, as Susan and I relinquished all navigating duties to Fessy.

I rinsed, spat in the sink, and walked over to the corner of the living room where Fessy was fast asleep.

I grabbed the map and compass out of his backpack and found a small hand radio with earbuds. I don't know what I had expected to hear—music, news, or survivors broadcasting, which was exactly what crackled in my ears. However, it was the last kind of survivor I wanted to hear from.

200

"'So whether we live or die, we belong to the Lord. For Christ died and rose to life in order to be the Lord of the living and of the dead'—Romans 14:8, brothers and sisters. The Rapture hasn't left you. It is not too late. Join us. We're at the New Windsor Private Academy."

It was hard pinpointing our location on the map, but I had a general idea of where we were—and where *he* was.

"Faysal!" I shouted while shaking him awake. "Tell me you didn't lead us here on purpose. Tell me you're not a fucking selfish, idiotic asshole!"

"What—fuck—what's wrong?" he said, and his eyes narrowed on the map and radio.

"What's going on?" Susan asked, her eyes wide with alarm.

"Faysal here," I began, pointing at him, "has been leading us to some psycho preacher in hopes of . . . I don't know."

"It's not like that! I swear we're on the best route or one of them at least," Fessy protested. "He calls himself Pastor Roman and claims the plague is God's plan. He's luring people, convincing them they should get infected—children, adults, babies. *Everyone.*"

Fessy's words hummed in the air, and his emotions pulsated the space between us.

"He's using Bible scriptures to warp their minds. Do you understand how many people are hurting right now? Lost people looking for something to believe in, and this piece of shit is preying on them, using a tool that's meant to heal."

"Faysal, I understand, but—"

"No! You don't understand, Susan!" Fessy interrupted.

His emotions prevented his outburst from sounding condescending.

"I know what these people are feeling because I *was* them. I was a lost kid. I hated people because they blamed me for a horrible attack that I had nothing to do with. They hated me because of my name, and the color of my skin, and what I called my god. I found a haven online. A place with others like me—or, at least, I thought they were like me . . . at first.

"Their ideology and teachings became more and more extreme. They told me blood had to be spilled for peace to reign—for my people to receive the world Allah had promised us. I had so much hate inside that I wanted to believe them. That year, one of my classmates came out as gay. The other kids ridiculed him, but instead of shying away, he shared his pain and loneliness with us. He started blogging about his struggles, and I read his posts every day. It let me know I wasn't alone. Gay, straight, Christian, Muslim, overweight, or handicapped—we all hurt."

Fessy's wave of emotion had receded, leaving a teary-eyed young man who didn't want to let people in pain make a terrible mistake.

Susan and I looked at each other and embraced Fessy.

While crying between us, he said, "I could've easily fallen prey to the worst of humankind. Pastor Roman can't win. When people like him win, humanity loses. Is that the world we're holding on to?"

"Okay, Faysal. You win. What should we do?" Susan said, volunteering me.

How long will this keep me from Alex? I wondered, selfishly.

"He's broadcasting from the academy's radio station," Fessy explained, sprawling the map on the floor. "We can cut through the academy's farm and follow the Hudson River north. But that's all I got so far. I was going to tell you guys about him this morning, hoping we could brainstorm a plan."

"You do realize we're not going there to protest outside his gate, right?" I said, looking deep into his eyes. "He's a fanatic, and his followers may be so convinced by his shit that they may see *us* as the enemy, there to attack their fearless leader. Faysal, you might—no, not *might*, you *will*—have to put an end to him, whatever that end may be. Are you ready to take it that far? Are you ready to live with the consequences?"

"Well, sir, if you were to put me and this here sniper rifle," he said, picking up his gun and doing his best *Saving Private Ryan* impersonation, "anywhere up to and including one mile from Adolf Hitler with a clean line of sight. Pack your bags, fella. War is over. Amen."

"I'm serious, Faysal," I admonished but smiled inside. I am a fan of levity.

"I can do it, Cole. Whatever it takes."

And with that, our plan was set into motion. We hoped it would just be a raving, lonely lunatic whom we could convince into becoming one of the creatures he deemed godly. But I doubted it would be that simple—life is complicated by design.

Monster or not, Pastor Roman was still a man. Sure, the idea of sacrificing one life for the lives of the many sounds defensible; however, in practice, such choices carry unforeseen ripples in one's soul. This experience would change Fessy forever. If it would change him for better or worse, that was up to Faysal.

Chapter 34

"Tell me again how we're selling this?" Susan asked. "Are we going full fanatic, ready to join the Rapture, or are we playing it off as doubters waiting to be convinced?"

"You're overthinking it," Fessy answered; his eyes and mind were on the rapidly darkening sky and distant thunder. "We're lost people looking for shelter. Let *him* sell us on it."

"Wait," I said, stopping us in our tracks. "'Do you hear that?"

The moans of the dead and rumblings of a storm were hushed by the cries of a child.

"It's coming from over the hill," Susan said, sprinting toward the wails.

It began raining as we raised after her, hoping to stop her from flinging herself into a desperate situation. However, it was Susan who stopped us, pulling us to the ground so we wouldn't be spotted.

The bawling child was actually a stereo with large speakers mounted on a tractor in the middle of a livestock enclosure. But instead of pigs, cows, or horses, Ol' McDonald had a farm of walking corpses.

The large pen had turnstile gates like a subway entrance. Zombies mindlessly followed the crying, the gates closing behind them, and the dead numbered in the hundreds. Their unison moaning and marching vibrated the earth.

"I guess the pastor understands his flock pretty well," I said, standing up and backing away from the edge. "Does he need to use a crying baby, though."

"I really fucking hate this guy," Fessy said, getting up and helping Susan back on her feet.

He led us back into the protection of the woods, and we walked east until we reached the river.

We didn't have to walk far; the radio station was visible soon after clearing the farm. Its tall antenna resembled a poorly constructed Eiffel Tower. The rain intensified the closer we got; combined with the cold, each drop felt like a hypodermic needle. The Hudson's brackish green water pulsated furiously, which made it appear as a giant anaconda splitting the land in half.

There was no one at the station; its broadcast played automatically on a loop. Fessy didn't know how to work the consoles, so he did the next best thing—destroyed any equipment that looked important. Our plan was to hide and wait for Pastor Roman to come investigate. However, the large antebellum mansion up the river road demanded our attention.

It was a beautiful whitewashed mansion. Once upon a time it had been the property's main residence. Then it was converted into the academy's administrative building. But currently, it served as Pastor Roman's unholy church. Chanting and blowing trumpets could be heard coming from the mansion. And every window was illuminated with a candle, like a lighthouse beckoning lost souls into hell.

We entered undetected through a side door, which wasn't hard to do because prayer in an ancient-sounding language accompanied by trumpets blared over every speaker in the house. We passed rooms filled with luggage, backpacks, tents, and clothing. And as we neared the center of the manse, the scent of sulfur got heavier and heavier.

Everything in me told me to grab my friends, turn back, and run. But it were as if the chanting had latched on to my inborn curiosity and wouldn't let go. I don't remember how long it took us to reach the large dining hall; I don't remember how Fessy got so far ahead of Susan and me; but I'll never forget the bodies lining every inch of the hall's walls.

There were seemingly hundreds of them, one atop the other. They were covered with white silk shrouds. There was no skin showing, but their shapes told us how young many of them had been. And at the end of the room stood a handsome tall man. He wore a black cleric's robe and was burning incense.

Pastor Roman was handsome in an "SS Nazi officer" sort of way. His eyes were *too* blue like arctic ice; his side-parted blond hair too yellow like a character from *Children of the Corn*.

I couldn't make out what Fessy was saying—he was too far—but I could hear the pastor. His voice perfectly complemented the trumpet's cadence.

"How can you say that the dead will not be raised to life? If that is true, it means that Christ has not been raised from death, then you have nothing to believe."

Fessy unholstered his gun and aimed it at the madman. I began walking toward them, when I felt Susan's death grip on my shoulder. The bodies had begun twitching underneath their shrouds.

"These loyal followers were not bit by the chosen," Pastor Roman rang. "Don't you see, brother? God's gift is *in* us. My flock drank the wine—the blood—of our savior. For just as death came to Him by means of a man, in the same way the rising from death comes by means of a man. I—"

The windows exploded all at once and bathed us in glass. Corpses poured in through every opening, shaking the foundation. They had been attracted by the noise and candles, and we had been too distracted to notice.

Pastor Roman's victims were reanimating, their naked bodies forming a wall between me and Fessy. Susan pulled me by the arm and led me out through the door we came in. The last thing I saw was Fessy chasing the pastor through a side exit.

The place had become a death trap as corpses blocked every exit. Susan and I cleared a path to the kitchen and out through the pantry's window. I emptied five clips and reloaded as if it were reflex. The rain poured, the wind howled, and the lightning and thunder confused the dead.

We climbed a steep hill to get a better view of the area. At first the storm made it impossible to find Fessy, but it were as if the universe wanted us to see it. The rain and wind lulled. We scanned the sea of dead; it was like a sick game of *Where's Waldo.*

"There!" She pointed at Pastor Roman's piss-yellow hair.

They were at the river's edge. Fessy aimed his gun at the man kneeling with arms outstretched to the heavens. Ten, maybe twelve, zombies were quickly encircling them. Fessy didn't seem to notice or care; his attention was on the lunatic praying to whatever god he had concocted.

Susan and I shouted, urged Fessy to look behind him. I know we were too far for him to hear us, but my mind has frozen the moment as it wants me to remember it.

Fessy swerved just in time for a zombie to miss him, and it fell into the river. He looked straight at us and smiled—a smile that said, "I love you. Keep going."

He turned back, and as he put a bullet through Pastor Roman's brain, the herd washed over Fessy, plunging him into the abyss. On the river's green surface there was a thin, snakelike strip of scarlet which dissipated when the rain returned.

The entire event is crystallized in my memory as if watching it in a snow globe.

We waited all night atop that hill. Faysal Spero Singh never resurfaced.

Chapter 35

How can I describe what heroin feels like?

Imagine you're nude, thrown out on the street, in the dead of winter, and someone covers you with the softest, warmest blanket you have ever felt. That's what it feels like.

However, we, humans, aren't supposed to feel *that* good all the time. Addicts run away from this truth or deny it altogether. We get stuck in a loop, constantly chasing the high—chasing the dragon.

My loop consisted of moments of clarity and sobriety, followed by action and accomplishment—getting my ducks in a row—then burn out. The low moments were always marked by an insatiable desire to escape—fix—-the energy-sucking sadness within.

It was during a weekly AA meeting in Green Haven that something finally clicked in my brain: Instead of rationalizing a relapse by seeing the pros and cons, why not just saying no to *everything*?

I didn't tell Alex I was adopting a *"no* across the board" mentality. Working toward sobriety while married to a fellow addict comes with extra challenges. I was at the mercy of his emotions, his cravings, his ups and downs, and the stress that comes with making a relationship work—especially in a desolate place such as prison. I needed time to strengthen my resolve on my own.

The first couple of months were torture. I'd pinch my thigh hard enough to leave a bruise every time I was asked to join the party festivities or lock myself in the bathroom where I would have one-sided arguments about the merits of saying *no*. Eventually the cravings became easier to deny, and I was ready to have the "let's get sober" talk with Alex when my father died.

Every inmate knows what it means when you're called to the cleric's building without previous warning. I thought one of the friends I hadn't talked to in a while must have been in an accident.

"Please, sit down, Mr. Trent. Your family contacted me this morning. I'm sorry, but your father, Jeffrey, died of a heart attack at 5:40 a.m. We can arrange . . ."

Time stopped. A tingle emanated from my toes and hands, spreading through my body. It felt as if my skin crawled with stinging ants. My face went numb, and while my tears went on autopilot, my breathing became an action I had to consciously control.

I could write pages—books, even—about this one day in early September. I've memorized every detail, from the way the deacon had misspelled my father's name on his pad (he wrote *Geoffrey*) to the way the butterflies danced as I walked through the yard behind the baseball cage to a small garden full of dandelions and roses. I fell to my knees, dug my hands in the soil, and screamed.

I've never screamed like that before or since. It was primal, tapped deep from a dark well. I learned a new level of grief that day.

Alex picked me off the ground and walked me back to my cell.

"Let's play chess," he said and set up the board on the stainless steel table.

Not having the mental capacity to do anything, I followed his lead. We played countless, mindless games of chess. And even though I cried as I played, there were also moments when I didn't cry.

There was crying that night during sex. I also cried the next day when he spoon-fed me breakfast, lunch, and dinner. I cried when Alex helped me shower, and I'd cry-laugh when he'd make fun of my horrendous breath since I wouldn't brush my teeth—or wash my face or follow any hygiene—for days at a time.

My pain suffocated me, preventing me from being much of a functional human being during my mourning. However, for the first time in my life, I also hadn't tried to escape my pain. The suffering was a reminder of the immense love I had for my father. Love and pain were one and the same; I couldn't have one without the other.

I found the duality in life. My drug use was rooted in my need to escape the bad and chase the good. But life is both good and bad, light and dark. Sadness wasn't something I needed to cure; it was something I needed to *feel*.

Once my tears dried, I shared my epiphany with Alex, and my sobriety became *our* sobriety.

"I have a surprise for you," Alex said on the night before our one-year anniversary and almost three months from our first full year of sobriety. "Meet me at the school's staircase, and make sure you're last."

Green Haven's architecture is a mix of 1950s psychiatric hospital and Stalin-era Russian—the four-floor, horseshoe school building favoring the latter.

"Close your eyes," he said, guiding me from one end of the horseshoe to the other where the library is. "Okay, open."

In the center of the school building, there's a courtyard where only grass grew.

But when I opened my eyes, a small tree covered in white blossoms was planted in the center.

"I had my boss champion the Catholic church for one of their trees," Alex explained, his hand on the small of my back. "It's a cockspur hawthorn."

He smiled.

"It's a perennial. It's here forever, like our love. Our lives will change. We'll weather storm after storm, grow old, and die—together and at the same time, of course. But this tree, like the things we'll accomplish, will outlive it all. It can handle every season, as we'll handle every season of *our* life, together."

I was speechless.

"I'm sorry. I hope it wasn't corny. I thought the gift for a first-year anniversary was wood, but that's for the sixth year. First year is paper, which fits since paper's made from—"

I stopped his nervous rambling by taking his hand and looking deep into his eyes.

"You're amazing," I said and moved to kiss him but stopped midway when I remembered we were on the fourth floor, surrounded by windows. I made up for it when we got to the library though.

Not only had he given me a living representation of our love but had managed to quote *Landslide* while at it—what Alex wanted, Alex got.

I thought about that tree while Susan and I waited atop the hill for any sign of Fessy. And as we ran through zombie-infested land, I thought about my sobriety journey and the life Alex and I will have built in this new world. I thought of my family and the island community they're building. I wondered if my niece will ever forgive me and understand why her mother did what she did. I thought about every person Susan and I left behind, wondering if we'll ever see them again.

I even tried remembering every time my dad told me to "get my ducks in a row" and distracted myself by guessing how the saying originated. (I think it has to do with the mother duck getting her ducklings in a row when they travel.)

I thought of anything and everything to keep me from thinking about the pharmacies we passed along the way and how *badly* I wanted to escape this godforsaken moment.

Chapter 36

The storm morphed into a hurricane, with gusts strong enough to knock us over. It were as if the tempest fed on our pain—and there was plenty to eat.

Anywhere we went, the dead followed. We had no map or sense of direction, so we found a red-brick Colonial-style apartment complex to wait out the weather.

It took us two hours to secure the floors—all six of them. I'd position myself at the bottom of the staircase, bang on the railing, and Susan, being the better shot, would pick the zombies off as they staggered to the stairs.

We heard moans and dead hands clawing behind apartment doors, but we didn't care; we didn't even bother moving the bodies off the stairs. Susan chose an apartment on the top floor, next to the emergency roof exit.

Using the butt of my gun, I rapped on the unlocked door and waited for the dead to come. No one answered. Somehow, the apartment possessed a sadder aura than us. A heavy gray film covered the neatly decorated space. The many picture frames told us the home belonged to a family of three: A handsome Asian couple and their young daughter who seemed to have been afflicted by some sort of breathing disorder. She's connected to an oxygen machine—in the earlier pictures, the tank is cylindrical and covered in star stickers; later, the clunky oxygen tank was replaced by a much smaller oxygen device—in almost every picture.

"Cole," Susan said, pointing at a compact, sticker-adorned oxygen machine sitting on the kitchen table.

Our senses sharpened as we raised our guns. The doors in the apartment were left open, which made securing the area much easier and faster—all the doors except one, the master bedroom.

"If you guys are in there," I said, after knocking on the door for over a minute, "we swear we're not here to hurt you. Just need a place to stay 'til the rain stops."

We didn't believe there was anyone behind the door, but neither did we want to be greeted with a gunshot.

I closed the door almost as soon as I had opened it. But it wasn't fast enough for the stench of rotting bodies and mothballs not to hit me—or for the image not to seared itself into my mind: a handsome couple laying on their large canopy bed, their young daughter nestled between them, their faces mummifying in an endless slumber.

I moved to push a small dresser in front of the door, but Susan stopped me and said, "We need dry clothes."

Bearing the horror, Susan ran into the room and grabbed a stack of clothes from the closet. She had been holding her breath and exhaled as she closed the door. Using her knife, she carved RIP on the wooden panel.

We changed into mix-matched sweatsuits and hung our clothes to dry in the kitchen.

"I'm gonna go inspect the other apartments for supplies and a map," I said while emptying my backpack of everything except ammunition.

"Okay. Please be careful." Susan's face was more pleading than concerned.

We did need a map, that was true. I also needed to channel my pain and anger over the loss of Fessy into something useful. However, there was more to my wanting to explore. A *more* that was hard to comprehend but has been familiar to me for over a decade.

Addicts call it "the monkey on our back." It's the ever-present echo in our subconscious urging us to get high and escape reality for a while. And its voice has only gotten louder since I came home, five days ago. There's no logic to my cravings; they're an inevitability I've had to learn to control and quiet.

I cleared one apartment after the other, putting my life in danger as I faced hordes of lumbering bodies—one bit my boot and narrowly missed my leg. All so I could check the medicine cabinets in bathrooms, kitchens, and night tables. I was ready to give up, remembering the nearest pharmacy, when I hit the jackpot— morphine and Xanax.

The drugs were prescribed to a Melinda Jones. And by the groans and scratching coming from behind a door, I guessed she wasn't going to be needing them. Telling by the pictures, Melinda looked to be three times my size. I was exhausted and couldn't risk a face-to-face confrontation. So I pushed a sofa in front of the door and opened it.

As planned, Melinda's corpse tripped, and I put a bullet through its skull. I hoped someone would do the same for me if I ever became one of them.

I stored the drugs in a hidden compartment inside my backpack but kept a few pills in my pocket. I had no plans of using any of it; they were just a safety blanket.

I left the apartment and headed back to Susan. A map, keychain compass, various canned and pouched foods, and a six-pack of bottled water safely packed away—all items found behind the second door, fourteen apartments ago.

Like I said, *illogical.*

Chapter 37

"I'm going to the roof," I said as I grabbed my backpack and a tiger-print fleece blanket I had found in the closet. "Keep an ear out for . . . everything."

Susan was almost asleep so she nodded and closed her eyes.

It was a beautiful October night. The rain stopped when the sun set, taking the cold with it. Stars blanketed the sky, and the moon washed the land in a ghastly glow. And there was silence. The flicker of the lighter when I lit my cigarette sounded like a mini explosion.

I looked over the map. It took two cigarettes' worth of time to find our location, and my heart sank when I realized we were almost eight miles away from the academy. As I stared at the stars, the moment Fessy went under played on a loop in my mind.

"Yes, he was swarmed, but you didn't see him get bit," I debated aloud with myself. "There was blood in the water though. The infected don't bleed—"

"What are you doing?" Susan asked, startling me and causing me to almost drop the map over the side of the building.

"Fuck, Susan! I didn't hear you enter the roof. I was studying the map," I said, glad to have finished smoking.

She remembered me as a heavy smoker, and I had been proud to tell her I'd quit years ago.

"Honestly, I'm looking for Fessy. I keep expecting him to jump out of the shadows or something. I know it's dumb—"

"It's not dumb," she interjected. "I looked for him the whole way here and was crushed when I realized how far we had traveled. But if he's out there, he knows the plan. He knows where to find us."

"So you are coming to Green Haven with me? Thank you," I said and hugged her. "Alex's family lives in Gowanda—Western New York, not Africa—we can take the Erie Canal together."

"Uh, I know it's not in Africa, Cole. I think that's racist to assume?" she said, making us laugh—the first since losing Fessy.

"Susan, it's my fault he's not with us. I was there when Fessy first heard the pastor on the radio. I saw the seed of an obsession on his face. And instead of taking it seriously, I was glad that he had something to keep him busy."

I turned from her gaze, stared into the dark expanse.

"You know, when I was in prison, every action, every decision had instant consequences. One careless word to the wrong person could get someone hurt. One lingering touch could have had Alex and I separated. I hated living in a state of hyperawareness. And when we got engaged, I sort of dumped the responsibility on him. He's so good with that stuff. He sees every angle and every outcome. I got comfortable believing all my choices didn't matter while Alex meticulously mapped out our next move. Of course, we can only plan until we can't. That's where I would come in. Alex hates unpredictability. I, on the other hand, revel in it. My dad used to say, 'Chaos is the mother of opportunity.'"

I swallowed hard and deliberately, slowing down my thoughts so I wouldn't lose them to nostalgia.

"Anyway, I got comfortable believing not every choice had dire consequences," I continued. "Then I thought it would be different once I came home. But I now realize there's no leaving that world behind. *All* choices matter. It was *my* idea to get on a boat. It was *my* choice to ignore Fessy's warning signs . . . and . . . fuck! I don't know what I'm doing! All I have is a dream. How could I have endangered your lives for a dream?"

Warm tears blurred my vision, and I turned away from Susan. She grabbed me by the arm and spun me around.

With a steel grip and cool eyes, she said, "I'm here because of that dream. Faysal knew the risks, just as well as I do. He made his choices. That's not on you. Cole, you gave us a reason to keep going. Look at this world."

She let go of my arm and made a grand gesture toward the darkness.

"I don't know if I'll find my brothers—I can't see how they'll survive in an apartment above a tattoo parlor. I hope they've gone north, to a place so cold these fucking cadavers freeze—"

"To death," I interjected. Couldn't help myself.

"Yes," she smiled. "Winter is coming, and I don't think they can handle it. They don't have circulation to keep them mobile. We'll wait until they freeze in place, and humanity has a shot again. 'Til then, all we have is *now* and *us*, which you gave us, Cole."

I had no words, just joy. I wrapped my arm around her and covered us with the blanket. I rested my head on her chest and listened to her heartbeat, as I used to do when we were kids.

"The weather has become unpredictable. It was below freezing a few days ago and now this lovely night," she said and breathed in the sweet tang in the air emanating from the nearby Hudson.

It was a reprieve from the sulfur and rotting meat stench to which we were becoming numb.

"So have you thought about how we're going to break Alex out of a maximum-security prison?" she said.

"It's obvious there's no government left to keep him in. If Green Haven hasn't been overtaken, then everyone is still in cages. Either way, Alex has enough supplies and know-how to survive until we get there. It's a thirty-foot wall, Susan," I said, looking her in the eye to see if she followed. "We can weather *anything* in there. We just need to figure out how to get in, not out."

Her mischievous smile told me she agreed.

"Look at all the constellations in the sky," she said, using her index finger to trace stars into shapes. "I've always heard about the effects of light pollution, but to actually see it—wow, we were really missing out on something beautiful. I wonder how the rest of the world is adapting."

"I hope to see the rest of the world one day," I said, allowing Alex to guide my thoughts. "My family owns a vacation home in Ancon, Peru. It's a beachside town between sandy mountains and the Pacific Ocean. Alex and I would fantasize about leaving everything behind and moving there—waking up next to each other underneath the southern sun, the aromas of jasmine, eucalyptus, and salt wafting through the windows . . . I know it's insane, but, Susan, I can still picture that life."

"There's nothing foolish about that. The world as we knew it is done, and like your dad said, there's opportunity in that. The future—any vision of it—is worth protecting. The love that you and Alex share the goodness and kindness in this world. Those things are worth fighting for. They need to outlast this pandemic," she said and threw a roof pebble at a lumbering emaciated corpse.

It wore tattered shorts, and its hands were sinew stumps. The creature groaned, arched its head in an almost 180-degree angle, and continued its vacant search for meat.

We chuckled—an empty, emotionless reflex since our minds still hadn't fully separated the monsters they had become from the humans they used to be.

Once the zombie disappeared behind a building, she continued, "And people like Alex and Faysal who risk everything to help dying men, save a little boy, or help a twenty-eight-year-old jailbird—"

"Hey!" I interjected, "*ex*-jailbird."

She smiled. "*Ex*—make it home. Those are the people we need to fight for. I'm done feeling sorry for myself. I'm ready. I *want* to survive. This world is going to be harsh. I don't think anything will be easy again—at least not in our lifetime—and we're going to have to do things we're not proud of. But I'm okay with that now. I know we'll have to make the hard choices because someone has to."

I nodded, taking her words in.

"Susan, back at Brooke's, Timothy—I mean, the boy—hadn't turned when we were overrun. He was going to, but he hadn't yet. I shot him. I killed him because I knew Fessy couldn't . . . or shouldn't. I don't know. I just knew it would change him forever."

"That's what I mean! You did what had to be done because not only did you want us to survive—you wanted to preserve the goodness in Faysal. That is laudable, Cole. We all have a role to play in this new world, and I think we have just begun to understand ours."

I smiled. I don't know if it was sharing the secret, or her response, or both. But my revelation felt better than pulling out an infected tooth. Alex (and I suppose my father too, if I count my dream) was right—*we all have a job to do.*

"Here, look at this," she said as she pulled a tube out of her pocket. "It's a laser target. I brought it in case we needed help with our aim."

She flashed the laser on a corpse's eyes and then pointed it at a wall. The fiend groaned and clawed at the green light. She pointed the laser up the street and into the woods, prompting the creature to mindlessly follow it.

"How did you figure that out?" I asked, amazed.

"When we were on the hill. It was hard to aim through the rain, so I used the laser to get a better shot, and those fuckers began chasing it. How did you think we were undisturbed for so long?"

I hadn't been thinking.

Going back to that day reminded me of something the pastor had said. It was connected to the ravings of the homeless-looking madman and went as far back as to what Alex had said about Oldman Danny becoming infected without being bitten—something I hadn't allowed myself to decipher because of its grave implications.

The temperature dropped sharply, and we went back inside. I decided not to share the dark seed germinating in my mind yet. It wasn't important tonight. What mattered was that we had purpose. We had goals and dreams. We had each other.

Chapter 38

The sun shone through heavy clouds, covering the day in gray. According to the map, if we cut through wooded hills, Green Haven was two miles up the Hudson. Susan and I were in agreement: We would reach our destination today, even if we had to walk in a blizzard or until our feet bled. We changed into our dried clothes and headed out.

"Hey, Susan, there's something I've been meaning to run by you," I said as I walked behind her down the hallway. "It's about what that crazy homeless guy and pastor—"

She reached the bottom of the stairs as I reached the first step. Her body constricted and her hands went up. Instinctively, I stepped back and hid behind the railing, my 9mm in my hands and ready.

"Looky, looky. What do we have here?" said a voice that sounded greasy and as if it were filtered through a meat grinder.

"Well, Phil, it looks like we've found ourselves a pretty bitch," the second man said, his voice slithering in the air like a snake. "We better make good use of her before Terrence calls dibs on this one too."

"No, don't," Susan screamed while trying to run back up the stairs.

The man with the greasy meat voice pushed her to the floor. I heard his boot kick her stomach, knocking the wind out of her.

I didn't have time to think; I saw my opening and took it. As soon as I heard Susan hit the ground, I turned to face her attacker and put a bullet through the head of the man standing over her. His lifeless body ricocheted off the wall.

Before the other man finished saying *fuck*, I put a bullet through him too. I aimed for his head but got his neck instead. The gunshot ripped half of his throat on to the wall. He was still choking on his blood as I picked Susan off the floor and made our way to the exit. But as soon as we pushed the door open, the sole of a tan boot kicked me in the face, causing me to fly backward and hit the wall.

I went in and out of consciousness. My senses were a pulsating kaleidoscope of colors and sounds. I heard Susan struggling against a voice that seemed too large to belong to one person.

"You're gonna fucking get it now, you stupid bitch," the gigantic voice boomed.

I regained my vision to see a linebacker of a man on top of Susan. With one hand, he held her down by the neck; with the other, he fumbled for the handcuffs in his back pocket. I reached for my gun but couldn't find it, and then the brute noticed me.

He rushed me and pushed me back on the floor, my sai holster excruciatingly stabbing my spine. He was on top of me, his sausage-sized fingers around my neck, crushing my windpipe.

Panic clouded everything. I traveled to a place beyond the pain, beyond light and dark—to a place where I could hear my heartbeat and nothing else.

I woke up in an apartment similar to the one Susan and I had stayed in, but this one didn't have a lived-in feel to it. The furniture was bland, the colors beige.

My head pounded at my slightest movement, as if my brain had disconnected from my skull. My breathing felt as tight as if I were sucking air through a straw.

Susan! my mind screamed, regaining my senses.

I tried standing but was yanked back down. My wrist was handcuffed to the radiator.

"Oh look who decided to join us. It's a fucking party now," he said.

He was at least six feet three and only wore gray sweatpants. The sight of him saddened me. He was handsome, the body of a Greek statue and the kind of face that differentiates a forgettable NFL quarterback from a superstar. And how this man could have sunk to such a low was a discouraging commentary on humanity.

"Terrence, I presume?"

My voice sounded as if I had smoked a carton of cigarettes and washed it down with a gallon of sand.

He recoiled at the sound of his name. I don't know if he was surprised I knew it or hearing it aloud reminded him of who he used to be and how far from that person he had become—assuming he was a somewhat decent man to begin with.

"Where's Susan, Terrence? What have you done with her?"

"Calm down, faggot. She's resting right here," he said, pointing at the sofa in the corner.

Susan lay lifeless, her hands bound and her pants off.

"Don't worry. Susan is just taking a nap. Must've choked the bitch too hard. I want her awake so she can really enjoy this," he said as he stroked his hardening dick over his sweatpants and licked his lips.

"You two really fucked shit up for me. Phil and Cash were fucking idiots, but they were useful. They deserved better than what you fucks did to them."

As I listened to Terrence's rant, I looked over at Susan and realized her hands were moving. She had been faking. I scanned the room for anything we could use to defend ourselves and felt my sai pressing against my back. The door to the hallway was wide open; Terrence's friend Cash lay dead in a pool of coagulated blood.

"Oh, those rapist fuckers were your friends," I said in hopes of distracting him. "Well, guess what? I shot them. One in the head and one in the throat. Would have shot their dicks off if I had had the chance."

"We got a livewire here, ladies and gentlemen," Terrence said, pulling his erect dick out of his pants and giving me his undivided attention. "You know, I was gonna save you for last, but, baby, you just do something to me. I like a bitch with a nice mouth—look how hard you got me."

He began jerking off, probably trying to ejaculate on my face. I saw Susan furiously working on the rope around her wrists, and I looked away as to not draw attention to her. So I focused on the door and the dead body on the floor. Except, Cash wasn't so dead. He moved.

He reanimated as all the infected had, but there was no groan since I had blown out its voice box. My instinct was to scream, warn of the danger silently crawling its way into the apartment. However, Terrence stood between me and the zombie.

Susan realized this as well. She stopped struggling with her binds and grabbed the laser pointer out of her coat. She flashed the laser on its eyes and then at the back of Terrence's leg.

I looked into Terrence's eyes, licked my lips, and then looked at the purple head of his throbbing dick. I wanted him to be in the moment, nowhere else.

"Oh yeah? You're a dirty faggot, aren't yah? You want this big cock in your ass, don't yah? You want me to fuck you raw? Oh yeah, baby, I'mma bout to c-c—"

Terrence's scream was high-pitched, like screeching car tires before an accident.

While Terrence wrestled with the corpse chewing on his calf, I grabbed my sai and drove it through the handcuff's chain link, twisting and breaking it. Once freed, I ran to Susan and used my sai to free her. The zombie was on top of Terrence, his forearm in its jaws.

"Just grab your shit and let's get the fuck out—"

A gunshot roared in my ears, and blood splattered on my face.

Chapter 39

Eight grams of metal changed the course of life as I had begun to know it, as I had hoped to know it. A single bullet managed to obliterate a part of me—a piece of my soul—without spilling a drop of my blood.

The bullet tore through Susan's chest, past a centimeter or two from my ear, and hit the wall behind us. Ignoring the hum in my left ear and the empty clicks of Terrence's gun while he screamed, I ran to Susan and held her in my arms before she hit the ground. I pressed my hand on her wound, but I couldn't stop the bleeding. Nothing could.

"Susan, please. No, please don't leave me," I cried.

"I . . . I," she labored to say as blood choked her words, "I don't want to die."

"Then don't! Don't fucking die, Susan. Please, just tell me how to fix you. Tell me what to do!"

"I . . . I want to stay . . . why can't I stay?" she said as her hand touched my face, her blood mixing with my tears.

"Please stay with me. Please, god, please stay . . . I don't know what to do," I cried and held Susan, watching as life left her eyes.

Rocking her back and forth, trying to will whatever life I had in me into her, I cried, "Someone please tell me what to do."

I stopped when I saw Cash lose interest in its friend and set its dead eyes on me. There was enough sense left in me to know Cash didn't kill Terrence out of altruism. It had been the empty hunger all the walking dead share. However, as I glanced at Terrence's mangled body, I couldn't help feeling a pang of gratitude toward the creature. I drove my sai through its temple and dragged the body into a small bedroom, closing the door behind me—the closest thing Cash will have to a funeral.

Terrence was beginning to reanimate as I put pants on Susan and propped her up on the sofa. I had thought that when Terrence came back, I would have an epic battle with it, destroy it limb by limb as I channeled my pain into violence. However, as he groaned back to "life," I just wanted him gone and out of our presence.

I stuck my sai through its nose and slowly pushed it into its brain. I dragged its body out to the hallway and crushed its face under my boot. Overkill, I guess.

I didn't know how much time I had to prepare, so I set out scouring the apartment for mine and Susan's stuff. I found our guns, holstering mine and putting hers in my backpack. My leather bomber was easy to wipe cleanish, but blood had soaked through my sweatshirt so I borrowed one of Susan's.

I studied psychology because the choice made sense to me. I was in prison, away from all the luxuries with which I had grown up and had taken for granted. In other words, I was stripped to my barest—unable to hide behind the pretty and shiny things most people use to distract others from seeing their authentic selves. And I wasn't alone; it was the perfect opportunity to find out if people who appear one way on the outside are another way on the inside.

Living among serial killers, rapists, and addicts, I saw every type of learning and social disability detailed in the *Diagnostic and Statistical Manual of Mental Disorders*. It was fascinating experiencing the dark side of sanity. At first, I focused on the obvious—addiction and the cycle of abuse. But I wasn't learning anything I hadn't read about in countless books. So I turned my attention to the infamous shit flingers.

People can spend years—decades, even—in solitary confinement. They're in a cage for twenty-three hours a day; their only respite is from one cage to a slightly larger cage where they can get some fresh air. Of course, tensions run high, and arguments can be heard from sundown to sunup; however, due to restricted contact, they can't channel their anger and frustration into physical violence. So some inmates attack their adversaries by throwing piss or semen but mostly feces.

When one gets hit with feces in the SHU, that person has two viable choices—become the damned and throw shit back or take it in stride and hope to forget it ever happened. The latter hold on to their sanity, while the former find a new reality where they're the sane ones and the rest, the non–shit flingers, haven't caught on yet.

I took that to be the key difference between the sane and insane—crazy people don't know they're crazy.

As I put on Susan's navy blue SUNY Oswego hoodie, looking myself over on the mirror and wiping caked blood off me, I knew something in my brain had snapped. And I could see, with my mind's eye, the proverbial gear breaking. I knew I had entered a place where reality and madness merged. But I was beyond caring.

I found the master bedroom at the end of the hall and set up Susan's possessions on the bare mattress, putting the laser pointer in my jacket pocket. Sitting Indian-style on the carpeted floor, I lit a cigarette and studied the map, memorizing the route to Green Haven.

And waited for Susan to come back.

Chapter 40

My brain had completed the puzzle as soon as I saw Cash reanimate. It all made sense—Oldman Danny turning without being bitten, how quickly the infection had devoured the world, the corpses' affinity for throwing themselves into flames.

"It's in us," the madman had raved.

The *Ophiocordyceps unilateralis* fungus is found in the Amazon jungle. It infects ants, hijacks their nervous system, and makes them use their mandibles to affix themselves to a major vein on the underside of a leaf where the host remains until its eventual death. Then, the fungus's spores rip through the ant's skull, and the cycle repeats itself. ACRES reminds me of that.

"ACRES! ACRES! ACRES!" I repeated it over and over.

It felt funny calling it that, seeing it had outlived the government who gave it that name. Humanity was going to have to call it something other than "the infection." It was here to stay. This wasn't a disease we would endure and adapt to. We humans weren't outliving anything anymore. You don't come back, period. The snow began to hit the windows. Wet, emaciated snowflakes; but the first of the season, nonetheless. I pressed my hand against the cold glass. I wanted it to hurt, but I felt nothing. I had the disconnected urge to punch a hole through the window, when I heard her.

"Susan," I called out with childlike expectation, like a kid who has heard mommy coming home from work.

"It's me, Cole. Do you remember *anything*?" I said, entering the living room.

I don't know what I had expected to find behind the dull glaze of her eyes. Humanity, I suppose. All I saw was hunger.

She lunged at me, tripping over the coffee table where I had set up some of the family pictures I found in her backpack. I pointed the laser in her eyes and led her toward the master bedroom.

I jumped on the bed when she entered the room. Her teeth snapped as fast as a mousetrap. Her hands were hooks, clawing at the air. As expected, she had trouble reaching me over the high bed. She tripped and had to crawl. I continued this game of "chase around the room," always making sure there were a yard or two between us and furniture for her to trip on.

"I'm sorry I was weak. I'm sorry for all the pain I caused and all the lies I told you. Even though I wasn't there for you, I've spent the last ten years imagining what you were going through and the hope that one day you'd tell me what I've missed is what kept me going. I built who I am today around you—on what you taught me.

"You were the voice in my head telling me to work harder. Do better. I'm not going to fail you. I'll find Alex and all the people we love. We're going to unite with other survivors and rebuild this world.

"You helped raise me, Susan. When our parents were out working late, it was you who made sure I had finished my homework," I began, slowly walking backward out of the room. "It was you who talked me into all those volunteer programs so I could add them to my college resume. The real reason I didn't go away to school was because *my parents couldn't afford it*. Dad made a few bad investments, and we were broke. We barely kept the house. I regret not telling you the truth. I know you would have helped me figure something out. Shame is a motherfucker.

"I love you, Susan O'Connell," I finished, closing the bedroom door behind me. "I'll be back. I swear."

Not ready to envision a world without Susan, I convinced myself that was the same as keeping her on life support after the doctor has declared brain death. I carved "DEAD INSIDE" in big, thick letters on the door and left the building.

Walking into the cold night, I realized Susan was right—winter was going to be our ally. If the dead were slow before, they were borderline catatonic now. I weaved through them without effort and stayed relatively unseen as I made my way through woods and grassy knolls.

The night went quick or, at least, it felt like it did. I had lost all concept of time and reality. I wasn't functioning on strength, will, or even pain. I was running on mania—a frantic energy born from when there's nothing left to feel.

Dawn began to change from gunmetal to a scarlet purple, and I spotted my first mark, the Newburgh Beacon Bridge. Its "WARNING! CONSTRUCTION UNDERWAY!" sign flashed orange through the early morning fog, beckoning not only me toward it but every walking corpse in the Hudson Valley as well.

Corpses tainted the horizon as far as the eye could see. I considered commandeering one of the many tanks the military had left stranded on the road, but nothing was going to be able to get through the shambling sea of decay. And I had no idea how to drive a tank.

I didn't need to get to the bridge; I had to get to the other side of the river. I thought about swimming across, but thankfully I still retained some semblance of sense. To me, the Hudson had become a living entity whom I hated—a monster that had swallowed Fessy and was now impeding me from reaching my destination, my purpose.

However, I reminded myself this was a tamed monster. I had passed many houses that called the Hudson their backyard. According to the map, this section of the river is a thousand feet wide so any floating device would do.

I canvassed the shore, moving from one empty dock to the next. The land was treacherous; gone were the grassy-areas and sidewalks, replaced by jagged boulders and haggard trees. I almost fell into the frigid gray river on more than one occasion; the only thing that saved me were the anemic, windswept branches reaching toward the water. And the dead were everywhere.

They moved north toward the bridge. Their swelling numbers droned the ground, like a beehive calling the cavalry. I was spotted but was able to escape through the yard of a large Victorian house. Exhausted, I almost missed the small motorboat. It was carefully concealed under branches and leaves. I didn't care to whom it belonged; such concerns had become trivial, a remnant of a time before.

I cut the rope and pushed the boat on to the shore, when I heard the crackling of dried twigs. It wasn't the sloppy movement of the dead; they were calculated noises—a person attempting stealth.

"Not another fucking step," I warned, turning around with my gun aimed.

"Woah, my friend. Please, don't shoot. I have a family. I don't want any problems," he said, his hands up and his face full of fear.

"If you don't want problems, what are you doing sneaking up on me?"

"That boat is all my family has. I have a baby, man. Only a few months old. We can't travel, so I scavenge for supplies. Please, winter is coming. We'll starve without that boat."

His face was windburned, and he sported a wild chestnut beard. His teal-colored eyes were pools of burden, and the warmth emanating from him said he'd do anything for his family. He reminded me of Alex.

My body began trembling and tears ran down my face.

"I-I'm sorry," I said. "It has just been too much—I've been through too much."

I fell to my knees and gasped for air—*anything* to help me keep going.

"I know, man. It's okay. I don't blame you. It's hard for everyone. But please calm down. Those monsters are everywhere," he pleaded.

His voice was fatherly, and it helped me gain control of myself.

"You can stay with us, if you want."

"No, I can't. I gotta cross the river, to Green Haven. I've come too far to stop now."

"Green Haven!" he exclaimed and mulled over his thoughts. "I'll take you there, but we must wait 'til dusk. We need the cover of dark. Name's Callum King. You?"

His house, a cozy ranch, was concealed with brown trees and overgrown dried ivy.

"How can you invite me into your home?" I said once he closed the door behind us. "I tried taking your boat and pointed a gun at you."

"I served in Iraq, Cole. I've seen what a shit situation does to good people. Right now, humanity is our most precious commodity. Everyone's worth a once-over. And you did have a gun pointed at my head. I could not *not* invite you in." He smiled, letting me know the past was forgiven. "Come meet my family."

He led me to the basement, which he had done his best to soundproof. Emma, his wife—a pretty brunette no taller than five feet—greeted us with a scowl.

"There ya gon' and done it agin, Call," she said, obviously not a native New Yorker.

"Em, this is Cole, and he's gonna help us. He's going to Green Haven."

Callum's younger brother, Stephen King (no relation to the author, I asked), worked as a correctional officer in Green Haven. Some of the locals had sought shelter in the prison. Stephen was supposed to find them safe passage, but the bridge and surrounding area were overrun. Callum hadn't heard any news from Dutchess County on the other side of the river, and they couldn't risk traveling with an infant.

"Don't worry, Callum, Emma, I'll find Stephen. Even if I don't, I'll send help somehow. I swear," I assured them. "You guys have enough supplies to last until help comes?"

They were running low on supplies. Callum had guns and rifles to spare, but their blast would alert every corpse in the vicinity. He couldn't risk getting swarmed; his family needed him. But safe scores were becoming harder and harder to find.

"Here," I said, reaching into my backpack and handing Callum Susan's gun and half of her ammunition. "The silencer should help."

I also gave them half of my food.

"I know it's mostly candy, but the jerky is protein."

Callum didn't speak, didn't stretch his hand out to me. He gave me a bear hug.

I wanted to return the emotion, tell him it's the least I could do, but I didn't. I had nothing left to give.

"Come meet my daughter, James," he said, pointing at a closed door.

James King slept in the bathtub of the small windowless bathroom. The walls were heavily insulated, making it the safest place to keep her cries from reaching the dead.

"No, thank you. I've been on the road too long, who knows what I could expose her to," I lied, sort of.

Yes I had been out there for what felt like years, but the real reason I didn't want to see her was that I didn't want to taint her with my presence. James is pure. She's everything that was worth saving in this world. I didn't know how seeing her would affect me, and I didn't have it in me to find out.

Although traveling by boat was better done at night, it was not recommended for traveling by foot. The dead don't need eyes to hunt. So we set out at an hour close—but not too close—to dawn.

Callum spent the night teaching me the safest route to the prison, an old railroad track that cut through the heart of Stormville. We rode in silence.

When we reached the Dutchess County shore, I hugged him and whispered, "I promise to come back. It's not just the bite anymore. The plague is in all of us. You die, you come back."

I got off the boat and ran into the cover of trees. I didn't wait or look back to see if Callum had understood my message. If he meant to survive, he had to learn to understand such things on his own.

Chapter 41

My skin couldn't tell if the air was warm or cold. I didn't notice the sun chase away the moon. I can't even say how many, if any, lumbering corpses I passed as I reached the center of Stormville. I mean, they were there, snapping their teeth, waiting for me to get closer. I just hadn't cared.

I felt older than ancient—a walking relic, a living memento of the way the world used to be. Every memory within me was a story I knew needed to be told but couldn't possibly bear to tell it in fear that there would be nothing left of me.

Life and death—simple terms to explain the same thing.

"What the fuck are you talking about, Cole?" I muttered.

My thoughts had become fragmented and unreliable. Every idea felt as if I had either found the hidden side of sanity or plunged into madness.

So perhaps it was the latter that protected me like when drunk people fall and never seem to get hurt. I was invincible, on a mission from the universe itself.

Only then could I rest. Alex would fix me; he would fix everything.

The buildings northward of the prison blazed, endangering the hills beyond but attracting most of the infected away from the south entrance. There was a lull between straggler zombies, and I seized the opportunity.

Banging on the forest-green metal gate, I waved at the security camera. No response. I tasted acid in my mouth, and my ears burned.

"Fuck! How did you not consider that maybe there wouldn't be any power to open the gate," I yelled mostly to myself, beating both fists on the cold steel and pleading at the camera.

All the entrances to Green Haven are made of exceptionally thick steel and can only be opened by a motorized pulley system. Or a bomb. I began searching my fractured mind for anything useful I had passed: abandoned tanks, military tent cities, SUVs in the parking lot, and the dead. Some—a lot—of the corpses wore military uniform.

Grenades are standard military gear, right? I wondered, when the chorus of the dead drowned out everything.

"Great place to brainstorm, Cole," I mocked as I unholstered my gun and counted heads.

Thirteen.

I shot at the gate, hoping to make a quick escape. But the bullet ricocheted into the pavement.

Breathe.

I picked off the closest six corpses, using body taps to get a clearer headshot. But my aim faltered on the seventh zombie. Its movement was too uneven—too unnatural—due to its missing left foot. However, it possessed speed, and it closed the distance faster than I could reload.

"Get some, motherfuckers," I said as I dropped my gun and kicked the fiend backward.

The corpse landed on two of its brethren, and they fell like bowling pins.

Unsheathing my sai, I rushed the fallen creatures and drove my weapons through their eye sockets. I ignored the third corpse—due to its missing arms, it was struggling to get up—and focused on the two lurking zombies dressed in black Kevlar riot gear. Their face visors were halfway down, making a clean blow through the eye impossible. I aimed for their noses, but their feral hunger made them lead with their gaping jaws. So I drove my sai through their mouths, upward into their skulls, annihilating them both simultaneously.

Without missing a beat, I twisted and pulled out my sai from their decaying skulls. The remaining two staggering corpses wore tattered evening gowns; their hair still held the semblance of a classic updo. Had I anything left in me to feel, I would've felt immensely saddened by them, perpetually stuck in a dead loop, cursed to scour for a gala that will never be. I kicked the zombie on the left in the stomach, knocking it down. Then weaved around the one on the right and drove my sai through the base of its skull.

The commotion had attracted every dead in the area. I was surrounded. I drove my sai through the other corpse in the evening gown and made my way back to the entrance, remembering to debrain the armless zombie who was still squirming on the ground.

As I neared the gate, I picked up my gun and wondered if that was the end.

Is this how the story ends?

I didn't feel fear though. I felt calm—either I was going to die or I wasn't. The simplicity was refreshing when I noticed the security camera had moved. It had followed me. Someone had watched me fight for my life.

"OPEN, NOW," I said and signed simultaneously into the camera.

I didn't know if the camera had sound or if whoever was watching knew ASL, so I covered all my bases.

"IF YOU DON'T OPEN DOOR, I WILL KILL YOU!" I said and signed again.

I remembered the two riot gear–wearing zombies I had finished, and although I didn't know if they carried grenades, whoever was watching didn't know either.

"OPEN OR I USE BOMB," I bluffed and pointed at the two corpses wearing Kevlar.

The herd was yards away, and panic enwrapped my chest, constricting my breathing. I didn't want to die; I wanted to fight, find Alex, and rebuild this world.

Looking for an opening in the herd, I raised my sai and began planning an exit strategy.

I could put on the riot gear and make a run for it, I thought. *Or I really could find a grenade. Breathe.*

I was ready to run when the entrance opened. It was a gap no bigger than two feet. I took off my backpack and slid it under the gate—diving headfirst behind it in case the gatekeepers changed their minds.

The entrance tunnel was dark and silent. I sheathed my sai, reloaded my gun, and put on my backpack. The tunnel led to a dried-up garden where I was greeted by twelve, fifteen machine gun–toting people.

"Put your weapon down, now!" ordered a tall, muscular black man.

He wore a green sweatshirt and blue jeans.

I couldn't tell if he was a CO or an inmate, and I was too exhausted to read the situation. Besides, it didn't matter who had control of the prison. I had come too far for anyone or anything to get in my way.

"I'm here for Alexander Oz. And *this*," I said, aiming my Beretta at his head, "this is my proof of release. So someone please get him, and we'll be on our way."

Four of the men, including the one I had my gun pointed at, began to snicker and chuckle—testing the last of my sanity.

"I'm not fucking playing. Where's—"

The crowd parted, and I saw Jack, followed by Rob, making their way toward me. Rob ran past Jack when our eyes met. Seeing a familiar face took the fight out of me. I lowered my gun and closed the distance between us.

Hugging Rob, I felt his thin arms wrap around me. I held him so tightly that I thought he would melt into me. Tears began to form, and I willed them away.

Not yet, I told myself.

I pulled away and made sure he could see my lips and hands.

"Alex, where?" I signed, remembering to scrunch my eyebrows to imply a question.

Rob looked down at the floor.

I shook him and forced him to look me in the eye.

Putting my hands on his bony shoulders, I asked again, "Where's Alex?"

"Sorry," he mouthed, shaking his head.

"No! Tell me where he is. Take me to him now!" I yelled, no longer just to Rob but to anyone who could hear.

"Cole, please, calm down," a disembodied voice said.

I held up my gun, searching for the owner of the voice slithering through the air.

"Woah, Cole, don't do some dumb shit," Jack said.

The traumatized mind works in funny ways. I should have been focused on all the machine guns pointed at me, their safeties long ago clicked off. I should have focused on the words being said and the familiar faces staring at me in disbelief. Instead, I focused on Jack's shiny bald head and the scent of his aftershave. He smelled like Alex.

"Fucking tell me where Alex is, Jack."

"He's not with us, brother. Please, lower your weapon."

"What do you mean? Where did he go? Back home?" I said, lowering my gun.

"No, Cole. He's gone. Dead."

"Get the fuck outta here, you're lying. He can't be dead. He's the strongest among us!" I yelled.

I either spun in circles or the ground underneath me spun. I'm not sure; it could've been an earthquake.

Still spinning, I raised my gun and shouted, "Why are you lying! What are you hiding?"

"Everyone calm down. Put your fucking weapons down," Jack's voice echoed from every direction.

Rob stopped me midspin, held me by the shoulders, and locked eyes with me. He may have mouthed it. He may have said it; he's deaf, not mute.

"He's dead, Cole. I saw it."

My blood turned into crawling ants. I lost feeling in my legs, and I fell. But not as if gravity pulled me to the ground; it were as if the sky turned a deep velvet and fell on me—plunging the world into the vacuum of the darkest void.

Part III

EVOLVE

Extinction is the rule, survival is the exception.

—Carl Sagan

Chapter 42

"Holy shit, Alex. These chicken wraps are delicious," I say, tearing into my third burrito.

"It's all about the seasoning," he says while collecting all the dirty dishes.

Alex can't enjoy his cooking until everything is cleaned and put away. I, on the other hand, don't mind dirty dishes left in the sink for the next day.

However, this dinner was different. Tomorrow, he'll be moving to the Hospice Unit, and I'll be released from prison. Tonight is our last night together—until he makes parole. Attention must be paid.

I put my burrito down, pick up the greasy pan and dirty pot he used to make the chicken filling, and follow him to the slop sink.

"Alex, I'm serious," I say as I squirt dish soap into the pot and pass it to him. "You're an amazing cook. You have the palate and skill for it. Have you ever considered making a career of it? You have the look for it too. Sexy, dangerous woodsman, without the ironic hipster vibe. Perfect."

His laugh fills the small space with warmth.

"Nah. I didn't find a passion for cooking until I came to prison. When I was home, people didn't expect much from me. I don't know. I didn't think about a career or what I wanted to do with my life. My parents were happy if I got a job at the local Coca Cola factory—figured that's as far as I needed to look."

Alex's vulnerability is intoxicating. In front of me stands a man who had never asked himself what he's good at but is on the cusp of figuring it out.

I must have gotten lost in thought because when my mind returns, the dishes are done and Alex is facing me with a smirk.

"Sorry, your culinary skills and attention to cleanliness is an irresistible aphrodisiac," I tease and get close to him.

With both hands, I cup his dick over his wet maroon shorts. His body matches my excitement, and I feel his hands cupping my ass. He picks me up, I wrap my legs around his waist, and he sits me on the sink.

My hands trace every muscle on his arms as he thrusts his hardness into me. Our kissing is passionate but with a tinge of desperation. It's as if we're trying to consume the other's life force.

"No, Alex," I purr while he kisses my neck and slowly pulls my pajama bottoms down. "Not here. We can get caught."

"*And*? They're gonna stop you from going home? Charge you with homosexual activity?"

"No, but they can give you a disciplinary ticket, Alex. Then you won't be able to work in hospice, and we need as many gold stars on your record as we can accumulate."

"Who gives a fuck?"

He lets go of me and picks up the dishes. His erection had instantly deflated.

"Who gives a fuck? I do, Alex. I know you're scared. I'm scared too—"

"No you're not," he interrupts. "You walk around with confidence like you got everything fucking figured out—like you know exactly what you want."

"Enough with the 'I'm a poor boy who doesn't know what he wants' routine."

I want to comfort him but can't. When disinfecting a wound, one must get it all—no matter how much it hurts.

"You have *everything* that matters in this world—health, family, good looks, smarts, and talent. And most importantly, a person who *really* fucking loves you. I'm crazy about you, Alex. I wake up thinking of ways to make you laugh and go to sleep wondering if I succeeded. You want to know why I get what I want? Because I know how to ask for what I want. I want you, Alex—*all* of you. I don't think our lives will be easy. I don't even know if you'll get paroled next year. I just know that I want to spend my life with you. The rest, we'll figure out, together."

Without saying a word, Alex sets the dishes down and, with the back of his hand, he caresses my face. I kiss his knuckles.

"I love you," he whispers. "How about we finish this in my cell? We can put the blanket up and celebrate our last night together—until I join you out there."

"Mr. Oz, wouldn't the neighbors know we're up to unholy acts? What will they say?"

"Let them talk," he says and leads me to his cell.

He covers the bars with a green fleece blanket. I undress and lie on his bed.

He undresses as well, but I stop him when he's down to his boxers.

"Keep them on for a bit," I say as I pull him on top of me.

Kissing my neck, he cups my chest in his strong hands. The feeling of my soft skin against the roughness of his body hair sends waves of ecstasy to every nerve in my body. With my foot, I push his boxers down and use saliva to lube his dick.

I wrap my legs around his waist, and he guides himself into me. It hurts as he enters me, and I bite his shoulder.

Then a white light engulfs us, and the cell becomes cold. Alex is frozen in time as the scene stretches in space.

Through half-opened eyes, I took in my surroundings—white walls, concrete floor, and the rough, thin mattress.

I heard bodiless voices floating in the ether:

"How the fuck did he make it here . . ."
"It's all that deaf fuck's fault . . ."
"What are we gonna tell him when he wakes up . . ."
"Jack will handle this . . ."

I turned off my mind. I didn't want to be in this timeline. I wanted to go back. Perhaps the place in the darkness was the real world and this place a dream. Closing my eyes, I willed myself to go back to where I had been. Maybe I could stay there.

"Alex, tell me what you want," I say while he lies on top of me, spent.

I love this part after making love. I love his chest hairs tickling my nipples, his body warming mine, and his softening dick brushing against my thigh.

"What do you mean?"

"Like what do you want your life to be?" I ask.

"I want you. I want us—forever."

The memory of our last time together began fading as the present chased away the final remnants of sleep.

My pillow was soaked with tears, and all I wanted to do was scream. I was wrong; I had one more thing left to feel—wrath.

Chapter 43

By the architecture and dull-green slacks I wore, I knew I was in Green Haven. But the cell wasn't familiar.

It was twice the size of a regular cell. Two of its concrete walls were whitewashed; the usual slab of steel bed bolted to the wall was too low to the ground. The metal sink-toilet contraption all prisons were infamous for was also different. It was smaller, with rounded edges, and connected to a small metal plate with a drain on the floor. I followed the metal plate up the wall and spotted a flat shower head on the ceiling.

A shower in a cell? I wondered, when I realized the other two walls were made of Plexiglas.

I felt like a goldfish in its bowl. And then I knew where I was—suicide watch in the Mental Health Unit.

"This explains everything," I said, laughing. "I must've had a mental breakdown! It was all a fucking dream."

I bit the back of my hand to control my laughter and sat on the floor. Through teary eyes, I saw a black backpack under the bed.

No . . .

A coldness washed over me—steeling me. It was pure hate. While madness was muddy and erratic, wrath felt crystalline and calculating. I knew I wanted to make someone pay. I just needed to figure out who.

I dumped the backpack's contents on the bed. The prescription bottles were still in the secret compartment, but a shirt had been wrapped around them and then wrapped again in a towel. Everything else was intact. But my gun, boxes of ammunition, and sai were missing.

Under the bed, on top of my boots, I found my clothes and a note:

> Your clothes clean. Take shower, you stink. Hot water stop after ten minutes. Toiletries and breakfast under green towels.
>
> All your stuff in backpack. No weapons allow— Jack's rules.
>
> Drugs not allow too.
>
> Meet Jack in hospital, listen to him, agree with him. After meet me at library. I show you everything.
>
> —Rob

Breakfast consisted of apple juice, water, three granola bars, and a Snickers. I guzzled all the liquids and nibbled on the granola bar while I reconstructed the timeline of events.

Prison is a pressure cooker—everything's intensified. A day lived in prison feels like a week lived outside like dog years. (Using that math, the 1,378 days Alex and I spent together feel like 26 years of us loving each other.) Now, as humanity dies, it feels like that but on meth.

I recalled the events on my notebook:

> October 10, Monday: Released. Met Fessy. Watched Brian's videos. Talked to Alex and read his letter (yellow rose). Last time I heard from my family. RIP Pilar Trent.
>
> October 11, Tuesday: Worked out. Fessy came back. Last time I heard from Alex ("I'm sorry, I was—"). 7-Eleven madman. Spent the night with Christina, Fessy, and Simon.
>
> October 12, Wednesday: Power died. RIP John, Jessie, Arissa, Gianna Hemburry. RIP Simon Green. Left

Christina with her family—-thank you for the sai. Picked up Susan. RIP Sharon O'Connell. Drove to Brooke's. RIP Timothy.

October 13, Thursday: On *Lady Lazarus*.

October 14, Friday: Reached NYC—fucking kids. Found empty apartment. Lights flashed on. Had a good night.

October 15, Saturday: RIP Faysal Spero Singh.

October 16, Sunday: RIP Melinda Jones.

October 17, Monday: Susan O'Connell.

October 18, Tuesday: Reached Newburgh Beacon Bridge. Met Callum, Emma, and James King.

October 19, Wednesday: Green Haven.

"Fucking less than two weeks," I murmured.

I had no idea how long I had been asleep for but didn't think it could've been for more than a day or two. Forget being in a pressure cooker—this felt as if I had lived ten lifetimes and circled back to the beginning.

My body ached, and I decided to shower. As I lathered under the warm water, I ran my fingers over my bruises and cuts. Each one had a story to tell; each one bore into my soul.

I changed into my black jeans and navy college hoodie. My clothes smelled like fresh laundry, and I allowed the scent to linger in my mind while I repacked. My boots had been cleaned as well, and I was reminded of just how useful Rob could be.

"Thank you. Pay you, I don't know how," Rob would sign after every Catholic service, using his entire body and face to emphasize how thankful he was for my interpreting.

I'd tell him there was no need to pay me. Now I could think of a few ways he could repay me.

My band fit too loose on my ring finger, so I pulled out a long thread from a towel and fastened it around the ring. After I finished brushing my teeth and tying my hair in a ponytail, I checked myself over on the metal mirror bolted to the wall. I didn't know what awaited me outside of this fishbowl, and I wanted to look my best—bruises and all. Some men dig the "damsel in distress, battered wife" look, especially in prison, and some things never change.

First, I needed to meet Jack and get it over with. I didn't know how such a person had risen so high up the food chain, but I knew two things—no one rises that high and fast without spilling blood and he was one of the last people to see Alex.

Then I'd meet Rob, get the real story, and find my weapons.

I put on my backpack and checked my pockets.

"Damn, you're thorough, Rob," I said, feeling the loose pills.

I reached into my back pocket and felt a small piece of paper—*my family's number*—and two wallet-sized pictures.

I ran my fingers over the pictures of Alex and my family, caressing them as if I could send them my love through my touch.

I pressed the sharp point of the heart on my ring under my thumbnail to keep myself from looking at the pictures. I swallowed the boulder forming in my throat and took a deep breath as I slid open the Plexiglas door.

Here we go, I thought.

Walking down the gray-white corridor, I wished I could skip the meeting with Jack.

I ran through everything I knew about him. Most, if not all, of what I knew of Jack came from Alex.

"He's one of those wannabe mafia dudes," Alex once said after we passed Jack in the hallway while flashing one of his toothy grins and pantomimed tipping his hat.

"So he's Italian?" I asked.

"Italian, German—who the fuck knows," Alex said. "The other day I heard him telling a CO he was Russian."

He stopped before we entered the Catholic church and looked me in the eye.

"He's dangerous, Cole. He's anything or anyone he needs to be to get what he wants. In the three years I've known him, he has told me he grew up in Buffalo, then it changed to Rochester, and just last month it was Syracuse."

"But don't you work out with him?"

"I don't work out or do anything *with* him—I tolerate him. Keep him close so he thinks twice about talking shit or selling me out. He's an inevitability of prison."

"Got it," I said. "What's his last name? That could tell us something about his background."

"Mehoff," he answered.

"I think that's German," I said, thinking of David Hasselhoff and the German's obsession of him.

"Jack Mehoff," I repeated, savoring every syllable as if it held the secret to his origin. Alex said nothing.

I finally got the joke halfway through the service. I stopped interpreting for Rob, looked at Alex, and mouthed, "Really, *Jack Me Off*?"

He laughed so hard, the priest paused his sermon to ask Alex if he was okay.

I never asked for his last name again. Who knows, it may be Mehoff.

—✳—

Entering the stairwell, I thought of different routes that wouldn't take me by the hospital. I noticed the emergency window exits but thought it would look suspicious if I went out the window when I spotted two men waiting at the bottom of the stairs.

As I neared them, I recognized the man on the left—tall, about six feet one, and a swimmer's built but with clumsy reflexes. I remembered him with a neatly trimmed afro, but he appeared to have shaven it and now wore a white kufi with red stripes.

What's his name, though. Mike? Milk? Mark? I wondered, and started firing off random details about him in hopes of remembering his name. *High-pitched laugh, around twenty-four years old, had a different girl visit him every week, was in the ASL class after mine had graduated but didn't complete it because his Puerto Rican father left his French-speaking Haitian mother—*

"Merci beaucoup, monsieur Merc," I said, in French since it had helped me remember.

"Why are you thanking me?" Merc said, smiling.

"Oh, I thought it was you guys who brought me here and left me breakfast," I lied.

"Nah, that was Rob. I helped carry you though. Uh, Cole—" he began but stopped, his eyes darting from side to side as if his brain had overloaded and was now playing a game of ping-pong. "How are things out there? Are people—"

"Jack," the other man interrupted, "wants to see you at once. He'll ask the questions."

His tone and aura were cold. I didn't recognize him or feel any familiarity toward him. He felt distant and standoffish, as if my presence offended him. He took the lead, and we followed. I couldn't imagine how a pleasant joker such as Merc could enjoy spending time with this assbag.

"Who is this guy?" I asked when we were past earshot.

"He used to be a CO in the watchtowers—graveyard shift. You probably never even saw him. His name is, uh, Stephen, but everyone calls him by his last name. King."

Fucking A.

They led me past six men guarding the commissary through one of the administrative buildings to the hospital. When I was transferred to Green Haven, all those years ago, I had expected everything to be different shades of green. It wasn't. All walls are beige, and the floors are gray or brown from decades of grime.

"You first," ordered Stephen as we entered the infirmary.

I gave him my warmest smile and nodded.

We passed several people—some were sweeping, some were guarding, and most were just pretending to keep busy. They all stared. I would have thought they were inmates except I saw women and . . .

Was that a kid or a little person? I thought.

"Are there kids here?" I asked Stephen.

I wanted to ask Merc—I should've asked him—but I needed to build rapport with King.

He ignored me, but by then, I didn't care. The sign reading "Hospice Third Floor" demanded all my attention. It took all I had not to push them aside and make a run for it. Instinctively, I reached for my sai and remembered they weren't there. I dug the end of the heart on my ring under my thumbnail again, drawing blood.

Stephen was too much of a robot to notice my turmoil, but Merc wasn't. He put a hand on my shoulder and gently squeezed. Any other time I would have welcomed this simple gesture, but now it felt almost as bad as seeing the hospice sign and not be able to do anything about it. My brain had cracked in so many different ways, it was impossible to guess how feeling my anguish would affect me. I had a mission. I didn't need to feel; I needed to act.

Ignoring the compassion in Merc's gesture, I focused on how he had also subtly nudged me onward.

"Cole!" Jack exclaimed as I entered the room. "Glad to see you back—in more ways than one."

He was all smiles, pleasantries, and platitudes. Nothing new, but the black Kevlar riot gear he wore was.

"Please, sit," Jack said. "I see you've met King, and I believe you already know Merc."

"Alex. Where is he?" I asked, clearing my mind so I could differentiate his lies from the truth.

"Dammit, I thought you'd remember. I'm sorry, Cole. He's dead."

Jack's face resembles a Wooly Willy; and his long, bushy eyebrows deflated as if they were dragged by the magnetic pencil.

"No. His body. Where is it?"

"Well, you knew he had transferred to the Hospice Unit, correct?"

I nodded.

"Danny, the old man, he brought that . . . that sickness into the prison. The guy working with Alex, Matt, and two others were bitten."

Truth.

"It spread so quickly. Alex was overwhelmed."

Truth.

"He wanted out of hospice, begged Sergeant Cooper to let him leave the company. But Cooper wouldn't have any of it."

"But how could they just leave Alex with all those infected?"

"I know, Cole. I pleaded with Cooper to let him out, but he refused. So I volunteered to help Alex."

Lie and truth.

"You! Jack," I said, reaching for his hand over the desk.

I could play his game too.

He took my hand and met my gaze. As if reflex, my hand recoiled from his greasy, cold touch. To deflect from my disgust, I put my head down and covered my face in both hands—only the tips of my middle fingers actually making contact with my skin.

"It was horrible," he continued. "The infected—they have this-this groan. One starts, and then the others join . . . I couldn't take it."

Truth.

"I begged Cooper to let him out, but he still refused. The infection had to be contained and I . . ." Jack turned from me and looked out the window to the rolling hills which appeared to be covered in snow but I knew it to be ash.

I took the moment to take in the hospital room. It was spacious, made for doctors or nurses to conduct follow-ups with handicapped inmates. The desk and counter were littered with Manila folders—some ruffled, some untouched. Inmate files.

Oh, Jack, you're fucking good, I seethed.

"I was ordered to choose a side—either I stayed with Alex or out with population. I chose Alex, but it was too late. I saw it, Cole. Somehow two of the infected got out, and they surrounded him. He fought them off—kicked one in the face—but the other four lunged at him—"

"But you said it was only two?" I interjected. "How would so many of them get out of their cells?"

Jack hated being interrupted, and he hated being questioned even more. I saw a shadow pass over his beady mole eyes, and I knew he was deciding how to handle me.

"I-I'm sorry," I said and allowed my emotions to envelop me. My tears weren't an act; hearing Alex's final moments was torture. "It's just too hard to hear . . ."

"I understand, kid." My crying disarmed his annoyance. "Some people must have been bitten and didn't report it. Anyway, they surrounded him, Cole. Fucking assholes biting into the person who was trying to help them. After that, Sergeant Cooper closed off the unit, and we haven't been able to get in since."

"You guys just *left* him there?" My tears stopped, and I tasted bitter bile rise.

"You don't understand the fragile position we were in," he huffed condescendingly. "All the administrative team had abandoned the prison. Most of the COs refused to come to work, and the ones who did come took an all-or-nothing approach. They wanted every inmate in his cell. We would've starved, Cole. We had to do something—I had the welfare of my brothers to consider. A few of us got together, and we have been able to wrangle control of the Eastside but barely."

Green Haven was really two prisons in one—Eastside and Westside. The Eastside, where Jack had assumed control, consists of blocks E, F, G, and H. It also holds the large school building with its library and gym; but most importantly, it contains the hospital, commissary, and armory.

The Westside has always been the more relaxed area of the prison. It's where the older, quieter inmates are housed. It consists of blocks A, B, C, D, and J. The Westside holds the churches and warehouse, with its seemingly endless supplies.

However, each side isn't autonomous. There's a main control room which governs both sides, and the West and East are connected by two main hallways. And then there's the mess hall.

Although each side has its own mess hall, they're connected by a central kitchen. The mess hall is a wide-open area the size of a school's gymnasium, a clear entrance into the heart of the Eastside. And the whole area is currently under the control of the others, on the Westside.

Chapter 44

The Westsiders, according to Jack, are the punishment-happy, duty-bound COs who see their way of life—and everything America stands for—endangered by the prisoners' uprising. The COs are accompanied by police, military, and civilians who believe the inmates need to be subdued and locked in their cells.

I couldn't have cared less about any of it; he could've called them Westies, and I wouldn't have noticed. I needed to see Alex, period. So while Jack continued his allocution, I traveled somewhere else.

—m—

"Jack's a rat. He'll tell on his best friend or family to get what he wants, and he'll chew right through anyone who stands in his way," Alex said as he passed me my cup of coffee.

Jack was the now topic in Green Haven, having been recently voted as inmate liaison committee president—the man chosen to fight for our rights. One of the president's duties was to report administrative corruption. Sometimes real justice was served, if the administrator's actions were abhorrent enough. But most times, it would just lead to administration labeling our whistle-blowing president a security risk and transferring him to another prison. Everyone doubted Jack would fight for us, yet he still won.

"You really hate him," I said and handed Alex a pile of Christmas cards.

"I don't hate him," he said and sipped his coffee. "If a shark bites you, do you hate it for following its nature? Jack is what he is. People like him can't help themselves. He latches on to any position that gives him the appearance of power so people won't figure out that he ain't worth shit. You know why I keep him close? Because with one whisper, he could have us separated."

"How do you know he hasn't tried?" I asked.

Realizing the delicate line our happiness straddled gave me goosebumps.

"I don't," he said and, seeing the worry in my face, placed his hand on my knee. "But I know he doesn't see me as a threat since I don't want anything he wants. He also knows if he does anything to one of us, he'll have the other to deal with. We're a team, babe, and there's strength in numbers. And he knows if he took you from me, I'd kill him."

He laughed that deep laugh of his. I used to tell him jokes or share funny ideas with him just so I could hear it—revel in it.

I smiled, and we went back to signing cards. This had become our tradition during the holidays: We'd meet at the library and sign one card after the other; I'd remind him of every person he needed to send a card to, and he'd bring the coffee.

I liked mine with a lot of milk and sugar. Alex took his black. Once, I snuck a sugar packet into his coffee, and he spit it out as if I had served him a cup of diabetes.

"Cole. Cole?"

"Yes—sorry. What did you just say?"

"Do you see the position they've put us in? We're fighting for our right to live. And we're not without allies," Jack said, allowing the word to linger as if it could awaken some latent truth within me.

"There was a big fight between us and the officers. The Prison Riot Response Team was called, but they weren't interested in putting us back in cages. They wanted to stay in here with us. There was more fighting, more death. And then *it* came."

"What do you mean 'it came'?" I asked in my sweetest voice, feigning concern.

"ACRES. It was everywhere. I can't explain it—the response team must have brought it in with them. One second everyone's fighting and then eating each other the next. We lost over two-thirds of the people in Green Haven that day, inmate and officer alike. And that's not counting our brothers on the Westside who are still locked up. As for our side, blocks E, F, and G are quarantined, with half of H block under a strict lockdown."

"That's hundreds of people still in cages!"

"Get off your high horse, Cole. You haven't seen what I've seen. That sickness—it doesn't follow a pattern! Some people get sick, some don't. And it's not just our brothers I'm protecting. There are civilians in here. Whole families. Not all the COs have gone to the Westside. You've met King. He's one of our allies, and there are many more like him."

Stephen flinched at the mention of his name. He was an enigma I would need to figure out later. Now, all I needed to do was bask in Jack's bullshit.

The pattern is simple, Jack Mehoff. You die, you come back, I thought.

Instead, I said, "I'm sorry. I get it—you're overwhelmed and trying to do your best to keep everyone safe. I was just surprised that so many people are still locked up. They probably feel forgotten and like they're worth less than the people who get to walk around freely. And then you expect them to rejoin us as if they haven't been kept in cages among those infected fucks."

It was more than I had intended to say, and I regretted it instantly.

"Cole, Sergeant Cooper left *me* in charge, and people look to me for guidance. I'm doing what's best for everyone. Only a very select few are allowed free range of the prison. If I were to let everyone out, half would try to escape, and the other half would fight over resources. It will be anarchy, and I can't spare any more men. Over three-fourths of my forces are busy securing the connecting points and mess hall."

His logic was like a woodpecker drilling into my skull—none of it made sense, and all of it gave me a killer headache. It baffled me that he could believe the people he has kept behind bars would simply fall in line when they got out. What was to gain from mistreating the people he'll have to live with? I considered that maybe he didn't expect to live with them—a "final solution" sort of deal—but he didn't have enough people on his side for such drastic measures. And what did he care if people escaped? That was less mouths to feed. Then it hit me: Jack didn't know the world has changed forever.

I wanted to laugh in his face, tell him we're all doomed to become walking death and that no government was coming to save us. Or judge our actions. Or reclaim the prison. But I didn't because I suspected the fear of the US government coming to exact justice was what kept Jack from going full tyrant.

Unsure of what to say or if I could hold in my giggles, I covered my face in both hands and said, "I'm sorry. This is just all too much to take in."

"I know it's a lot, but, Cole, you've been out there. Please, tell me what you've seen, what you know. You're the first outsider—well, that's not quite right. You're still one of us," he said as he flashed me a sharklike smile. "What I mean to say is that you're the first person we've seen from the outside in over a week—"

"A week?" I interjected. "The date. What is it?"

"Saturday, twenty-second."

"I've been asleep for three days," I mumbled.

The room became very small, and the air felt heavy and dusty, like a closet filled with furs and mothballs.

"We weren't sure if you were going to wake up. People feared you were infected—something about failing the black light test—but Rob refused to leave your side. He stayed until you showed signs of recovering. That Rob, he's been a real help. Shame what happened to his friends."

"His friends?" I said, regaining control of my breathing.

"Yes, they sought refuge in the main administrative building . . . and, well, it's Rob's story to tell. You'll see him soon enough. Now, please, tell me what you've seen."

"I came home to a dying town and an empty house. Two of my friends threw me a small welcome-back party. It was hard to celebrate anything though. People were dying all around us, and the military police made regular door-to-door visits.

"My family called me at night. They were stuck in Florida, and the phones and power grids had begun failing. Thankfully, the military had provided them with a satellite phone. I carry their number in case I find a working line. My sister-in-law was infected. She died within hours. The rest of my family found refuge in the Keys. It's where I'll be heading once . . . I'm able to travel.

"I also got a call from Alex, but I wasn't home to answer it. The last thing I'll ever hear him say is his name on an automated message. I'll never forgive myself. I called the prison, but no one answered.

"By Wednesday, the twelfth, the military was losing control of the situation—too many infected, too many looters. The authorities sectioned us off by zip code, then streets. This created its own chaos since the wealthier areas got preferential treatment. My friend Brooke lives in a mansion on the water, and she invited me to ride out the plague with her and her family. She also invited our friends Susan and Christina and their families—strength in numbers. We packed into a van and drove horse trails and forgotten roads so the military wouldn't stop us.

"Last Saturday we were informed that the government was building a stronghold at West Point, in Orange County. The military offered to evacuate the entire area by way of the Long Island Sound

261

and Hudson River. Some people left, but most didn't. I was the only one in our group without family there. I felt lost, so I was on the first boat out.

"West Point was and wasn't what they had promised it would be. Yes they had walls, weapons, soldiers, and plenty of room for civilians, but they ran the place like a prison. Aside from all their strict rules, they kept civilians busy by having us reinforce the complex. Once I had time to decompress from all the horrors I had witnessed, I began feeling a void within my heart. I needed to get to my family in Florida, but how could I do it on my own? I found a map and saw I wasn't far from Stormville—from Alex.

"I overheard soldiers talking about prisons being overwhelmed by the plague and inmates escaping. They said the situation is so dire that it'll take a while for the government to regain control, and by then the escaped prisoners will be impossible to find—or for officials to even know who's alive or dead. Right then I knew I needed to find Alex and maybe we could help each other find our families. I made friends with a soldier in charge, gave him everything of value I had on me in exchange for weapons and a small boat, and made my way here.

"How was I planning to break Alex out of a maximum-security prison? I didn't know. I had a gun, and I hoped the rest would work itself out. Crazy, I know.

"New York City? The infected? Yes, the city was in bad shape. I don't know exactly how bad, though, because I only traveled by water. As for the infected, they were everywhere, but I avoided them by trekking through the woods.

"My wounds? Blood on my clothes? All that happened when I came ashore. This area is teeming with the infected. It's the sign on the Newburgh Beacon Bridge—they're attracted to its light. There are thousands of them up the road, and more are coming."

Looking down at the floor, I swallowed as if I had ate an apple whole. I wasn't sure how convincing my story had been (I shouldn't have lied about not talking with Alex), but the pain was real and had overtaken me, and I began crying.

Life taught me a lot, and one of those lessons is that men don't react well when seeing someone crying. It makes them uncomfortable.

Flustered, Jack shifted his weight on the chair and said, "Thank you, Cole. You should grab something to eat."

Soon he would find the holes in my story and realize there won't be a calvary arriving from West Point or officials to tell him what he should or shouldn't do. But for now, he was satisfied.

"Get some rest, kid. King or Merc will—"

"I appreciate the offer," I interrupted. "But I've slept enough, Jack. I'd like to see Rob and thank him. If you don't mind, of course."

I sniffled and with the back of my hand wiped my eyes.

"I can't imagine what he has been through."

"Yes, of course. He stays in the library. You shouldn't have a problem finding the place, correct? As I recall, you and Alex used to spend a lot of time there," he said with a gigantic smirk on his face. What a fucking douche.

I wanted to inquire about my weapons but decided not to because in his attempt at humor, he had given me free range of the prison. I nodded and rushed out. I didn't get far though because I was stopped by one person after the other.

"Have you heard from . . . Albany . . . Staten Island . . . I'm from Yonkers . . . You passed through . . . New Jersey . . . Pennsylvania . . . the city . . . upstate . . . any word from . . ."

I was drowning in cacophony of questions.

"Sorry, I didn't pass through there. No, I don't know," I responded, not wanting to lie to them.

Their desperation for any news was suffocating. I was ready to scream out the truth, tell them everyone and everything was dead or dying, when a strong, authoritative voice quieted the crowd.

"Let him through! He'll tell us everything he knows in due time!" Stephen scooped me by the waist and, with the wave of his hand, parted the sea of people.

He led me out of the hospital and escorted me through the corridor. We passed the entrance to the mess hall where eight or ten men carrying machine guns stood. They took a step toward us but relaxed when Stephen gave them a nod.

We didn't speak as we walked, but gone was the dickhead vibe I had sensed earlier. He's about six feet tall, give or take an inch, and heavily favors his older brother, Callum. But Stephen's features are more defined, angular, and his hair is a lighter shade of brown. His eyes are a green hazel; they're kind eyes, just like Callum's . . . like Alex's.

"Thank you, Stephen," I said as we neared the school building's entrance. "I got it from here."

"Uh, yeah, but there could be more people waiting for you—"

"I'm okay," I interjected. "Knowing Rob, he has probably cleared the building and set up arrows for me to follow."

He smiled. He wasn't an assbag—he was hurting.

Fighting the urge to reveal everything, I said, "Stephen, would you please wait for me down here? We *must* talk, one on one. It's important."

"Sure, but why can't we talk now?" he asked, impatience showing as he gritted his teeth.

"Rob kept me alive. I need to talk to him. I'll be quick. Promise."

"Okay. I'll be here."

Pushing the school's door open, I said, "Stephen, you wouldn't happen to own a King James Bible, do you?"

I turned and ran upstairs before he could answer.

Chapter 45

"Look, a murder of crows, Alex," I said, pointing at the flock of large, black birds descending on the hawthorn and scaring away the brown rabbits.

On our way to the library, we would always pause to take in the growing tree.

Our anniversary gift was thriving. It stood at least twelve feet. Its white blossoms had been replaced by scarlet-bronze leaves and red-orange apple-like fruits, which provided sustenance to a plethora of animals. (The rabbits were my favorite.)

"Those aren't crows, babe. They're ravens—an *unkindness* of ravens," he said, in his nonchalant way, as if everyone has seen a raven and knows a flock is called an unkindness.

"Alex, do I really need to meet your parents? What if they hate me or blame me for turning their youngest gay?"

I had dreaded having to meet them from the moment Alex had gotten on one knee.

His parents were from a deeply conservative part of New York. And although Alex's mom and I had exchanged many letters and cards throughout the years (we were both fans of the lost art of thank-you cards), we had never discussed gay—anything. I was not looking forward to breaking the news that she shouldn't expect grandchildren from her baby Alex.

"Cole, don't worry. They'll love you," he said, looking into my eyes. "How can anyone not?"

That happened a week before my release date. The ravens and rabbits were gone now, replaced by two large snowy owls and a smaller one hiding in the foliage.

A *family*, I guessed.

My strength began to waver, and my knees buckled as thoughts of family—mine and Alex's—flooded me.

"I can't," I whispered. "Not yet."

Steeling myself, I decided I had to stop this collection of memories. It were as if my heart needed to accumulate all the pieces Alex and I had left behind in order for me to stay alive. Everything reminded me of him. This place looked the same—the Plexiglas windows were still dusty, the wallpaper was still sterile and dull—but it *felt* different, as if it were all covered with a somber see-through shroud. It's strange seeing a place exactly as you left it but knowing you'll *never* experience it the same way.

I took a deep breath, peeled my gaze off the hawthorn, and marched down the gray corridor. The white ceiling had speckles of brown of what looked like dried-up ketchup or blood—or both. The evening autumn sun shone through cracked windows, washing the hallway in rose-gold strands of light. A faint odor of burnt hair and bleach hung in the air. I focused on every minute detail so I could ignore the small broom closet where Alex and I had had many quickies or the corner where Alex had picked me up by the waist, pressed me against the wall, and kissed me. He had been overtaken with pride after I had aced my college finals.

Turning the corner, I saw Rob through the library's window. His face was buried in a book; but on cue, as if he could sense my arrival or feel the vibration of my steps, he looked up, and we shared a sad smile. Life was about to change for us, again.

Suddenly, I felt exhausted and weak as I pushed the door open. "A *parliament* of owls," Alex said it was called.

Robert Johansen—his family calls him Bobby Jo—twenty years old, brown eyes, dirty-blond hair, about five feet five, with a splashing of freckles on his face. His large, square-shaped head and small, pointy nose always reminded me of a Christmas elf.

He enjoys jigsaw puzzles and watching movies. He spent his childhood working on his family's farm; raising chickens was his favorite part. Rob's life was a solitary one, being the only deaf person in his small town. He's from Perry, a farming town in Western New York. Alex's mom is from there too.

My brain fired off these details about Rob as we walked toward each other. (It's a habit of mine; if I don't do it at the beginning of the meet, I'll do it throughout the conversation and not pay attention. Rude, I know.) He wrapped his wiry arms around my midsection, and I felt his thin but well-built body relax against me.

I pulled away, looked into his eyes, and said, "I'm sorry."

He took a step back and signed, "Me too."

Rob has the type of face that even at ninety years old it'll hold its youthful appearance, but it was now marked with dark circles and creases around the eyes.

His perfect posture was weighted down around the shoulders, and his breaths were heavy, as if sighs would follow. They were all signs of a person who had lived a lifetime in the span of a week.

"Everything tell me," I signed.

He ran to the counter and reached behind a stack of books. The library had a lived-in smell, not musky or offensive but homey like pumpkin spice. On the sofa under the window was a nest of blankets and pillows, and the floor was littered with candy wrappers and juice pods.

Rob came back with a stack of CDs, and signed, "Show you."

When ACRES overtook the prison, the COs abandoned Rob and the rest of the deaf guys, Harry, Joe, Greg, and Chris. Being the best communicator among them, Rob became their de facto leader.

He decided they couldn't stay in J block on the Westside. The main administration building is in the center of the prison, connecting East and West. It's also where the prison's central command room is located. Both Eastside and Westside have their own control room, but central command overrides everything. Rob and his friends believed it would be the most guarded and safest area in the prison and thus where they needed to go.

Officers were openly shooting inmates in the halls, and inmates were using whatever weapons they could find to attack officers. Chris was shot in the head, and Joe had his throat ripped open by an infected. Harry and Greg reached their destination, but Rob fell behind when he was attacked.

The inmate's—the creature's—prison slacks were bloodied and tattered; a splintered officer's baton was lodged through its chest. Rob grabbed the baton by the handle and moved it around the creature's body in an attempt to puncture its heart or lungs. Nothing happened. The zombie pushed Rob to the ground and got on top of him. In his desperation, Rob pulled the splintered baton out of its chest and rammed it through its eye. It worked. The corpse deflated, but its dead weight pinned him down.

He struggled to get it off him, especially since he had to stop and play dead whenever anyone—inmate, officer, or infected—came close enough to notice him.

When he finally broke free, he felt the ground shake.

Rob ran through the administrative building upstairs to central operations. The gates were locked and the switchboards ablaze. People were dead, and the dying couldn't get out of the burning room. A female officer ran toward him. They struggled with the gate, but it wouldn't budge. She passed him a black case made of hard construction plastic. It was labeled "BACKUP."

Rob told me the woman said something. Rob's one of the best lip readers I've met, but even the best struggle with such a precise and difficult skill. The flames had reached the woman, and the combination of pain and fear made her words almost unintelligible.

He believes she said, "Show them." Rob took the case and held her hand until she stopped screaming and his arm hair was singed. He showed me the wounds where her nails had dug into his hand.

A herd had formed downstairs, so he escaped through an emergency window exit.

The roof led him straight to the school building. He broke in through an old plastic skylight and made his way to the library, which was where Jack had found him. But not before Rob had a chance to examine the black case.

It was filled with CDs. And when he put them into the computer, Rob realized it was the backup memory for every camera in the prison.

Chapter 46

Rob had carefully curated the story he wanted to tell with the security videos.

The first was of the central control room. It was time stamped October 11, 5:35 p.m., and it showed the officers in chaos. Buttons on the switchboard flashed, and people yelled orders. Rob fast-forwarded an hour, and familiar faces popped up.

Harry and Greg were huddled in the corner. Then six men stood by the entrance.

They formed a tight perimeter and showered the room with bullets. They shot another round into the consoles, poured some sort of accelerant on them, and lit it. The video ended there.

He reached for a CD labeled "Armory," but I stopped him.

"Later, show me. Now show me Alex," I signed.

Rob nodded and skipped over four CDs. I took a deep breath and readied myself.

The screen split into four sections, providing a 360-degree view of the Hospice Unit.

It was stamped October 10, 8:00 a.m. Alex appears picking up breakfast trays, and his friend Matt is helping him The top-left screen shows them at the front of the company—oblivious to what's awaiting them in the back. The bottom-right screen shows Oldman Danny biting into Manny's face.

"Fucking run, Alex!" I screamed at the screen.

I was no longer watching the past—I was living it.

It occurred just as Alex described it, except he had told me there were five infected men. I counted seven.

After securing the situation, Alex is pleading with Sergeant Cooper. Alex loses his tempter and kicks the gate. He walks to the phone and dials. His hands are trembling, and he's wiping tears from his eyes. He hangs up and redials over and over again. Frustrated, he punches the concrete wall. The time was 1:15 p.m.

"Pause," I signed and ran to the window.

The sun was a fading orange sphere, and the moon was a ghostly figure in the sky. I dug the sharp end of my ring under my nail—anything to keep me from falling apart since I wasn't sure I'd be able to put myself back together. My brain was firing in all directions:

What if I had been home when he called? Couldn't I have stayed one more day? Why didn't his family answer the phone? How . . .

"Fuck!" I yelled and kicked Rob's sofa.

My steel-toe boot cracked its left leg, and the couch drooped forward.

"Sorry," I signed and walked back to the computer. "Continue."

Matt lies in bed while Alex tends to him through the gate. Manny and Danny are locked in their cells, clawing at the air. The two other infected inmates, the ones Alex had counted, are sitting in their cells praying or crying. Plus the six other inmates in their cells make a total of eleven men locked in. Four inmates are sitting at the table by the TV. They're praying and talking among themselves; and two of those men are infected. I saw it—one was nipped on the hand when Matt wrestled with Manny's corpse; the other had been nipped on the forearm when Danny had tired of chewing on Manny's face.

"Alex! Can't you see them? They're hiding their fucking arms under their sweatshirts," I said to the monitor.

Alex is running back and forth, mopping blood off the floor and passing food trays. Various nurses appear at the front of the tier throughout the day. The staff pass medications and supplies to Alex, who dispenses everyone's appropriate dosage. He's in his element, helping people. All are looked after—everyone except the two assholes who are visibly succumbing to their fate.

Jack shows up at around 5:00 p.m. He's talking to Alex through the bars.

Although only the back of Jack's head is visible in the video, they appeared to be having a good conversation. He even pats Alex on the back. Then Jack leans in and whispers into his hear. Wrong move. He recoils from Jack. Disgust is visible on Alex's face. Jack is waving his arms, appearing to plead his case. Alex doesn't flinch and walks away.

At 6:00 p.m., five more inmates are allowed out of their cells—to watch TV or shower, I suppose. That's a total of ten inmates on the tier, including Alex. The two infected are at the back table. They're slumped on each other, seemingly asleep.

Alex is at the phone, the biggest smile plastered on his face. I knew then he was talking to me. As he talks to me, he goes through a range of emotions—relief, confusion, anger, sadness, happiness. The call drops, and he redials again and again. Then the sleeping inmates get up.

They lunge at the closest two people. The man with the walker doesn't stand a chance. The zombie grabs him from behind and tears into his shoulder. It's chaos, and the people who attempt to get the zombies off their friends only succeed at getting bit. By the time Alex makes it to the back of the tier, four inmates have been infected and two lie on the floor, dying or dead.

Alex moves with military precision. He uses a mop to push the two zombies into one cell and locks the gate. He drags the dying men into their cells and orders the rest to lock in. An old man suffering from lung cancer is in fetal position underneath the metal table. His name is Johnny, I think. He's not infected, but everything he has seen has broken his mind. Alex kneels next to him and takes his hand.

Johnny grapples onto Alex's arm and slowly pulls himself from under the table. Getting behind Johnny, Alex wraps his arms around him and lays one hand on Johnny's chest while searches Johnny's pockets and pulls out an inhaler with the other.

Johnny is not just having a mental breakdown; he's having an asthma attack as well.

Alex places the inhaler up to Johnny's mouth and presses down. Then, using his hand as support, Alex takes deep, slow breaths to help guide Johnny's own breathing.

Alex stays with him until Johnny can get up and walk to his cell.

"Pause. How is he dead?" I yelled. I wanted to sign but couldn't focus. "How can a person like him be dead and someone like me be alive? What kind of world do we live in where good people like Alex perish, but people like me thrive?"

I wanted to cry, but no tears came.

Rob shook his head and said, "You alive because you strong. Alex strong too. Just . . . *different*."

He pointed at the monitor, which was a screenshot of Alex looking straight into the camera. His hair was sleek with sweat, and his face and clothes were blood splattered. He looked tired, and his blue-green eyes had a faraway appearance, beyond pain and fear—to a place where life's torture holds its own serenity.

I kissed the palm of my hand and laid it on Alex. My fingers caressed his face, tracing the lines on his forehead, the rough edges of his reddish beard.

"Ready?" Rob signed.

I nodded, and he pressed Play.

Alex steps out of the shower, nude, taking his time to dry himself. He puts on his prison greens and black boots. His wet hair is sticking up like a rooster's crest.

He's back on the phone. I follow his index finger dial my 631 area code, but the call won't connect. He dials his house, and his body relaxes as he talks to his family. He calls them three times, and between each call, he tries my number.

At 11:00 p.m., the CO calls Alex to the gate. While they talk, only Alex's face is visible.

"Read lips, can you?" I signed.

Rob didn't look at the screen; he had already studied it.

"No, I won't leave Matt," he said.

Alex returns to his cell, puts on his headphones, and picks up two tablets. I had left him mine, with its extensive music collection, before I went home. He spends the night listening to my music as he types on his tablet. Whenever he nods off, he wakes up startled and covering his ears.

I scanned the other cells and counted twelve moaning and clawing corpses. Plus, there were two uninfected inmates—Johnny and a wheelchair-bound man who hadn't left his cell since it all began. And then there was Matt.

He was infected. His wounds hadn't stopped bleeding, and Alex had helped change his bandages. But as Rob fast-forwarded to Tuesday, the eleventh, Matt hadn't turned yet.

While anger doesn't need a target to exist, wrath needs it to feed upon. I should've been impressed with Matt's endurance—hopeful, even. Perhaps there's a natural immunity to ACRES, and from that, a vaccine may come. However, as I watched Matt fighting for his life, there was only one thing on my mind:

You're the reason Alex is dead.

Alex doesn't believe in sacrificing one for the many—every life matters. The world needs more people like that. I couldn't blame him for being himself.

Matt succumbs to the infection at 2:00 p.m. Alex is distraught, throwing food trays at the zombies and using a broken broomstick to stab them through the bars.

"Is this what you left me for?" I whispered with venom in my voice.

He runs to the phone. His fingers ware dialing too fast for me to identify the number, but I didn't need to see it to know who he was calling.

"I love you. I'm sorry, I was—" he had said to me.

"You were so *what* Alex?" I yelled at the screen. "Stupid? Selfish? You know what you were? Fucking wrong—"

The words choked in my throat as I watched every cell door suddenly open.

Thirteen corpses staggered onto the tier.

Three zombies devour Johnny, and two attack the man in the wheelchair. Alex grabs the broken broom and swiftly sweeps two corpses off their feet. Two more zombies lunge at him, and he evades them by jumping on the table. But he's surrounded.

He holds them back with the broom as he yells for help.

"Through the brain," I muttered, and as if magic, he drives the broom through the eye of the closest zombie.

The corpse deflates and falls. Understanding takes over Alex, and within seconds he has disposed three more.

He's going to make it!

Like pride or hope, the will to survive has a perceptible aura to anyone who has experienced it. Muscles tighten and become defined, the eyes sharpen, and the person breathes slowly and deliberately— using the lapse to calculate options.

Alex jumps over two corpses, jams the splintered broom through a zombie's eye, and uses the body as a shield to push the rest back. He reaches his cell.

You're almost there.

He throws the lifeless body and dives into his cell, turning midair to slam the gate shut.

Oh my god. You're alive! I thought.

Except, it doesn't close. The gate bounces open. Alex rushes to close it. He slams it over and over, but the mechanism won't lock. He grabs a textbook and jams it between the bars to prevent the gate from sliding back, when a crawling body grabs his hand and sinks its teeth into his flesh.

"Stop," I signed, and Rob paused the video.

Alex is on the floor, holding his bleeding hand, his eyes wide with dread and disbelief.

I rewound and watched the moment Alex was bitten on a loop, slowing it down frame by frame. Not only did I want to be certain of his injuries, but I also wanted to identify who bit him. I don't know why that was important at the time.

No matter how much I slowed down or zoomed in, the identity of Alex's attacker was never visible through the rest of the bodies. But Alex's fate was clear for all to see—he made sure of that.

After securing his gate by jamming the metal door of his locker through the bars and fastening it with a sheet, Alex makes a sharp weapon from the remaining locker pieces. He understands the creature's vacant hunger now and drives his makeshift spear through their eyes as they bite the bars. Once all the zombies are finished, Alex stands on his bed, faces the camera, and points at his bleeding hand. He picks up his tablet and holds it in front of him, making a hand gesture on the screen.

I paused and rewound until there was no doubt about what I was seeing—one finger, four fingers, three fingers.

"One, four, three? Mean what?" signed Rob.

"It's something my friends and I used to write," I said, feeling slightly guilty about signing only the words my shocked brain could remember. "I taught it to Alex, and we'd use it whenever saying goodbye. It's an old beeper code—*one letter, four letters, three letters.* I love you."

Chapter 47

"*How?* How! How . . ." I repeated in various degrees of tone and intensity.

The library was pitch dark, and the light from the monitor created a bubble around us.

Pacing back and forth, I said, "How is Alex dead and I'm alive? How is it that he fought with all his might and *still* failed? How will I go on . . . But more importantly, how the fuck did all the gates open and stayed open?"

Rob's face crumbled, as if all the air had escaped him. His shoulders slumped, his lips pursed, and his eyes flickered as if he were attempting to solve a mathematical equation.

"Watch," he signed and rewound the video to October 11, 2:15 p.m., the last time I heard Alex's voice.

Rob pointed at the top-right screen and answered my question.

Outside every company, there's a lockbox which controls the cells' lock mechanism. Only COs have the key to open it; however, the shadow figure sneaking up to the box, unlocking it, and pulling the Release All lever looked *nothing* like an officer.

It was Jack. He stole the key. He pulled the lever and locked the gates open.

He killed Alex. And now my wrath had found its target.

"But how . . . *why?*"

"Because he did as Cooper told him," a deep voice hollered from behind us.

"What the fuck," I said and ducked behind a bookcase.

Rob unplugged the computer, plunging the library into complete darkness.

The voice didn't stir, only its steady breathing was audible, as if wanting to assure us of its presence without further shock.

When my eyes adjusted to the dim light of the cloudy night, I saw Rob and the CD case had disappeared. The voice had a shape now, a tall man standing by the entrance.

"How long have you been there?"

"Long enough to know what you were watching," Stephen responded.

"I know something about you as well," I said, standing up and meeting his gaze.

"I know that your family is waiting for you. They need you, Stephen. And you're going to need all the help you can get to reach them."

"That's your best move?" he mocked and walked closer. "We all have or had family waiting for us."

"Yeah, but in your case, your brother, Callum, *really* fucking thinks you're coming for them. He can't risk looking for you. He's all Emma and James have."

"How . . . how do you know those names? Who told you!" he yelled as he rushed me and tried grabbing my arms.

Using my forearms, I knocked his hands aside and raised my right leg to kick him in the groin. Stephen saw it coming and closed his knees around my ankle, whirling me around and pressing his body atop of mine.

"I don't want to fight you," he said through labored breaths and pinning me against a bookcase.

"It's hard to tell," I said, squirming underneath him.

My leg was trapped between his thighs, and both my arms were pinned by his. I was more angry than worried. I spent the last week fighting for my life, and somehow I let this asshole overpower me— his larger size was irrelevant.

I stopped struggling and softened my voice.

"Okay, you win. Stephen, we're on the same side. Please, you're hurting me. Let me go."

"Why? So you can try to kick me in the balls again? You're secured. I'm not hurting—"

A blur of red and blond flashed in my peripheral. And before I could acknowledge it as Rob, he was on Stephen's back. He got on his feet and pawed at the child-sized figure clawing at his neck.

My initial instinct was to finish what I had started—kick Stephen in the groin, subdue him, and take it from there. But as I watched him gently trying to push Rob off—Stephen is twice Rob's size and could've easily thrown him aside—I remembered fighting hadn't always been the answer. And trust goes both ways.

"Enough!" I barked and pulled Rob away.

"We are *not* enemies," I said and signed simultaneously. "Stephen, you can't tell Jack what you saw—"

"Fuck all that right now. My family. How do you know their names?"

"Everything I told Jack was a lie—*almost* everything."

I walked to the window, and they followed. There was enough milky light to illuminate our faces and bodies. I needed Rob to be included because not only would it be rude to exclude him from the conversation, it was also dangerous. Our fates were entwined now; he deserved to be a part of every decision.

"The world is dead," I continued. "No one is coming to save us. The Newburgh Beacon Bridge is overrun with corpses—"

"Corpses?" Stephen interrupted. "There was a battle?"

"The infected. They're dead—uh, well, undead."

"You're kidding, right?"

"Ha! Makes sense. You guys have been sheltered in here, and I doubt anyone has gotten close enough to the infected to take their pulse. It was simple before—the bite kills you, and the bite brings you back. Now, let me guess, there have been random infections but with no clear source of contagion?"

I allowed the question to linger.

Rob looked down, as if he had already solved the puzzle and didn't care to replay it. But Stephen's gears were churning; the events of the past two weeks distorted his expression, like a computer melting.

"Okay, another guess," I added. "No suicides, right? Peculiar how the world goes to shit, but no suicides. I mean, people have killed themselves over less."

"It's in us," Stephen said. "The sickness is in everybody."

"Bingo," Rob responded.

Glad to know Rob was following, I continued, "The bridge was impassable. I scavenged the shore for a boat, and the one I found just happened to belong to your brother, Callum. I told him I needed to get to Green Haven, and he offered to help. We need to rescue your family, Stephen. I gave them half of my supplies, but more and more corpses show up every day. They're attracted to the flashing sign on the bridge."

Stephen's body deflated, and he leaned on the window for support.

"I thought I had more time . . . It's hard enough trying to figure out how to travel through this shit with a baby, but how do I get out of here unseen?"

"Why unseen?"

"No one is allowed to leave, Cole. You don't think Jack bought your West Point story, do you?" he sneered and looked into my eyes. "Sure, it gave him a *little* pause. If the government comes back, he wants his bases covered, like the people who don't believe in god but pray when death is near—just in case. He doesn't care about anyone escaping. He just doesn't want people leading anyone here. Green Haven has everything we need, but how long do you think he can hold on to it?"

Stephen got close to me, and I felt his breath on my face.

"He was going to let you die, you know. It was *him* who convinced Jack to open the gate," he said, pointing at Rob.

"How?" I signed, and Rob shook his head.

"Oh, he didn't tell you?" Stephen said, turning his poisonous pain toward Rob. "That's Jack's little pet. He does whatever he's told, and I guess he had done enough favors to ask for one of his own—"

"Stop it," I interrupted. "I get it, Stephen. You're hurting, mind-fucked with no idea how to reach your family. Shit, you're probably wondering if they're alive. I know that pain—we *all* do. But lashing out at each other won't solve anything. Rob did what he had to do to survive—another thing all of us have in common. Rob is no friend of Jack's. He was actually showing me the truth."

I stopped, remembering how all this began.

Turning to Rob, I signed, "CDs where?"

"Hide CD," signed Rob. "Police, I want show to, but—"

"None police to show to." I laid a hand on Rob's shoulder and turned to Stephen. "Wait, you said Cooper told Jack to open the gates. What did you mean?"

"Sergeant Cooper wanted an excuse—a security breach—that would allow him to assume authority of the prison over the administrative team."

"Like an outbreak in hospice," I said. "Giving him carte blanche to 'secure' the prison any way he deemed suitable."

"Exactly. The rest is murky. All that's known is Cooper was bit and Jack ended up with control of the armory and hospital."

"I know how Jack won the armory," Rob said. "Can show you."

"Show us later," I said. "It's not important how Jack got rid of Cooper and gained control. What matters is that he's in charge now and we're running out of time."

I paused and took a good look out the window. The fires smoldered, and the silver moon was beginning to peek through the pewter clouds. I had to be sure of what I was about to say, that the words were coming from what *needed* to be done and not what I *wanted* to do.

At least that's what I choose to believe I cared about at the time.

Looking at Rob and Stephen, I said, "We have to kill Jack."

Chapter 48

In prison, resources were limited, so I learned to differentiate *wants* from *needs*.

It was a skill that I translated into every aspect of my life; however, it's easy for things such as friendships and relationships to get lost in translation when survival is the only goal. This black-and-white mentality had a numbing effect, and it was Alex who snapped me out of it. He showed me everything can't be put into lists and categories. Our love existed in a place where it was forbidden and the odds were stacked against us—it was neither what we needed nor wanted, yet it was perfect.

Now, in this dying world where every decision, action, emotion is on steroids, the lines between *want* and *need*—wrong and right—are becoming blurred to the point of obscurity. But if there's any hope for humanity, for us to hold on to the best parts of us, some lines cannot be forgotten. They can't be ignored.

My wants and needs included Alex, help Callum, go back for Susan, and find my family.

Stephen's wants and needs: Rescue his family and make Green Haven an actual haven.

So yes. For all this to occur, Jack Mehoff had to die. That I would be his demise was just an added bonus.

There wasn't much time for planning; the longer we waited, the sooner Jack would see us coming. And it wasn't as simple as cutting off the head of the snake. Like a hydra, cutting one head would spawn three more.

Jack Mehoff had done an excellent job of surrounding himself with like-minded psychopaths—but much less cunning and intelligent, of course. Killing their führer would create a power vacuum, plunging this already fragile microcosm into chaos—again. Which wouldn't be so bad if the only goal were to leave. No, we needed a stable-ish place to come back to after rescuing Callum.

"We can't take over the hospital and the armory on our own. And we can't win if we don't take them both at the same time," Stephen said. "I'll round up the people I trust and who want to overthrow the current regime."

I hated having to rely on strangers, but I couldn't argue Stephen's logic.

"Okay, what I still don't understand is why Jack chose the hospital as his base. Isn't the place too big to defend and isn't almost every window an emergency exit?" I asked.

Not only were the emergency window exits the old kind that open on both sides, but there was also a lack of gates and bars.

"The water and power controls are in the hospital's basement," he explained.

Valid facilities to protect, I thought. *But not enough reason to make it his lair.*

"And the drugs," he added. "Jack decides which diabetic gets insulin, whose asthma requires an inhaler. Heart problems? Mental health issues? *Any* ailment. Jack's your one and only doctor. Let's not forget recreational users. Want an escape? Call Dr. Feel Good."

"Got it."

As for the armory's importance, that was obvious. Although Jack kept most of the small weapons—such as my confiscated 9mm—at his base, the armory still held high-caliber artillery, the bulk of the ammunition, and riot response equipment such as Kevlar suits, tear gas, tasers, etc.

"How are we going to keep his goons distracted long enough for us to make our move?" Stephen asked.

I rummaged through my backpack and placed the orange medicine bottles on the counter.

"I have enough Xanax and morphine to knock out a gang of buffalo," I said. "Find the people who will be a problem during our coup d'état and drug them."

Stephen was confused about form of delivery and dosage.

"I'll crush the pills," I instructed. "You pour the powder into a bottle of strong liquor and start sharing the good times with your brethren. As for dosage, use it all. Everyone won't be knocked out, but it'll make them slow and stupid."

Rob's contribution was threefold (although I wish he had stopped at two):

1. He drew a map of the best route by way of the roof into the hospital, making sure every step and danger was accounted for. I would slip unseen into the room adjacent to Jack's.
2. While Jack kept the remaining inmates behind bars, Rob had kept them well-fed and aware of exactly who was keeping them locked up. Rob and I made a list of people we knew would join our fight. He'd recruit Merc, and together they'd free the aforementioned prisoners.
3. Our takeover's success hinged on Jack being in his room at a precise time.

"Calise," Rob suggested, sealing her fate.

His final—and arguably most useful—contribution will haunt me for ages to come. At least I hope it does. It must. If it doesn't, it'll mean I have changed into someone I wouldn't recognize. No, that's not correct. If it doesn't affect me, I'll know *exactly* who I have become, a person willing to sacrifice anyone for the greater good. And all it'll mean is that I wasn't able—or cared enough—to have changed course.

Calise, nineteen years old and a rare beauty, was tall, had porcelain skin, and had long black hair. Or at least that's how Rob described her to me. I never got the chance to meet her, the real her. Calise had sought refuge in Green Haven after losing her father, the only family she had, during the early days of the plague.

She had been involved in a terrible car accident as a child, which left her deaf in one ear and encouraged her to learn ASL in school. Rob had naturally gravitated to her, but that wasn't why they met.

Above all, Calise was a survivor. She knew how to use her beauty and knew she'd be stupid not to use it in this harsh new world. It was not clear who made the first move; it didn't matter, really, since these kinds of stories tend to be boiled down to cliches—Jack, the sex-starved fifty-something-year-old man in a position of power; and Calise, the lovely ingenue who had lost the only family she knew. Rob didn't know if she was actually sleeping with Jack or any of the other men in command. He never asked, and she never said. All Rob did was escort her—at her request—to whosoever room she wanted to visit without being seen. And that was how he knew Calise could keep Jack busy for a few hours.

I argued against trusting her, but Rob vouched for her. He said she hated Jack as much as anyone else. So we compromised. Calise wouldn't know the exact nature of her mission, only that she must keep him occupied while Rob breaks into the pharmacy to retrieve some much-needed medication for an ailing friend. And it all had to be done at a precise time to avoid being caught by Jack's patrol. I gave Rob a handful of morphine and Xanax. Perhaps Calise could sneak it into Jack's drink or she could use it herself and go on autopilot.

We synchronized our watches, which Stephen provided since I've never worn one, and gave each other three hours to prepare. Stephen left for a few minutes and gave me a present when he came back.

"Here," he said, laying my sai on the counter. "You'll need them. Remember, we have people counting on us. Everything we're doing is for a better world."

"I know. Thank you, Stephen. Oh, I almost forgot," I said and reached into my pocket, pulling out the laser sight. "Use this if the infected surround you. Flash it in their eyes and then point it wherever you want them to go. They'll follow it like cats."

"How did you ever figure that out?" he said as I handed him the device.

"My friend, Susan. She, uh, she showed me."

We exchanged empty smiles, and then he put his hand on my shoulder and nodded. Before the three of us left the library, we discussed what to do about the Westsiders. They could use our coup as their chance to assert their dominance. And there was also the question of how to hold control of the prison while away rescuing Callum and his family. But the conversation was cut short.

"One problem at a time," we concluded.

The Westsiders were a threat as dangerous as Jack, and his fate had been decided. So perhaps the discussion was stopped because we knew what had to be done—how far we were willing to take it. If no one talked about it, then whatever it was hadn't been planned, just more casualties of war. Absolution could be ours in the eyes of others. And if we tried really hard, we may even be able to justify our actions to ourselves when we're alone and taking stock of the life we've built.

Or perhaps the discussion was cut short because we had *hope* in our hearts—hope that since humans have become an endangered species, the distinctions of the past (*us* vs. *them*) will disappear. And the labels that divided people—race, sexuality, socioeconomic status, religion, etc.—will become as superficial and interchangeable as the clothes we wear. If humanity was on its way out, maybe we'll finally accept we're part of the same family and share the same goal: live well.

But I'm getting ahead of myself. None of this, as my regret over Calise, came into play during our decision-making process. In hindsight, it's easy to trick myself into believing on some level I must have cared about the fate of humanity—the price our actions will tax our souls. I didn't.

As I sat in the dark, preparing my mind and body for the upcoming battle, all I could feel was hate forged into the sharp edge of wrath. It was the fire that fueled me and would ultimately destroy me. I mean, isn't that how hate works? Motivates us into action, keeps us going when we have nothing more to give—all the while poisoning and consuming us from the inside. I knew our mission could fail. I knew, whether justified or not, no one has the right to take a life. And I knew either I was going to kill Jack or he was going to kill me.

Human cost be damned.

Chapter 49

If you want to make God laugh . . .

Did everything go as planned? If it all amounts to the desired outcome, does it make it a victory? Too many people died; but according to Stephen and Rob, whom I saw briefly, the mission was a success. However, if I asked a Westsider or one of the many people who lost family and loved ones during the takeover, would that person agree?

I wish I could comment more on the specifics of the battle, but I wasn't there. Given time, surely the story will be composed (a history told mostly through the eyes of the victors). Heroes and villains will be decided and sins either absolved or condemned. But that comes later when the healing begins. For now, this is what I know:

Stephen mixed the Xanax-morphine powder in a jug filled with vodka, rum, tequila, gin, and Coke (which I think constitutes it as a Long Island iced tea). He shared the concoction with the men guarding the hospital's entrance and some civilians who were hanging out at the post and didn't get the hint that *maybe* they should hang out somewhere else.

Several people passed out soon after drinking; some overdosed, reanimated, and ripped the throats of the sleeping guards. The other drugged persons panicked, couldn't shoot straight, and were quickly disposed of by the resistance Stephen assembled. He made sure no one was shot in the head, using the hordes of walking dead to overwhelm and distract the rest of Jack's forces. Except, death doesn't discriminate. It was a massacre. Much of the fighting population, friend and foe alike, were left either dead or undead.

Rob freed the prisoners, and they took the armory. Jack's men never even had the chance to raise their weapons. After, led by Merc and Rob, they armed themselves and headed to defend the Eastside from the Westsiders who, using the chaos, had bombarded the mess hall and two connecting corridors.

Not many people from either side survived the confrontation; apparently they were overrun by herds of wandering zombies. No one from the battle at the mess hall made it out. The question left unanswered, for now, is how such large herds were able to strategically strike three places almost simultaneously. Some say they were attracted to the gunfire. And I would accept that, if the bulk of the herds hadn't consisted of the men who had been stationed at the hospital on the opposite side of the prison. The other less-known rumor is that the zombies were guided there using laser pointers.

But again, I'm getting ahead of myself. During all this, I only had one mission, one concern. It was where mine and Calise's paths crossed. I don't know how history will remember her role or if it'll even be told in the tale of the big picture. But what I do know is that if it weren't for her, I wouldn't be telling this story.

There was no philosophical awakening as I made my way through the roof from the library to the hospital—no second thoughts, no foreboding feeling that I was heading down a path I'll regret later. I was going to kill a man, and there was a serene detachment that came with not needing to rationalize my actions. Wrath was all I knew.

Forced by the gunfire, I ditched entering through the room adjacent from Jack's and broke into the hallway instead. The whitewashed walls and gray linoleum floor were dimly lit by the emergency lights on the ceiling. They were spaced several yards apart from each other, creating pockets of darkness.

I unsheathed my sai and crept toward his door, thankful that it was in the shadow between lights. I knelt to look inside his room when I heard footsteps coming from behind his door and had to quickly scurry into the nearest doorway. Hidden by the dark, I flattened my body and listened as his door swung open.

Jack, wearing Kevlar and revolver in hand, passed by me; and for a microsecond I considered letting him walk away. I could find the master key, go to the Hospice Unit while everyone was preoccupied killing each other, and fulfill my original mission. But no—I owed him pain.

"What the—" he said as I emerged from the shadow and drove my sai into his hand.

Jack's gun skidded across the floor, and I shoved my elbow into his solar plexus, putting all my weight behind the blow.

The force pushed him against the wall, but his suit absorbed most of the hit. An electrifying sting coursed up my arm from my damaged elbow. I tried catching my breath, but he rushed me and knocked me to the ground.

Jack smelled of sweat and vodka, and he weighed as much as a moose. My body was trapped between his massive thighs, and my upper arms were pinned under his knees. They felt like bowling balls crushing my bones. Breathing became constricted, and it were as if the more I struggled beneath him, the more my frame melted into him. Without saying a word, he wrapped his stubby fingers around my neck.

As Jack crushed my windpipe, I had the disconnected feeling of déjà vu.

Why do assholes love choking people? I thought.

However, the panic I felt when Terrence had done it was gone. Either I was going to die or I wasn't. Simple.

I thrashed my head from side to side, loosening Jack's grasp enough for me to sink my teeth into his hand. I tasted blood and heard his bone snap as I ripped off the tip of his pinky.

Pain swept over him, but it was panic that caused his body to recoil in shock—a bite is a death sentence in this new world.

I spat his finger and blood on his face. Before he collected himself and realized I wasn't a zombie infecting him, I drew my leg up and drove my heel into his groin.

290

Once he was off me, I reached for my sai, but I lost all feeling and movement in my arms. My hands felt as if they were made out of gelatin, and I couldn't close my fingers around the handles when Jack landed a sharp kick to my abdomen. It sent me flying several feet across the floor. I puked warm bile and blood.

I tried getting up, but a swift kick to the back of my head took the fight out of me. All I heard was gunfire, the moans of the dead, and Jack picking up something metallic off the floor. And I was okay with all of it.

Laying my head on the cold linoleum, I began to think of Alex—willing my consciousness to travel every plain of existence in search of him.

Science states that nothing can be created or destroyed, only transformed. An act of kindness, a crime driven by hate, a moment shared with a lover—all cause ripples in the world. Our memories, our feelings, our souls have a palpable force. All that energy must go somewhere.

And as I resigned to my fate, I had the horrible premonition that something was wrong. What if this new existence, this walking death, prevented our souls from moving on, like being trapped in a restless coma.

What if no one frees Alex? I thought, realizing my job wasn't done.

My eyes stung, and everything felt as if I were underwater. I saw Calise's lifeless body on the floor of Jack's room. She was nude but for a white sheet tangled around her legs. Her eyes resembled dead fish's; her hair was matted and wild, covering her mouth. Calise's porcelain skin was turning gray. And then her arm began to spasm.

Bingo.

Quickly, I got on my back and faced Jack. He had his revolver pointed at my head.

Click.

My body jerked, expecting the end.

Click. Click. Click.

"Fuck, you broke my gun," he said as he continued pulling the trigger. "I was gonna kill you quickly, but I guess I'll have to make it hurt."

Jack holstered his weapon and walked toward my sai.

"Serves you right after what you did to my hand, you rabid bitch."

I dragged myself on the floor and rested my back on the door across from Jack's room.

"Why?" I shouted.

"Why what? You're the one who attacked me! After I offered you shelter," he said and knelt to pick up my weapons, never taking his dead shark eyes off me.

"Why did you open the gates in hospice? Why did you kill Alex?"

His eyes widened, and his gaze fell to the floor. I watched his jaw muscles constrain as he tried to figure out how I had known.

"Who . . . how . . ."

Shots blasted nearby, and Jack shook his head.

"It doesn't matter. Is that what this is about? You're here to avenge your faggot boyfriend? Ha! That's a fucking good one. I mean it. You've shown real commitment, kid."

"Why, Jack? Please. You've won. I've lost everything. Just tell me why he's gone," I pleaded.

He walked toward me.

Using my elbows, I slowly inched away from the door as to not draw attention to the twitching corpse in his room.

Déjà vu indeed.

"I liked Alex, I really did. He was one of the good ones," he said. "But Cooper needed an accident to occur, and hospice was already doomed. I even asked Alex to join me. Told him to let the sickos bite the others so they could eat each other while he locked in the front. I promised I'd get him out. And I would've too. I'm a man of my word. But motherfucker looked at me as if I had asked him to kill newborn babies. Anyway, I had to do it. I needed to gain Cooper's trust. And when the infection overtook the prison, I made sure he was the first to go. You see, Cooper was a snake. He would've left us all locked up and starved us or outright killed us. Alex's sacrifice gave us a fighting chance."

Jack stood in front of me, and I spat at his feet.

He smiled and said, "I don't expect you to get it. Perhaps if you hadn't thrown your life away fighting for a ghost, you could've seen the bigger picture. It's all about survival—and there's levels to this shit."

"You really are a cocksucker, Jack. And you talk too much," I said, loud enough to muffle the sounds of a moan and shuffling steps.

"That's rich coming from you. I should've left your faggot ass to die outside," he said, raising my sai.

"Yeah, you should have," I said, smirking.

And before Jack could strike, Calise bit into the back of his head.

His scream sounded like a bursting steam pipe. Terrified, he turned away from her, and she ripped his ear with her jaws. In the struggle, Jack dropped one of the sai. I caught it midfall and thrusted it through the base of his skull, into his brain stem.

Jack's body convulsed and fell on top of Calise, pinning her to the floor. I picked up my other sai, and while she continued chewing on his face, I knelt beside her and swiftly drove it through her temple. Calise's body went limp, and I dragged it into a room, closing the door behind her.

While searching Jack's body, I wondered what had killed Calise—OD? Jack? Or was it us? It had been our choice to put her in harm's way. But without Calise, there wouldn't have been a victory. There wouldn't have been a me.

The tangle of thoughts and guilt gave me a headache that pulsated more furiously than my throbbing elbow and bruised ribs. I hated to admit it, but after all the things Jack had said, he was right about one thing—there are levels to this surviving shit.

I found the prison's master key and headed to the stairwell at the end of the hall. The third floor was desolate, and instead of an emergency light every few yards, there was one light for each long corridor.

Traveling down several dark and littered hallways, I thought how ironic it would be if a zombie were to attack and kill me right there.

"Imagine, after everything you've endured," I said, giggling to myself. "To come this far only to die at the door."

I broke out into a deranged laugh that reverberated across the entire floor. Fortunately, the biggest struggle I faced was finding the right key to the wide metal hospice door.

The stench of decay escaped as if it were pushed out of a balloon when I entered the unit. I locked the door behind me and turned on the lights along the catwalk, flooding the tier in a soft glow. Using my sai, I banged on the gate. Nothing stirred, so I fumbled for the right key and entered the company, locking each gate behind me.

It took everything I had to stop me from hopping over the rotting bodies and racing into Alex's cell. He had covered the bars with a fleece blanket; and when I called out his name, an unnatural, gurgled groan answered.

I still don't know if I didn't push the blanket aside because I knew only death awaited me or I wanted to hold on to the hope that *maybe* it wasn't him. Whatever the reason, like a recovering addict breaking sobriety, I prolonged the moment.

I dragged every corpse into the cell next to Alex's, piling one atop the other. Then I pushed a stainless steel table in front of his cell and placed a few morphine pills on the tabletop.

Although my entire body felt as if it had been pummeled with a meat tenderizer, I had no desire to get high—yet. I wanted to be in the moment, with Alex. Whatever I was about to feel, I wanted it to be authentic, not something a chemical was telling me I should feel.

"Hello, lover," I said as I pulled the blanket.

Chapter 50

His arms flailed. The bandage on his hand slipped off, and his toes dangled inches over a pool of coagulated blood. The belt was looped through the air vent on the ceiling and tied around his neck—the pressure causing his eyes to bulge as if ready to explode.

My mother fell in love with my father when they were in their teens.

"I never felt old," she said, one night on the phone. "Because every morning I woke up next to him and saw us as we were when we married. But after he died, I looked in the mirror, and it were as if my reflection fast-forwarded thirty-plus years and the old woman I had become was staring back at me."

That's how it was for me when I saw Alex hanging from the vent—his death reflected my own. Like when Oscar Wilde's Dorian Gray sees his portrait and he's destroyed by the reflection of the price paid for his sins, my two timelines melded into a single present.

In one timeline, I'm a recently released twenty-eight-year-old with fears, dreams, responsibilities, goals, and an entire life ahead to figure it all out. My heart desires for atonement and purpose. And love—I have it. Not the cure-all, knows-all kind of love seen in movies. Our love was work and sacrifice. It wasn't given to us; we took it. We faced the impossible and told the universe, "Bring it. Home is anywhere we're together."

In the other timeline, I'm also recently released. But even though I'm twenty-eight, I look and feel like a man who has outlived his better years. My family is lost. I've watched my childhood burn to ashes. Friends have died, and people have become monsters— including me. My hands are bathed in blood from decisions made in the name of love. Or at least that's what I tell myself outwardly. Deep inside, the truth lies.

Love hasn't kept you *going,* my conscience whispers. *Self- preservation has kept you alive. You've killed not for love but for the life you believe you're entitled to.*

This was the timeline I existed in, obliterating any traces of the former.

Standing in front of his gate, I watched Alex swaying in place— his arms struggling to reach me.

"You don't need to bite me, love," I said. "We're both the monsters now."

I took my jacket off and let it drop to the floor, never breaking eye contact.

"You left me, Alex. Do you know what I've done to get here? Faysal. Susan. They died helping me, and for what? So I can have a conversation with the dead?"

Reminding myself to breathe, I reached for my sai and held on to the handles. I dug my nails into the leather to keep me from unsheathing them.

"I've killed for you. Timothy. Phil. Cash. Terrence. Jack. Calise. I fucking *hate* you."

I'm a logical person. I knew he wasn't in there anymore. But as hot tears ran down my face, I had to find purpose to the obscene sense of loss I was drowning in. If I didn't, I risked losing myself to the dark hate that had fueled me thus far.

And neither logic nor death was going to stop me from having one last row with Alex.

I earned it.

"You were my everything. My whole life was planned around you—around us. I don't know what to do, where do I go from here . . ."

I knelt down in front of his gate and held on to the bars. It was all I could do to keep me from falling to the ground as I cried and hyperventilated.

"How do I live without you?" I managed to say through gasps.

My body felt light, as if I could float and dissipate into the ether. Looking back, I think if I would have closed my eyes at that moment, I may have never opened them again.

As I struggled to breathe and through the sounds of Alex's choked snarls, my mind registered the white envelopes tied to the tablet on top of his bed. I grabbed the package and crawled to the table.

Composing myself, I sat on the stool.

Breathe.

My broken body began aching all over, and my heartbeat thumped in my ears. I stared at the envelopes and then at the pills on the table.

"No," I said. "I'll be in the moment with you, my love."

With my arm, I swept the drugs off the table, and they scattered on the floor.

One envelope was labeled "To my parents" and the other "To Cole Trent." My address and phone number were written on the back, in Alex's neat handwriting.

Breathe.

My eyes began to water again, and the sound of my tears smacking on the paper seemed to echo through the tier. I couldn't hear Alex's strangled growls. He was frothing from the mouth, and his face contorted from vacuous hunger. However, looking into his eyes, steeling myself in preparation to read his final words, I saw the man he had once been. The man I had fallen in love with.

His blue-green eyes shone with life; his tangled blond hair looked as if he had just gotten out of the shower. The smile I had lived to put on his face had a crookedness at the edge of his lips, giving him a mischievous charm. And his white tank top, showing off his well-defined arms, was soaked with sweat, not blood. That was how I saw him—that's how I choose to remember him.

Breathe.

Chapter 51

Hey Beautiful,

I'm sorry, my love. I was wrong. Thought it was a passing plague, that I could beat it, that civilization would find a solution. And I wanted to be part of the cure.

Things will never be normal again, I understand that now. And I'll protect you until I die. I can't risk turning into one of those monsters and hurting you or anyone else, which is why I've chosen to end it on my terms. Please forgive me.

You have—and always will be—my inspiration. I live in awe of you. Your accomplishments, the way you conduct yourself on a daily basis. You're an impressive person, Cole. Even though I'm older than you (by like a hundred years), you have so much of life figured out. I've learned things from you every time we were together. And now it's time I share you with the world.

Babe, take the pain you feel and *use* it. I know this life won't be easy. It's going to beat you down and make you wonder how or why you're still standing. But I *promise* I will always be with you, through all your good and bad times.

I know the cynic in you is asking how I can make such an outrageous pledge. But I know I'll be with you because so much of me is you and vice versa. We're the best parts of each other, and I will be in everything you do. You made me believe in myself, and I'm here to do the same for you.

Cole, you always said that I'm a better person than you, but that's not true. You showed me the hidden beauty in life when we love a person more than we love ourselves. You gave me hope that there's more to this life than what we see or know. As I write this, I know you're on your way here. There's no explanation to how I know, doubt science has an answer, but I can feel you with me. Our love is like a key to a secret dimension. A secret only a select few get the opportunity to unlock.

You gave me that life. You *are* life. This world is going to need you to put itself back together. I know it's a lot to ask of you, but I know you can do it. We all have a job to do, babe. Yours is to live, and mine is to help you do it. And when the work is done, we'll be together again.

Last night I wrote you something and saved it on my tablet.

Read it over and over when you don't think you have anything left to keep you going. I'll take all our memories, all the perfect love we shared, and live within your heart. Let's make a home there.

I know you're angry. I can feel your pain. You taught me to always look for the beauty in the darkest of places, so don't let this world define who you are or want to be. You're bound to make mistakes. Don't beat yourself up when it happens—it's the price that comes with being the one who has to make the hard choices others can't or won't. Whenever you're lost and don't know what to do, all you have to do is look within.

Everything you need is there.

I wish I could stay a little longer, but I feel the change coming. I miss you so much. I'd give anything to see your face one more time, see the way your eyes light up when I say I love you.

Don't ever forget—you're strong and a good person. The best person I've known. It's been an honor to call you mine. You do more than outshine the world. You're my shooting star.

See you when I see you, Chicabear.

Love always & forever ever,
Alexander Oz

I took his letter and pressed it close to my heart as I cried tears that seemed to come from the deepest well.

Alex became more ferocious, the leather belt stretching to its limit, and I knew it was time to let him go.

But how?

I considered staying in there with him, perhaps join him in his new state of being. I didn't know what I wanted. I wanted him. I wanted the life we had planned and dreamt about. I wanted to feel his embrace and the comfort I had known from loving him. I may have failed at everything, but at least I knew how to love him. *That* I did right. How does one say goodbye to that?

With my right sai, I removed the block Alex had made to keep his gate from sliding open. I stood at the entrance and couldn't formulate the words to describe what I felt in my heart.

"No, I can't," I said and walked back to the table.

I turned his tablet on and looked for the file Alex had left me.

The whip of the belt snapping roared in my ears, and before I could register the danger I was in, Alex was on me. His claws dug into my shoulders, and I moved my head fast enough to keep him from sinking his teeth into my neck. The tablet bounced on the floor, and the disconnected fear and anger I felt from it possibly breaking gave me the push I needed to fight back.

I swerved to his right and elbowed his side, the force of the impact knocking him back a few feet. It only gave me a second-long reprieve before he lunged at me again. But that was enough time for me to unsheathe my other sai.

He landed on me, and we fell to the floor. Even in his undead state, he was so strong. His movement was clumsy and uncoordinated, but his weight kept me pinned down. I drove my sai into his sternum to keep him from biting my face off. It held him back, for a little while. Alex continued pushing himself into the sai. It was only a matter of seconds until the entire weapon was in him and his teeth in me.

"I thought honoring you meant joining you," I said, looking into his eyes. "But you were right. I need to survive and keep going."

His jaws were centimeters from my face. And with all the love in my eyes, I raised my other sai and pushed it into his temple.

"I love you, Alex. I'll honor you by living. I'll keep you alive by staying the person you fell in love with. You're my home base."

Chapter 52

I lay on my back for what felt like infinite lifetimes, Alex's body atop of me.

His head rested on my chest as I combed my fingers through his hair, untangling the kinks. It's true, we remember the people we love by being the person they believe we can be. Alex will live on in every kindness I commit; I'll see him in the face of every person I save. However, the dead take a piece of us with them as well.

Once I get back on my feet, I'll wrap Alex in a clean white sheet and bury him underneath our tree. I will bypass my mourning and head straight into the fight for control of the Haven but with renewed purpose—save the families, children, and survivors. That was Alex's gift to me. He gave me vision.

But I also know a part of me will never leave this company. There is no letting go of Alex, no moving on—only a new way of being. The person I was, before my heart was encased in scar tissue, will be buried with him.

So in my attempt to stretch my last moment with my husband, I inched my arm and picked up his tablet.

I kissed his forehead and said, "See you when I see you, my love."

I opened the file labeled "[6.29-4E] 143" and began reading the words of a man who had hope in his heart:

This is how a kiss changed my life forever.

A few summers ago, I'm walking around the yard with a friend of mine, when out of nowhere I see the hottest person I've ever seen in my life. He had long, dark hair (a weakness of mine). Beautiful brown—check that, it was more of a caramel hue—skin tone. And an eccentric personality. My mind raced through what I wanted to do to him, but it could only remain a fantasy (that I played out in my mind on many lonely nights).

He walked into my life in winter. Before then, I had only admired him from afar, but I knew I couldn't let him leave the library without introducing myself. Boy, was I nervous. I helped him find a book on sign language. Our conversation flowed smoothly, and I noticed right away that he was an easygoing person, far from arrogant, which is rare for a person who possesses beauty as he does. He was taking college courses, and I enrolled as well, which I only did so we could spend time together. Talk about a chase. How many men can say they got a degree *just* so they can have an excuse to talk to someone. But through it all, I maintained my yearnings secret.

But then I started to get to know him. He became so much more to me than a sexual fling. He ended up becoming my best friend. I finally found someone I could trust and confide in. I don't think he understood how hard it was for me to open up to him. Life had taught me to never fully trust anyone, not even my parents.

I wanted to tell him how I felt, but I couldn't. See, all my life I've been taught that gay was wrong. And hanging out with homos in prison was a big no-no. It opens the door for cats to slander your name. So can you understand my dilemma? How do I make something happen without anyone finding out? He wasn't like anyone I had ever met. He is so intelligent and always sees the best in everyone, even though he sometimes fails to see the best within himself, maybe because of his past or because of this environment. I also saw his potential.

I know he is one of the rare people in the world who can accomplish anything he puts his mind to. That's how special he is.

It's spring and an opportunity arises. We're tucked away in our spot, I pulled him in and kissed him. It was in the heat of the moment, but little did I know the lasting effect it would have on me. My stomach was in knots for weeks after. He was all I could think about.

June 29th—two become one. I go for it. I'm super nervous. I hope he doesn't notice. I drop to one knee and pop the question. He says yes. I'm in there. Love is official. God has truly blessed me.

I didn't want to believe the world was ending. I should have listened to you. And now I'm trapped, my only hope is that you'll come get me. Of course you will. I can't explain it. I close my eyes, and I can feel you here. I also know my Chicabear can't pass up the chance to tell me "I told you so!" :) So I ration my food and water and wait.

I hear your voice calling me. You're on me before my gate has fully opened. God, you're magnificent. Your hair is a bit frizzy and tangled from your journey, but your skin is soft, and you smell like morning dew.

After the excitement of reuniting wears off and countless rounds of sex, we have to answer a pressing question—where do we go from here?

We argue about it, a lot. You want to go get our families, and you call me a heartless asshole for not agreeing. I want to start over, just the two of us, knowing a journey to Gowanda and Florida would be too dangerous. I don't know, you'd probably find a way to manipulate me into agreeing with you. But this is *my* vision, so let's pretend I finally won an argument.

So it's just us, and the world is ours. Don't get me wrong, it's not an easy life. It's full of pain, loss, and regrets. But it's also new and full of opportunity, and we live every second as if we're on borrowed time. I live to see the sun set on your face.

Years go by and we've avoided people as much as possible, except for helping the occasional straggler we run into along the way. I see the way your face lights up every time we help a kid or a family; it melts my heart. And I begin to wonder that maybe our time to join the bigger picture has come.

We traveled through forests and prairies, stayed close to the coast and rivers. we were aimlessly roaming. But I had a plan the whole time.

I've been slowly leading us to the place we used to go to in our dreams. It wasn't easy traveling to another continent in monster-infested land, but nothing that's worth something comes easy.

You begin to recognize the mountains and the aroma of jasmine on the ocean breeze. (And knowing you, you probably figured out what I was planning long before we arrived but acted surprised just to make me happy. Thank you.)

Ancon, the place between the ocean and mountains. The natural barriers have kept this place relatively safe, and it'll be a great spot to finish out our time.

We're old, but when I look at you, I only see the beautiful person I fell in love with all that time ago. Our last years are spent sharing what we've learned with our neighbors, especially the kids.

They're the ones who will inherit the world we've built and carry the torch once we're gone. And our love, like the monuments humans have been building since the dawn of civilization, will outlast everything. However, unlike monuments built of stone and concrete, our legacy is made up of the lives we've touched and the love we've shared.

Now, Cole, do you see why I can feel at peace, no matter what? You are one of a kind, and you're with me. The world can go to shit, but I can't complain because

I've already won so much. You always said we found what most people spend their entire lives looking for. Cole, with you I found what I didn't even knew existed. And when I close my eyes, I see our life.

That's what I see when I think of you. Now, close your eyes and let's go for another ride.

Beautiful, ain't it?

Epilogue

"Be a good boy and come back inside, Pan," Dora pleads while standing in the back porch behind the locked door.

Any other time she wouldn't bother calling her one-year-old feline friend back inside, but tonight, she can't endure being alone. Pan wasn't Dora's usual house buddy—he's too independent. Her companion had been Pan's brother, Peter.

They had been the only boys in the litter, two orange Maine coons, and their mother's name was Tinkerbell and father's was Hook. Dora couldn't have named them anything but Peter and Pan. The similarities ended there though. While Pan loves open spaces to explore, Peter never strayed too far from Dora.

She scans the yard for any signs of Pan, and she's amazed at how well her eyes have adapted to a world without electricity.

"Pan, please, get inside," Dora pleads once more, hearing the desperation in her voice.

She wants to scream his name, but she knows *they* are attracted to sound. And she won't make that mistake again.

Dora, the youngest of three, knew her destiny was tied to the family's farm along a tributary of the Hudson River—land her ancestors had called home for generations. While her older sisters had married and moved out of state as soon as they were old enough to drive, Dora had gone to school to become a veterinarian.

Her dating life had been nonexistent during her teens since she was homeschooled. Then during her first years in college, she found the sudden male attention overwhelming. After a few awkward dates, she decided she liked the sex more than the romance and focused on her studies—only taking a recreational approach to men.

She was enjoying spending her twenties away, but that life came to an end a year ago when she got a call from her oldest sister informing Dora their parents had died in a car accident.

After the funeral, her sisters discussed selling the farm and splitting the profits. But unlike her siblings, Dora felt the primal connection humans make to their land—as if her bones and the ground were made of the same minerals. She couldn't envision her life anywhere else.

Dora convinced them to let her run the farm, at least for a year or two. Her plan had been to hire farmhands while she finished her veterinary studies so she could open her own practice and attend to the animals in the surrounding areas. But her reality had been much different—the endless bureaucracy behind farming had made her want to burn the wheat fields to ashes. And there had also been the loneliness. Her closest neighbors were miles apart, and her dependency on Peter and Pan had begun to give her flashes of a lonely life filled with cats.

But all that became irrelevant when the world changed and the word *dead* became a relative term. And then her world changed again, six days ago, when the man washed ashore and Peter was killed.

Dora was inspecting the mill by the stream for damage from the storm when Peter and Pan caught his scent and ran off. She chased after them, screaming their names. Peter stopped at the sound of her voice and circled back, but Pan kept going.

The man was on his back. A pool of blood had formed underneath him, flowing from the gash on his face. Pan stood on the man's chest and pawed at his neck. She grabbed Peter and began running after Pan but slipped on the sleek grass as a second person washed ashore. Except it was no person.

It wasn't the first time Dora had encountered these demons. One had stumbled into the stable last week.

"Shoot them in the head," the sheriff had posted online, before the power died. And Dora had done just that, blowing the creature's brain into so many pieces it had taken her four days to disinfect the barn.

However, as she cowered behind a shrub so the monster that had emerged from the water wouldn't spot her, all she could do was curse herself for leaving her .22-gauge rifle in the kitchen. The monster was emaciated and nude, with skin the color and texture of marble. It trudged toward the house, and Dora exhaled in relief. And then Pan hissed at it.

"No, Pan! Run, boy," she barked, instantly regretting it as the demon turned its focus on her.

She ran to Pan and picked him up, clutching both cats under each armpit.

The man moved.

Dora must have been entranced by this sign of life because when she turned to run, she felt a cold clawlike hand sink into her shoulder.

It pushed her to the ground. Peter and Pan landed on their feet, hissed at the fiend, and lunged. It grabbed Peter and sank its putrid teeth into his hind legs. The cat screeched and went limp.

During the commotion, the man had pulled out a black Ranger knife before passing out again. Dora seized the weapon and plunged it through the demon's temple. She brought Peter and the man into the house. Peter succumbed to his wounds soon after, but the man clung to life.

His eye had been gouged out, and he suffered from hypothermia. Dora did her best to patch him up, but her veterinary skills were limited and the animal antibiotics and medicines could only do but so much. The rest was up to him.

And live he did. His will to survive was unmatched. The bluish tint of his skin disappeared after the first day, and his fever broke two days later. He had been unconscious, sometimes mumbling unintelligibly in his sleep. However, he had stirred all day, and she knew he'll be awake soon, which is why she's desperate for Pan.

Giving up, she leaves an open can of tuna on the floor and props open the kitty door.

"Don't be nervous, Dora," she says, walking down the hallway. "You know a lot about him. He's a good guy."

While changing him into dry clothes, Dora had gone through the man's pockets. He had written letters for his brother, parents, friends, and stuffed them into his wallet. Dora hadn't meant to read them, but if she had left them in the wallet, they would have been ruined.

"He'll thank me when he wakes up," she assures herself.

She also found his driver's license. Dora still can't believe he's only twenty years old, not that he looks old. Even with his patched eye, his dimples and round face give him a boyish handsomeness. She just finds it hard to believe he's that young because the man's aura—combined with the adversities he has detailed in his letters—is of a person who has lived many lives.

He's lying in her parents' bed. She didn't want to bring him there, remembering her parents would have made her a chastity belt if she had ever brought a boy home. But it's the biggest room and there's a fireplace. The temperature had improved after the storm, but the cold had returned with a vengeance.

Dora closes all the blinds and lights a small fire. As she fans the embers, Pan swaggers into the room and jumps on the bed.

The man stirs, and his eye flutters.

This is it.

Dora braces herself, remembering the "welcome back" speech she had been practicing for the past three days. She had thought very hard about what she would say when he woke up, finally settling on complimenting his name. Not only would it help her know if his memory worked, but she really did like his middle name. It means "to hope" in Latin. There's a shortage of hope right now, but she knows it's the only thing that can rebuild the world. His name reminds her of a story her mom used to read to her as a child; something about a box that was opened and unleashed every malice onto humanity, and the only thing left in the box was—

"Pan!" Dora shouts as he jumps into her arms, startling her and waking up the man.

"Hi. It's just past midnight so it's Sunday, the twenty-third," she says, wincing at her awkward greeting.

Taking a deep breath to calm her nerves, she continues.

"I—well, Pan here found you at the river's shore six days ago."

"I . . . remember," he says.

His voice is strained, and his body is in so much pain that all he wants to do is go back to the darkness. Which, he does, closing his eye and falling asleep.

"Rest," Dora murmurs.

She places Pan on the floor and checks the man's forehead for a fever.

"You'll need all your strength. I have a feeling your journey has just begun, Faysal Spero Singh."

CPSIA information can be obtained
at www.ICGtesting.com
Printed in the USA
LVHW090406290821
R16921000002B/R169210PG696168LVX00015B/11

9 781956 010251